I0522500

He was on his way home, when his life was changed forever…

Adam awoke slowly, feeling dazed and confused from his drugged sleep. His head was pounding. It felt like it was being hit by a jackhammer. He had no idea where he was or what he'd been doing? Brief snippets of recent events appeared in a rapid sideshow in his head. He remembered playing football…he could picture the inside of a car, a referee…after the picture in his head of a referee, everything went black, and he couldn't remember anything else.

None of it made sense. He stood up unsteadily from the bed he'd been lying on and leaned on the hard, dank concrete wall of the cell he appeared to be in. The wall felt cold and clammy.

Suddenly, his legs became unsteady, and he hurriedly sat back down on the bed. This time, he didn't risk standing again. Instead, he just sat still trying to get his bearings.

As his eyes started to clear, he could see he was in a four-walled cell, with a locked gate in the middle of the rear cell wall. It was solid and well-constructed and looked impossible to escape from. The only piece of furniture in the cell was the lumpy bed. As Adam lay on the bed, wondering what was going on, the wall in front of him suddenly lit up with a black and white movie projection of a Nazi Nuremburg rally. Loud Nazi marching music suddenly pounded through speakers outside the cell. Adam sat up abruptly and stared outside the cell to a spot where he was sure he'd just seen someone move in the shadows.

The sound of the deafening marching band music abruptly halted. "I'm glad to see you're awake, Adam," a cold analytical voice said.

“Let me go!” Adam demanded.

“All in good time, my disciple. Before I let you go, there’s a lot you must learn first to enable you to have the ability to fulfil your destiny.”

A terrorist bombing at a summer carnival on the Brighton sea front causes mayhem and murder. Detective Inspector Sarah Machin and her colleague, Detective Sergeant Morgan Roberts, recently transferred to Counter Terrorism Command, are sent to investigate. After discovering the bomber, a teenage boy, had been kidnapped and had no connection with any terrorist group, a baffled Machin starts a frantic hunt for the ones behind the awful crime.

With the recent rise of the English Patriot Party, a far right organization fronted in Sussex by local leader, Ian Bailey, Machin looks at them as major suspects. When ex-copper Bailey denies all knowledge and claims the bombing was, in fact, carried out by the militant left in a bid to destroy the well-supported EPP, Machin's case is thrown into disarray. As the investigation unfolds and more terror attacks are carried out by what appear to be brainwashed boys, she realizes that she's locked in a fight with evil killers who have no compunction about taking human life.

KUDOS for *Bailey's Land*

In *Bailey's Land* by Paul Howard, Detective Inspector Sarah Machin and her partner, Detective Sergeant Morgan Roberts, have been transferred to Britain's Counter Terrorism Command. They are sent to investigate a terrorist bombing carried out by a kidnapped and brain-washed teenage boy. Their chief suspect as to who is behind the crime is Ian Bailey, a leader in the far-right political party, the English Patriotic Party, or EPP. Bailey vehemently denies any involvement and tries to throw suspicion onto far-left militant groups. Pressure on Machin to solve the crimes increases and more terrorist attacks are carried out by recently kidnapped and brain-washed teenagers. She begins to have her doubts about Bailey's involvement, but as she searches for the truth, she soon discovers that she is dealing with a singular evil, and nothing is as it seems. Fast paced, tense, and compelling, with a subtle international flavor, the book will grab your attention from the very first page and hold it all the way through. A great read. ~ *Taylor Jones, The Review Team of Taylor Jones & Regan Murphy*

Bailey's Land by Paul Howard is the story of England's Detective Inspector Sarah Machin who we met in Howard's first book in this series, Soul Mates. Machin has just been transferred to the Counter Terrorism Command when a series of terrorist attacks hits Britain. The attacks, carried out by teenage boys who have recently gone missing and are clearly brainwashed, are targeted at Britain's minorities and immigrants, and the boys shout "Britain for the British" as they fulfill their deadly missions. This leads Machin to believe that the people responsible for the attacks are members of a new far-right political party called the English Patriotic Party

(EPP). One of the leaders of this new party is a former policeman named Ian Bailey. Machin brings him in for questioning, but Bailey denies any knowledge and claims that his party is peaceful and prefers to make changes through the electoral process, not by murdering innocent people. Machin doesn't believe him, but without any evidence against him, her investigation stalls. As the bodies pile up and Machin digs deeper for the truth, she uncovers betrayal of the worst kind. *Bailey's Land* is both timely and compelling, a thought-provoking look at how far some people will go for their ideological beliefs, even so far as spilling innocent blood. A story of fanaticism, betrayal, and bigotry, it's one you won't find easy to put down. ~ *Regan Murphy, The Review Team of Taylor Jones & Regan Murphy*

ACKNOWLEDGMENTS

Thanks to Lauri, Faith, and Jack, at Black Opal Books, for their support.

As usual, a special mention for Jack Phillips for his belief in me.

Faye, as usual, your input was invaluable.

BAILEY'S LAND

Paul Howard

A Black Opal Books Publication

GENRE: MYSTERY-DETECTIVE/THRILLER

This is a work of fiction. Names, places, characters and incidents are either the product of the author's imagination or are used fictitiously, and any resemblance to any actual persons, living or dead, businesses, organizations, events or locales is entirely coincidental. All trademarks, service marks, registered trademarks, and registered service marks are the property of their respective owners and are used herein for identification purposes only. The publisher does not have any control over or assume any responsibility for author or third-party websites or their contents.

DEDICATION

*To Anna-Maria, my love, always.
I hope my mother and father, Mike and Hilda,
deceased, would be proud of the book.*

CHAPTER 1

The evening was hot and sultry, an August evening, the clammy type of evening that got inside the pores of your skin, making you sweat in the most unimaginable places. The salt smell of the sea wafted on the air in the light evening breeze. Brighton sea front was alive with music, full of expectation, and cheerful crowds were standing behind metal railings, watching the slow procession of colorful floats along the sea front. It had been hailed in the press as the carnival of the union, a title the organizers had proudly announced a few months previous. With recent ethnic tensions over immigration issues, it was a chance for the people of Brighton to take an expansive view of mankind's multicultural diversity—that was what the brochure advertising the carnival had claimed.

The heat brought out certain ailments in the old and a unique irritation in the young, and, under certain circumstances, it could be the cause of the worst kind of lunacy. In the heat, there was always the possibility of a weirdo on the horizon. You might not notice them—some of them had the ability to slip off the radar. Whatever they did, they were always watching, waiting, looking for the moment when they could unleash their own particular brand of mayhem on an unsuspecting world.

Today's weirdo was in the shape of a teenage boy called John, who was dressed in an overcoat. John in his overcoat, and with a studious disposition, looked totally out of place among the happy T-shirted revelers smiling and waving as each float in the procession drifted past. As he rudely pushed his way to the front of the crowd, John received angry grumbles from those he elbowed out the way.

The glazed, fixed look in his turbulent, gray-green eyes was that of a zealot, a look that would inform anybody willing to pay attention that he wasn't listening to their feeble protests. John only ever listened to one person in his life. That person had ordered him to get to the front of the crowd and to stand with the masses at the moment when the heart of the carnival procession went slowly by.

"Do you mind?" an irritated man with a laughing child on his shoulders snapped, as John pushed rudely past him and squeezed through a tiny gap in the barrier that had been left for emergencies. Once free of the encumbrance of the crowd, John found a new lease of life and strode confidently out into the middle of the road.

Along the road, a community police officer in charge of crowd control for this sector of the carnival procession suddenly became aware of trouble and strode angrily up to John. "Please go back behind the barriers, sir," she ordered, trying to keep her tone impassive, so as not to ruin the party mood of the crowd.

But John didn't listen—the policewoman was not the person that John obeyed. There was only one person now that John followed, and he had told John what to do. John ignored the fresh-faced community policewoman and walked toward a float called the Caribbean Queen. As he stood next to some jigging West Indian transvestites blowing whistles in his face, the policewoman, irritated by John's actions, pushed the transvestites aside and angrily grabbed his arm. John didn't put up a fight. He just turned and looked into the policewoman's deep blue eyes with a blank, vacant look of incomprehension.

"You have to go behind the barriers, sir," the policewoman ordered, finding it hard to mask her irritation as the boy seemed determined to ruin the pleasure of those around him.

"Britain for the British!" John shouted loudly and then wrestled himself free of the policewoman's grasp.

The policewoman angrily grabbed John's arm, in a last desperate attempt to quell the boy's ardor. As she touched his warm flesh, John detonated the bomb that was strapped to his midriff. The bomb killed quickly. John and the policewoman died in a millisecond, as their blood, flesh, and bones disintegrated. The Caribbean Queen was no longer living the Jamaicans' dream. Their skin and bones were ripped to pieces as the force of the blast quickly spiraled outward. The father and son by the railing and everybody within the float's immediate vicinity could not escape the wrath of the blast. As they all fell, the road was soon awash with the dead and wounded.

A car alarm shrilled a ghostly wail, breaking the eerie silence of the bomb's aftermath. As the dust started to settle and the scream of ambulance sirens could be heard on the wind, the angel of death seemed to hover over the ghoulish scene. He hovered for a reason. Tonight he had come a calling, looking for helpless souls to replenish his legions. He didn't care about age or infirmity, didn't give a fig about life's absurdity. As he looked at the dead that now lay before him, he knew that, thanks to John, on Brighton sea front this warm sultry evening, his work was done.

CHAPTER 2

DI Machin and DS Roberts weren't sure what they were going to find when they arrived at the crime scene. It was almost dark, and the public had been quickly cleared from the area as the police were worried there might be another bomb. Hours after the bomb, and with the sea front covered in the blanket of darkness, the bomb squad finally decided that the area was safe and that their investigation could begin. DI Machin's transfer to the Counter Terrorism Command was meant to be one of calm transition after her promotion to this exciting new post, instead, because of this evening's events on Brighton sea front, it had turned into a bludgeoning assault and meant her being thrown in at the deep end.

They stepped under the flapping crime scene tape where police officers in white overalls were carefully at work, combing the bomb site for evidence. DI Machin skirted along the edge of their work, closely followed by her lapdog, Roberts. One condition of the transfer to Counter Terrorism Command was that Machin could take her sergeant with her. Machin and Roberts worked well as a team, a fact they'd proved when they'd recently put an end to the evil reign of terror of the serial killer, Peter Rivers.

"This is crazy, ma'am," Roberts said, studying the blood and dust that was caked all around the bomb site. "They say it was a teenage white kid—witnesses report that he walked calmly up to a carnival float and detonated a bomb strapped to his body."

Machin was shocked. After her boyfriend Nick had been gunned down by the serial killer, Peter Rivers, she'd thought there was nothing left that could shock her—that was until tonight. How could a teenager coldly maim and murder like this? She thought about the obvious, the New IRA or Islamic fundamentalists. There was something about all this that didn't sit right. If it was the work of any of the major terrorist players, why hadn't they come forward and claimed responsibility for the act? These people thrived on publicity, keeping their cause in the public eye, yet nobody had so far come forward with anything.

Machin needed to view the sea front CCTV footage. She'd have to see the last acts of this crazy kid before he'd murdered all these people. It was a suicide bombing, carried out by a boy that nothing was going to stop. Who was the boy? It was a question that they needed to find the answer to fast.

They'd found no serviceable ID from his splattered body, would try for dental records once they'd pieced together what they could of his jaw-line. So far they had no name and nothing to link him to any organization. As Machin looked across at the desolation and mayhem the boy had caused, all she could think was that the boy had to have a reason, for nobody murdered like this without a cause.

"It's going to take a while for forensics to piece this one together, ma'am," Roberts said gloomily.

"That's it, Roberts, look on the bright side."

"I'm being realistic, ma'am."

"Forget realism, can't you lie to me for a change, Sergeant?"

Machin's mobile phone rang. She answered it. It was DCI Khan, head of her section. They'd had a break, there'd been a call from a family who'd seen the pictures of the Brighton bomber on the news, the family reckoned that the bomber looked like their missing son. Machin grabbed Roberts and dragged him back to the car. The crime scene could wait until after they'd spoken to the parents.

When Machin and Roberts sat in the humid police interview room opposite the unfortunate parents of the suicide bomber, John Chambers, the room was racked with a putrid mix of loss and tension. Machin didn't know where to start. Talking to the distraught parents about their dead son was never going to be easy. When people had suffered loss, particularly in such a violent fashion, Machin had seen in the past how impossible it was to comfort them. She started at the beginning by asking, "How long has John been missing, Mr. Chambers?"

"It was four weeks ago tonight," Mr. Chambers said. "He went out with his mates to the skateboard park near our house. After he had separated from his mates to come home, he disappeared."

Mrs. Chambers started to cry. Mr. Chambers tried to comfort her, and the room lapsed momentarily into an uncomfortable silence.

"If you'd like to take a short break," Machin said.

"I don't want a break, I want to find out what happened to John," Mrs. Chambers pleaded.

Machin nodded and then continued. "You've seen the CCTV footage just before the attack. From that footage, you ID the bomber as your son?"

"The bomber's, John," Mr. Chambers reluctantly

admitted with a look of abject misery on his fraught, freckled face.

"John never had a violent bone in his body," Mrs. Chambers said. "This is all a mistake."

Mrs. Chambers couldn't accept it. Machin decided she was still in a state of denial. "This is no mistake, Mrs. Chambers, John walked out from the crowd and detonated a bomb strapped to his body near a carnival float."

Mrs. Chambers began to cry again. Mr. Chambers interjected, "Maybe I should speak to the officers alone, Kathy."

"Don't try and freeze me out, Lee!" Mrs. Chambers angrily rounded on her husband , an inflection of despair in her voice that told a stunned Mr. Chambers this wasn't up for debate.

"I'm not trying to freeze you out, darling," Mr. Chambers assured her.

"This must be awful for both of you—let's take a break." Machin gave the Chambers coffee, and then Machin and Roberts left them alone for a few minutes. Outside in the corridor, Machin quickly came to a bleak conclusion. "Apart from identifying their son, they're not going to know anything that could help us."

"Why would a supposedly normal kid from a middle class background do this?" Roberts reflected.

"That's what we're paid to find out, Sergeant."

"Witnesses say that he shouted, 'Britain for the British,' just before he detonated the bomb."

"Then we've got to be looking for far right extremists. We need to find out if John Chambers was political, whether he was sympathetic to neo-Nazis, or if he was involved with neo-Nazi groups." Machin looked at a text message on her mobile phone. "DCI Khan says that another one of the wounded off the float has just died in hospital, that makes ten dead, including John Chambers."

There was a moment's sad reflection. "John Chambers was only sixteen," Roberts pointed out, "the same age as my nephew, Hayden."

"It's best not to think about it, Morgan," Machin said.

Roberts noted that Machin used his Christian name, a rare occasion in their work together, and the use of it showed Roberts how deeply all this was affecting Machin. "Someone supplied him with the bomb," he said.

"Obviously, but who?"

"This isn't the organized far right. The modern fascists try to slip under the political spectrum, put themselves over as legitimate democrats," Roberts remarked.

"I agree. We're not looking for established loonies, everything points to a loner," Machin stated. "What we're looking for is someone who's pissed off with the far right's inactivity and wants direct action." She was thinking more of an individual like the London nail bomber, a nutcase with a grudge.

"We'll look at everything, ma'am."

"Because of what Chambers shouted, don't get too restricted, Sergeant. His shouting of a Nazi slogan might've been a ploy to throw us off the mark." Machin wasn't going to be blinkered and would look at everything possible, until it was proved otherwise.

"Why would he want to create a smokescreen?" Roberts asked. "If the bombing was a political message, surely the bombers want us to know what that message is."

"He stepped over the barrier when the West Indian float was almost upon him," Machin reflected. "Numerous floats passed him by, and yet he targeted that float in particular."

"An obvious racial attack, ma'am."

"Not necessarily. If you wanted to kill a specific person and for the hit to go undetected, what better way than to detonate a bomb near the float that they're on. By making it look like a terrorist attack, you could fool everyone."

Machin had a point, Roberts decided. "So, you want me to look in detail at the backgrounds of all the people killed on the float?"

"We have to look at everything, Sergeant. Because of all the deaths, the press will have a microscope on this. We need to be seen in their inevitable backlash to have been covering all our bases." Machin remembered previous mistakes in past cases, like when she'd wrongly accused John Douglas of murder when the real murderer had been the serial killer, Peter Rivers. The press had made a big issue of police incompetence when John Douglas, an innocent dupe, had been found not guilty in a courtroom. Machin had vowed that day in court never to make the same mistake again.

They went back into the interview room to find that Mrs. Chambers had stopped crying and seemed more in control. This time their interview was calmer and more structured. After repeated denials that their son was involved with neo-Nazis and the fact that the Chambers genuinely seemed mystified by what had happened to their son, Machin came to the conclusion that Mr. and Mrs. Chambers knew nothing of what had gone on here and that Counter Terrorism Command's limited resources would be better off utilized elsewhere.

CHAPTER 3

The steamy mud-splattered changing room was silent as Adam Reid dried himself with a soft towel after his lukewarm shower. As Adam started to put on his crumpled clothes, everybody around him was silent. Adam knew the reason for the silence—he had the misfortune of missing a penalty in the last minute of the match for his amateur team, Henton United. It had been the cup semi-final and had meant that Henton had lost the game. By the way, the rest of the team had reacted since the final whistle, it was plainly obvious to Adam that the other players, because of the penalty miss, blamed him personally for the defeat.

Adam was furious at their attitude, hurriedly got changed, and left. Outside, he started walking angrily toward the bus stop to get a bus back into town. Why he'd ever gotten involved with playing for a bunch of sulkers such as Henton was beyond him. It was a friend of a friend who'd told him they were looking for players. They said that he'd be guaranteed a game every week. When he was promised a game every week, nobody told him he'd soon become a pariah to the Henton half-wits just because of one penalty miss.

Anger meant he was walking quickly, so quickly that he didn't notice anything going on around him. When a Skoda car pulled up alongside him and stopped, he thought it might be one of his team mates stopping to apologize for their over-the-top overreaction. As the car window slid down, he saw it was one of the refs from the park still wearing his ref's kit. It wasn't the ref from Henton's game, so it had to be a ref who'd been refereeing one of the other matches. Adam hadn't been looking, so he didn't really know.

Through the open window, the ref asked, "You live on the Hampton Estate, don't you?"

Adam said he did.

"I thought I'd seen you around the estate. I live a couple of streets from you—get in, I'll give you a lift," the ref said.

Adam couldn't remember seeing the guy about, but the fact that he knew him was good enough for Adam. Adam got in the front passenger seat, belted up, and then the man drove off. As they drove, the man took out a packet of toffees from the glove compartment and offered Adam one. Adam hadn't eaten since lunchtime, so he greedily accepted. As he sucked on the sweet, his head started pounding and, suddenly, the car seemed to become stuffy and suffocating. As the ref slid the car to a halt in a quiet lay-by, it was at that moment that Adam couldn't focus anymore on anything, and suddenly everything around him went black. As the ref leaned over him and asked Adam if he was okay, Adam could no longer hear him as at that precise moment he blacked out.

CHAPTER 4

The conference room at the police station was cramped and charged with tension. DI Machin and DS Roberts stood at the front of the room beside a board, on which all the information that had so far been discovered about the Brighton bombing was written. A group of officers sat eagerly in front of Machin, waiting for her to begin. Children had died in the blast, and that, combined with the fact that the bomber himself was only sixteen, meant that Machin was standing and addressing a group of very animated officers.

"Since the bombing, we've had nobody contact us claiming responsibility. It means that we've still got no idea whether the bombing was a random act of an individual or the act of a terrorist group," Machin commented.

DC Kylie Jacobs in the front row of seats said, "Before he detonated the bomb, the lad shouted 'Britain for the British,' that surely must mean far right undertones, ma'am."

"Maybe. If it was a far right terrorist attack, then we have to work on the theory that the bomber was part of a neo-Nazi terrorist group that's going to embark on a campaign of terror," Machin said, adding, "If that's the case, then there's a likelihood that they've now got a taste for it, and they enjoy the power over life and death that such random terrorist attacks give them." She paused while they took in what she told them. "Every connection with white supremacist organizations, no matter how seemingly insignificant, needs to be looked into. They killed six people on that float, several in the crowd, plus our colleague who confronted the boy."

There was a moment's reverential silence as they considered the dead police officer. Machin continued. "I've spoken to John Chambers's family, not one of them told us there was any hint of his involvement in far right extremism. Everybody who knew him told us that he was a fairly normal kid who had plenty of friends, and that there was no abnormality in his behavior."

"I've talked to his friends," DC Kylie Jacobs said. "All of them said he wasn't a violent kid, a couple of his friends are Muslims. If we work on the idea of him being in a far right terror cell, we're barking up the wrong tree, ma'am."

DS Roberts was irritated. He didn't deal in hearsay but preferred to work with facts. "He shouted 'Britain for the British' just before he detonated the bomb, Jacobs, I think that alone merits giving the far right some of our attention."

A red-faced Jacobs went silent after the rebuke. Machin, pacified, remarked, "What he shouted points to the far right, Jacobs, and at the moment we've uncovered nothing that contradicts that line of investigation."

"He could've been brainwashed, ma'am," Jacobs said, adjusting her thin-rimmed glasses. "I've studied stills of the CCTV footage of his actions prior to the bomb detonating, and, to me, he's acting in a robotic fashion. It looks like he doesn't have a will of his own."

In the brief time that Machin had worked with DC Jacobs, she'd found her bright, intelligent, and enthusiastic. Jacobs had also been a member of the team studying the CCTV footage from the Brighton Council sea front CCTV cameras. "Okay, Jacobs, let's say that you're right, and John Chambers was brainwashed…"

"I am right, ma'am," Jacobs interjected. "A non-violent, easy-going teenager doesn't turn into a brutal killer like this without outside intervention."

Machin mulled over what Jacobs said. If she was right, then someone had kidnapped this boy and brainwashed him to be used as a weapon. It left Machin with a big problem, which meant she had a controlling extremist out there who was prepared to brainwash teenage boys into committing mass murder. At the moment, they had no links or leads to go on. If Chambers had been brainwashed by a terrorist group, was this attack the first in a series of brutal attacks, or was it just a one-off act of evil?

At the moment, Machin had no idea. After the mayhem the bomber caused on Brighton sea front, one thing she knew for certain was, whatever was going on here, Counter Terrorism Command needed to find out, and they needed to find out fast.

CHAPTER 5

Adam awoke slowly, feeling dazed and confused from his drugged sleep. His head was pounding. It felt like it was being hit by a jackhammer. He had no idea where he was or what he'd been doing? Brief snippets of recent events appeared in a rapid sideshow in his head. He remembered playing football…he could picture the inside of a car, a referee…after the picture in his head of a referee, everything went black, and he couldn't remember anything else.

None of it made sense. He stood up unsteadily from the bed he'd been lying on and leaned on the hard, dank concrete wall of the cell he appeared to be in. The wall felt cold and clammy.

Suddenly, his legs became unsteady, and he hurriedly sat back down on the bed. This time, he didn't risk standing again. Instead, he just sat still trying to get his bearings.

As his eyes started to clear, he could see he was in a four-walled cell, with a locked gate in the middle of the rear cell wall. It was solid and well-constructed and looked impossible to escape from. The only piece of furniture in the cell was the lumpy bed. As Adam lay on the bed, wondering what was going on, the wall in front of him suddenly lit up with a black and white movie projection of a Nazi Nuremburg rally. Loud Nazi marching music suddenly pounded through speakers outside the cell. Adam sat up abruptly and stared outside the cell to a spot where he was sure he'd just seen someone move in the shadows.

The sound of the deafening marching band music abruptly halted. "I'm glad to see you're awake, Adam," a cold analytical voice said.

"Let me go!" Adam demanded.

"All in good time, my disciple. Before I let you go, there's a lot you must learn first to enable you to have the ability to fulfil your destiny."

"What am I doing here?" Adam snapped. "Why have you kidnapped me?"

The Voice laughed. "All will be made plain to you, my disciple, all you have to know for now is that I'm the man who's going to save this land."

"Save what land?"

"Adam, I'm disappointed in you. I've brought you here to give you the chance to do something for your country."

"What are you talking about?" Adam asked.

The Voice laughed. Through the sound system's acoustics, it sounded like a ghostly echo. "Never mind, Adam, all will shortly become plain to you, you just sit and watch the movie and get acclimatized to your new home."

"If you're not going to let me go, then I'm going back to sleep," Adam told the Voice, then he lay back on the bed and shut his eyes.

"You need to watch the film," the Voice ordered.

"I'm not watching that black and white shit," Adam grumbled.

"The volume can be turned up much louder," the Voice calmly threatened.

"If you turn it up, it doesn't mean I'm going to watch it," Adam said.

The Voice sighed. "I was going to give you the chance of watching the film of your own volition, but because of your poor attitude, it looks like I'm going to have to give you some encouragement. When was the last time you ate a meal or had a drink, Adam? You were playing football yesterday, your body must be dehydrated after all that exercise, it's only a matter of time before your body's thirst for fluids will force you to cooperate."

"Why are you doing this?" Adam asked nervously, the realization of how precarious his position was slowly knocking some of the feistiness out of him.

"It's irrelevant what I'm doing, all you have to understand, my disciple, is that I'm doing it, and you need to obey me. One thing is certain, Adam, if you want to eat or drink again, you need to watch this film. When the film is finished, I'm going to ask you twenty questions about it, if you don't get ten of those questions right, then you don't drink, if you don't get fifteen right, then you also don't eat. Is that simple enough for you to understand, my disciple?"

"You drugged me—I've got a headache!" Adam moaned. "How can you expect me to study the film when my head's pounding like this?" When Adam didn't receive an answer to his question, he added, "Anyway, I was always rubbish at history at school."

"I'll tell you this once, Adam, so please listen. You're no longer back in the cosseted world of the schoolroom. In my study room, no excuses are accepted for not doing your homework. You're now in the real world, Adam, a world where you need to try and remain focused. Remaining focused and studying hard is the only way to ensure that you ever eat or drink again. Do you understand what I'm saying, my disciple?"

Adam understood, all right. "You're a raving fucking loony!" he shouted.

The Voice laughed, letting his laugh's echo hang in the air. "I'm not a lunatic, Adam, I'm just a patriot trying to save this country. And by the way, in future when you address me you will call me sir. I'm afraid that lapse in etiquette means that you need to be punished, and you'll therefore get less food even if you get fifteen questions right."

"That's not fair—sir."

"You'll find nothing is fair in Britain in 2019, Adam. Is it fair that Slovaks bombard us from Eastern Europe with economic migration? Is it fair that Poles get the jobs in Britain that young white Saxons should be getting? Let's not even start on Somali gangsters and Yardi criminals. Anyway, Adam, you've got plenty of time to learn about such things, and trust me, Adam, if you want to live, you'll learn."

With that, the Voice ended his sermon. Adam was going to try and sleep, and then he felt his stomach rumble, and the dryness of his throat made him realize how dehydrated he was. Adam sat up and started to watch the film. From his position in his CCTV enclave, the Voice watched and smiled, thinking about how his new disciple had just taken his first step on the road to his soul's salvation.

CHAPTER 6

The house was a normal suburban house on a residential street. DS Sandy Offord and DC Andrew Platt got out the car, walked up the cracked concrete garden path and knocked on the paint-flecked front door. Adam Fowler, the missing teenage boy they'd come to see the Fowler family about, had been missing for three days, and his parents were distraught. In the Scandinavian-themed living room, Mr. and Mrs. Fowler sat next to each other on the cream sofa, while DS Offord stood and talked and a seated DC Platt wrote notes.

"And you say he never came home after playing football?" Platt asked, clarifying Mr. Fowler's statement before he wrote it down.

"He's been missing for three days," Mr. Fowler stated. "It's so unlike Adam. He always tells us what he's doing, where he's going."

"Has he got a girlfriend?" DS Offord asked.

Mrs. Fowler nodded. "I've checked with Kirsty. She hasn't heard from him since Saturday morning."

"They're always on the phone with each other," Mr. Fowler offered.

"None of his friends from college have seen him either," Mrs. Fowler told the detectives, having already made some enquiries.

"Has he been unhappy about anything recently?" Offord asked, desperately looking for something that would unravel this mystery.

"Adam is always happy, easy going—the model son," Mrs. Fowler said.

"Would he have any reason to run away?" DS Offord asked.

"Of course not!" Mrs. Fowler snapped, angry at the inference her son wasn't happy.

This was the part of the job Offord hated. Asking families about disharmony, looking for reasons why their son would run. One look at the hard stress lines on Mrs. Fowler's tight-lined face showed Offord how stressed she was, and Offord quickly concluded this was a family torn apart. Offord didn't want to add to her anxiety. "Please don't get uptight with me, Mrs. Fowler. In the case of a missing person, we always have to ask these questions."

Mrs. Fowler's face softened. "I'm sorry, Sergeant, I'm under a lot of stress."

Offord understood. What parent wouldn't be when faced with the ultimate horror of all horrors, a missing child? "If you could give us a list of all his friends, write down his interests. Tell us anything he likes to do. Anything you can give us, no matter how seemingly insignificant, might help us in our search." Offord made sure he said, might. He didn't want to give the Fowler family false hope.

The Fowlers took the notebook that Platt gave them and wrote down everything they could think of. When they'd finished and handed the notebook back, Mrs. Fowler said, "Adam isn't a boy that goes off doing things without telling us, Sergeant. Acting like this is so unlike him, so out of character."

Mr. Fowler hugged his wife. "Let's not jump the gun, love."

Yes, let's do, Offord thought. *When kids do something unusual, disappeared, because of the cruel society we live in these days, I always think the worst.* He tried to give Mrs. Fowler some hope. "Try and keep an open mind, Mrs. Fowler. Maybe your son has been seeing another girl, and he's run off with her."

Mrs. Fowler's face reddened and suddenly filled with horror. "Adam and Kirsty are besotted with each other. There's no way Adam would cheat on Kirsty."

"Adam and Kirsty are strong," Mr. Fowler confirmed. "Don't waste your time on that angle, Sergeant."

Offord was going to keep an open mind. The last time Adam had been seen was in the changing room after he'd finished playing in a football match Saturday afternoon. There'd been no sightings of him since he left the changing room. At the moment, they had nothing. Offord and Platt, by going through the list of friends, would at least be doing something. Offord had found out in other cases over the years that hope could be a fleeting thing and was something that could be snatched away instantly by a horrific discovery of a body. Offord hoped, for Mr. and Mrs. Fowler's sake, this wasn't going to be just such an occasion.

CHAPTER 7

Adam had slowly edged to a position close to his cell door, was currently pulling and prodding at the bars, looking for signs of weakness. The door was solid, the aging brickwork of the cell walls had been reinforced with concrete so that, without some kind of tool to loosen the concrete, they were impregnable. There were no weaknesses Adam could find in his prison, no chink in his prison's armor enabling him the opportunity to escape. As Adam studied the bars in great detail, the cell's speakers suddenly crackled to life, and his captor's voice suddenly boomed from them, "Get away from the bars, Adam!"

Adam slowly stepped back from the bars, explaining, "I needed to stretch my legs, sir."

The Voice momentarily laughed and then said, "I'm not an idiot, Adam. Please remember that in this cell you're under constant CCTV surveillance and that any attempt at trying to escape is pointless. As a punishment for your act of defiance, I'm going to stop your water for twelve hours."

"I was only stretching my legs, sir," Adam pleaded.

"I'm not stupid so don't treat me as if I was, boy.

Twelve hours without water as punishment for your feeble attempts to escape will hopefully make you understand that your will is now my will, that you now do what I want you to do."

"I'm trying to do what you want, sir, please don't take my water away," Adam begged.

The Voice laughed again. "You've no idea what I want, my disciple. The young have no idea what they want. You're like a rudderless ship adrift on the ocean. I have so much to teach you, my boy, lessons that I'm willing to teach you so you can embark on your mission for the good of the nation. Did you learn anything from my teachings so far, Adam?"

"I've learned that I need to obey, sir."

The Voice lapsed into silence, quietly contemplating what Adam had just said. Unquestioning obedience was the only way that the new world the Voice was aiming for was going to be achieved. It could only be achieved through ruthless efficiency. Adam learning the necessity to obey his captor was a small first step on the road to true enlightenment. "We've got a long way to go, Adam, but I'm pleased with your progress to date. If you keep making progress at such a good rate, then soon you'll be ready for Stage Two of your training."

"What's Stage Two, sir?" Adam asked. He was trying to keep the Voice talking in the hope of finding some humanity inside this kidnapping monster.

"Stage Two is where you get to become a part of the glorious revolution. Stage Two is where you get the chance to serve your country, Adam." The Voice let his call to arms hang in the air a moment, adding: "Are you ready to serve your country, boy?"

"I'm ready, sir!" Adam said, standing to attention for the benefit of the camera.

"A good answer, my disciple. Such clear dedication

to the cause won't go unrewarded. For giving me such a clear message of your devotion, I shall only deprive you of your water ration for ten hours instead of twelve."

"Thank you, sir," Adam said, as he showed how far his understanding of his situation had developed. Adam had learned that he had to tell this psycho whatever he wanted to hear if he was going survive.

"Now, Adam, it's important that you study the film carefully. To get to Stage Two, you need to prove that you're worthy of the trust that the British people will be putting in you. I've decided that you need to study harder, learn with the intensity that's necessary for the path to salvation. From today on, you need to up the intensity of your study. From today on, you need to get seventeen out of twenty questions correct to earn your food ration." The Voice was expecting his disciple to erupt into a fit of fury. When he didn't and blandly acknowledged what the Voice said without protest, the Voice was extremely pleased.

The Fuhrer blasted out another speech to the massed Brown Shirts listening at a Nuremburg rally. At the end of Hitler's speech, the Brown Shirts cheered with the raucous fury of true believers. The Voice listened and watched Adam's reactions on the TV monitor. The Voice knew that the time was rapidly approaching when he'd start slipping scopolamine into the boy's food. After a few weeks of brainwashing, his new disciple would be ready. Adam, carefully studying the projection on the wall, had no idea what awaited him. He had no idea that very shortly, as the Voice's new disciple, he would be unleashed on an unsuspecting world.

CHAPTER 8

The police interrogation room was quiet, as DI Machin and DS Roberts sat opposite Ian Bailey, leader of the Sussex branch of the far right English Patriot's Party. A former police detective, Bailey showed an irritating indifference to being brought in by the police. He knew how the police worked, understood that after a violent terrorist action the Counter Terrorism Command needed to be seen to be doing something. Bailey, who resembled a sergeant major, remained silent.

Machin decided to knock him out of his reverie. "I gather you know why you're here, Mr. Bailey."

Bailey sat back and stared hard into Machin's clear blue eyes, trying to assert dominance. "I've got no idea. The EPP is a law abiding party, so when the police ask me to help them with their enquiries, I'll always willingly come forward."

Machin calmly held his stare. "You must've seen the news about the suicide bombing," she pressed.

Bailey shrugged. "The media in this country is no longer run by the British. It has long since been infiltrated by Asian academics. Why would I listen to their propaganda?"

"I take it you know the details of the Brighton bombing," Machin pushed, finding it hard to remain neutral.

"I heard about it," Bailey admitted. "That poor kid, resorting to this desperate solo act of defiance against the government for failing to listen to white kids' problems."

"Why am I not surprised that you defend the bombing?" Machin remarked.

"I'm not defending it. The kid was obviously sick of everything he saw going on around him. Something in his head must have flipped, and he thought that the only way he could draw attention to his plight was by this desperate act." Bailey reflected for a moment. "The government should be looking at the reasons why the boy felt the need to do this? Why he felt that the country was in such a state that this was the only way he could get his voice heard."

"This was an evil act of terrorism that has now killed twelve people, Mr. Bailey. Surely as an ex-copper, you're not defending this heinous crime," Roberts said.

"Of course, I'm not!" Bailey snapped. "All I'm pointing out is the need to understand the circumstances that could lead a boy to do this."

Machin let the mood cool a moment then said calmly, "The EPP are our number one suspects for being involved in this."

"Ridiculous!" Bailey said.

"Ridiculous that a party that's always shouting off white supremacist claptrap and preaching racial intolerance could be involved in this," Machin quickly retorted.

"You can think what you like about the EPP, but one thing you have to realize is that we're a party of the ballot box. We're certainly not involved in violence. As you pointed out, as an ex-copper, I'd never be involved in breaking the law."

Machin calmly read from a sheet in front of her.

"Your party was taken to court last year because the police thought that you petrol bombed a Polish builder's yard in Worthing."

Bailey sighed. "Exactly, the police thought we were involved, but if you'll note, the jury decided otherwise."

"You were still suspects," Roberts stated.

"We proved in court we were innocent," Bailey said, unruffled.

"Lunatics who petrol bomb a builder's yard are capable of murder," Machin said.

"The builder's yard attack wasn't by the EPP, so please stop making it sound like it was," Bailey told her.

"I was just generalizing, Mr. Bailey," Machin stated. "Okay, let's say that we believe that you didn't bomb the builder's yard."

"Considering we were cleared by the court of all involvement, that's very good of you, Inspector," an irritated Bailey remarked.

"The fact is, you're around people with far right views. Being around such people, you must hear things. If anybody can tell us if this is a far right terrorist group, it's you." Machin let Bailey take in what she'd said. "If you've heard any rumors, or if you know a group out there who's capable of this, then please let us know now, Bailey."

"This was the random act of a misguided soul, Inspector," Bailey concluded.

"The bomb was detonated by a teenage boy, a teenage boy who doesn't know enough about the world to commit a random act like this. To take such action, this boy must have had outside help," Machin stated convincingly.

"Well, if he did have help, the EPP didn't give it to him."

"I'm not saying you did, but you probably know a man who did," she pushed.

Bailey was irritated. The EPP always kept inside the boundaries of the law, and yet the police were always hassling them. It was time he made things clear. "Nobody I know, or anyone involved with the EPP, did this. If you keep making unsubstantiated allegations that we're involved in this, then I'll have to consult my lawyers." Bailey paused so Machin could digest what he said. "At the EPP, we're a legitimate political party that do things through the ballot box—"

"The ballot box!" Machin snapped. "Don't make me laugh."

"In the local council elections recently we gained a lot of seats. The EPP are making strong electoral gains among the voters. A random terrorist act like this is abhorrent, Inspector, and is something the EPP would never be involved in."

"Well, someone is involved in it," Machin countered.

"Whoever it is, it isn't us," Bailey stated confidently.

Machin didn't know what to make of Bailey. She was trying to understand the man and his motivations, to see whether his party was capable of terrorism. Could an ex-copper turn to the dark side of terrorism? "So, the EPP is a party of politics. That being the case, I need you to tell me of someone on the far right scene who isn't into politics, someone who champions more direct action."

"I can't think of anybody," Bailey said.

"This isn't going to go away, Mr. Bailey. Now that the far right has been linked with terrorism, you can no longer sit on the fence. The threat of violence by the far right will decimate your electoral support as people turn away in horror from your politics of hate. If you ever want to be taken seriously as an electoral party, it's in your interests as much as ours to stop things like the Brighton bombing from happening."

"I can't help you with something I know nothing about," Bailey grumbled.

"Maybe not, but we need answers," Machin suggested. "Because of the loss of life, the press will show vitriol toward your party over this. The police have to give them something. I'll have to tell them that we've been talking to you and show them that we're looking where we should be."

"This is virtually blackmail, Inspector!" Bailey snarled. "You're making it sound like the EPP might be involved when we haven't done anything. You're destroying my political career just when it's taking off—"

Roberts laughed. "A council seat on a run-down Brighton housing estate, it's hardly Number Ten, Downing Street, Mr. Bailey."

"It's a seat where I can make a difference," Bailey declared. "Now that I'm on the local council, the EPP can try and make some worthwhile changes involving local issues."

"I'm sure you'll change the world," Machin remarked sarcastically.

Bailey remained resolute. "Every politician has to start somewhere. I wasn't born into the right circles, wasn't given a hand up like Cameron, Johnson, and some of the other political mainstays. What I've got, I've earned through hard work and diligence."

"Before you leave here, you're going to write down anybody on the fringe of fanaticism in far right circles who you think might have been capable of this," Machin demanded.

"Nobody I know is capable of this."

"If you're not involved in the bombing, you've got nothing to fear by talking to us, Mr. Bailey," Machin pressed. "Your help would mean that instead of being a suspect you suddenly would become an invaluable information source on the Brighton bombing."

"And my name would stay out the press?"

"Provided I find that the EPP has no involvement in this heinous act, then I'll do my best to keep your name out the press," Machin reluctantly agreed. She didn't like making any kind of deal with people with such prejudiced views as Bailey's, but in this case, if it led to them finding out who'd brainwashed John Chambers into evil acts of murder, then she was willing to make a deal.

"It's hardly a cast-iron guarantee," Bailey grumbled.

Machin sighed. "It's all you're going to get."

Bailey leaned forward and rested his weary head on his hands. After all the police had put him through in recent years, it now looked like they'd successfully enlisted his help. "After years of the IRA and Islamic extremism, the British people have made it plain that they want politics, not violence. For any of my party to be involved in this would be madness, Inspector."

"Just help us, Bailey," Machin pleaded.

Bailey took a notebook and pen and reluctantly began to write down anything he could think of that might help the police. Machin decided that Bailey was backed into a corner, and it was the only thing he could do to save his party's reputation. She concluded that Bailey had shown all the assets necessary to make it in the cutthroat world of politics, and that was by following the mantra that every time there was a whiff of scandal, always look to save yourself.

CHAPTER 9

ounter Terrorism is too dangerous," movie director Clay Thompson told his girlfriend, DI Machin,
when she'd arrived home late in the evening after
nearly twenty-four hours on her feet.

"Please, Clay, not tonight." Machin was knackered
and in no mood for an argument and one of Thompson's
infamous lectures.

To his credit, Thompson sensed her mood and his
bulk wandered off into the kitchen to make them tea.

Machin sat on the sofa and rested, momentarily closing her eyes and contemplating the horror of her recent
life. She'd joined the police force not just as a career, but
to genuinely make society a better place. It was certainly
a better place after she'd killed the serial killer, Peter
Rivers. The press had dubbed Rivers the ringmaster after
the discovery of a selection of wedding rings from his
victims' fingers found in a silver tobacco tin among the
killer's possessions. Rivers had a number of aliases, and
never stayed in the same place for any length of time, and
Machin had come to the conclusion that the police would
never get to the bottom of all of his crimes. A line had
been drawn under the investigation, and they'd all moved

on. The mental scars Rivers had left all of them with did not mean it was a better place they'd mentally moved on to.

She awoke from her doze with a start as Thompson gently shook her awake to give her the tea he'd made. Machin drank it and contemplated recent events. The murder of Thompson's wife, Jodie, by a mugger and the murder of Machin's boyfriend, Nick, by Rivers had made an unbreakable bond between the couple. Outsiders who hadn't suffered the violent losses Machin and Thompson had suffered would never understand it. The suffering and need for revenge had led Machin to dark places, places where avenging Nick's death was all that mattered. She'd questioned her right to go on as a policewoman after gunning down Rivers in cold blood—a murder witnessed by Thompson that he'd vowed never to mention. She had serious doubts about what motivated her in her job since then.

"The newspapers say the bomber was a fifteen-year-old kid," Thompson said, sitting next to her on the sofa and putting a reassuring arm around her tired shoulders.

"His name was John Chambers, and he disappeared on the way home after a visit to a skateboard park with friends. There was a missing person's report out on him. His parents say he wasn't a troubled child, was happy in his home life. They couldn't think of a reason why he would run away." Machin stared into Thompson's warm, sensual eyes, and at this moment of her greatest need, his chubby face seemed to hold a depth of kindness and understanding that she badly needed in these awful times.

Thompson held her in his arms while she cried. These were the tears that Machin would never let her colleagues see. Any sign of weakness would be frowned upon by her juniors, and Machin had no intention of showing any to them. When Thompson led her to bed, Machin didn't protest. As his calming, delicate touch brought out sensations in her body she'd never known were there before, she knew in those moments she could briefly forget all that had gone before. His bad-boy Hollywood reputation in the years before his marriage to Jodie was fully justified, Machin reckoned, because no man could be so good at making love unless in the past he'd slept with numerous ladies.

When Thompson's phallus searched deep inside her, it found what it was looking for, the depth of her soul, the essence of everything that made up Sarah Machin as a woman. As he ejaculated, she knew that after a year with Clay Thompson, legendary British film movie director, she was in no doubt about being in love with him, and that love meant she couldn't imagine a life without him.

CHAPTER 10

The toilet was a bleach-smelling relic of Victoriana. It was from the days when public convenience structures were built to last and also had a certain authority and style about them. Bailey carefully made sure that nobody was following him and then entered through the mossy concrete doorway. Inside the porcelain palace, Jimmy Clayton, a man Bailey turned to in delicate situations, was waiting.

Clayton's tight-lined smoker's face was edgy. Rumor had it, from those in the know, that he'd just returned from a well-paid mercenary operation in the Middle East. Bailey didn't know or care about Clayton's military activities. All that concerned Bailey was that he could utilize Clayton's abilities to help him now.

Bailey glanced around, licked his lips, and wrung his hands. He was sure he was being tailed by the police. If he wasn't, after the Brighton bombing, then the police were being deficient in their duty. "Is the toilet clear, Jimmy?"

Clayton smirked. "It's clear, Bailey, don't wet yourself."

Bailey ignored the slight. Clayton had always been a

man of harsh words and direct action. "The EPP have got a big problem, Jimmy."

Clayton laughed. "I could've guessed that myself by the fact that you wanted to meet me. Nobody brings me in unless they've got a big problem."

"The police had me in to talk about the Brighton bombing. They're trying to pin this atrocity on the EPP. If they succeed, then it could put the far right's cause in Britain back a generation." Bailey tried to, but couldn't, keep the fraught sound of desperation out of his voice, and mad Jimmy Clayton was not a man who you wanted to sound desperate to.

"Two generations, if you're lucky," Clayton predicted gloomily.

"As the police have had me in for questioning, I'm assuming they must be following me."

"Undoubtedly. I trust you took all the proper precautions when you came here." Clayton had long ago decided that the EPP were bungling amateurs, but had quickly put aside his doubts about them since their money was as good as anybody's.

"Don't worry, I know what I'm doing," Bailey said. Clayton doubted it but didn't comment. "If I can't prove that the EPP weren't involved in this, then I've got no chance of ever being re-elected."

"And are you involved in this?"

"Of course not, Jimmy. How could you think that I'm involved in this shit?"

Clayton stared at Bailey and wondered how such a violent activist from the past could become this weedy third-rate politician. "I remember how wild you used to be in the old days, Ian."

"The old days were a long time ago," Bailey curtly told Clayton. "Anyway, even at my wildest, I was never this stupid."

"You were reckless, Ian. You might try and close the book on it and invent a fictitious past, but someday a reporter is going to uncover the darkness, old son. When they uncover that darkness, your party will be finished."

Bailey was lost in a moment of silent reflection. He had done some things back then he'd rather forget about. He'd never been arrested, and there was no film footage of him having been involved in violent acts—all the things that stopped you from having a successful police career or hindered a man's rise in politics. "Whatever you want to call those days, they're well behind me, and I'm now a legitimate politician who's going to stand for the EPP in the next general election in a Brighton Ward."

"Something you won't be able to do if some mad terrorist group has come along and blown all your good work away."

"Exactly—and, for this reason, I've brought you in, Jimmy."

"So what makes you think the boy wasn't just a pissed off patriot acting on his own?"

"Don't use the word patriot in reference to this lunatic," Bailey grumbled. "If he was a patriot, he wouldn't be involved in this shit. Patriots don't ruin the far right's cause just at the moment when we're starting to make an impact in British politics."

"You might protest at what he did, Ian, but we both know from the past and your dark side, that deep down you agree with direct action."

"I'm a politician. Of course, I don't agree with murder," Bailey countered irritably.

"Okay, Ian, if that's your political stance then you stick with it," Clayton said, though Bailey couldn't help noticing the cynical smirk on the man's face as he spoke.

Clayton walked to the entrance and looked out the door, checking for police surveillance. Bailey said he hadn't been followed, though Clayton decided there was no harm in making sure. When he was happy, he came back to Bailey. There was a momentary silence when all that could be heard was the cold drip of cistern water and the distant rumble of traffic from the nearby road.

Bailey finally broke the silence. "Enough chit-chat, if the police are following me and they saw me come in here, they're going to wonder why I'm taking so long," Bailey said.

Clayton agreed.

"What I want from you is a list of fringe lunatics of the far right in Britain that might be capable of this atrocity, and I need that list fast, Jimmy."

"It won't be easy," Clayton stated.

Bailey took an envelope from his pocket with two thousand pounds in it and handed it to Clayton.

"That's your expense money. When you give me a list of names, there'll be a further two grand for you," Bailey said. "You have far right sympathies because of your past, Jimmy. You, of all people, know how important this is to the EPP that we prove we've got nothing to do with this."

Clayton knew and had been quietly pleased that the far right, under the leadership of Toby Henson and his EPP, had gained a scattering of seats in the recent local council elections. If they couldn't prove non-involvement, then the limited support they had would be gone. Even if they could prove it wasn't them, Clayton wasn't sure after this far right atrocity that the EPP vote could be saved.

"Chambers didn't act alone," Clayton stated. "I've looked at the CCTV footage on the internet of the boy before he detonated the bomb, and he looks like he's on drugs. In my travels, I've seen people brainwashed and tortured, Ian, and from what I can see of the footage, this boy, when he committed this act, didn't seem to have a will of his own."

In his mercenary days, Bailey had no doubts that Clayton had seen the depths of depravity that man was capable of, so when Clayton said that Chambers had been drugged, Bailey took note and listened. "So where does this leave us, Jimmy?"

It left them with a big headache, Clayton concluded. The whole attack reeked of fanaticism—fanaticism the boy with his social standing and becalmed school life shouldn't have been capable of. As Clayton sat in the toilet cubicle and waited for Bailey to be well clear of the area before he moved, he reckoned the way the attack had been carried out had cleverly avoided any connection to the real attacker. It meant that whoever had carried it out was bright and intelligent. Were they bright enough not to make any mistakes? If they were not, then Clayton was soon going to find out.

CHAPTER 11

Adam lay on his lumpy bed, watching grainy black and white Nazi images being projected from a camera outside the cell onto the dank concrete wall. From the speakers, Hitler's voice boomed with his usual rhetoric of hatred and non-compromise. Adam was desperately trying to read the subtitles translating what Hitler said. Unlike at school where he'd been a bit of a ditherer, today there was no time for dithering. All that he learned from the film needed to be enough to get most of the questions right in his captor's quiz that was soon to follow. Adam had never been any good at history, but he was good at simple mathematics. After another of the Voice's lectures, he quickly understood that not giving enough correct answers equated to failure in the eyes of his master and would mean he'd receive no food or water that day.

Suddenly, the film cut out and the cell was locked in a tense blackness and silence. In the background, Adam could hear the static from the cell's sound system, a sound Adam was now getting acquainted with. It was a sound that always heralded the arrival of his tormentor. Adam tried to sit up. His head was spinning, and this was making him unable to think straight. In a short while, his moment of destiny would come in the form of a quiz where, if he didn't get enough questions right, it meant that he could easily die.

"Are you ready for your questions, Adam?" the Voice asked, though Adam realized it wasn't really a question as there was no option other than to answer.

"You drugged my drink, I feel ill," Adam said weakly as he looked for ways to stop this mental torture.

"It was just a sedative to help you relax, my disciple, there was nothing in the drug that can do you any harm," the Voice lied as he thought about scopolamine, nicknamed devil's breath, and what it could do to the mind if administered correctly.

"My head is spinning, sir. I don't think I'm capable of answering the questions feeling like this."

"You have to be strong, my disciple. For the task that lies ahead of you, there's no time for weakness. What I've given you will only help you. The only meaning in your life, Adam, is to fulfil your destiny. You've now seen the movies, learned the facts, have seen how ordered and controlled life can be when you don't mix the races. Your people are becoming the minority in their homeland, Adam, are you happy with that?"

"I don't know, sir," Adam mumbled, feeling very unwell.

"You don't know!" the Voice shouted. "You don't know about the mess that your country is in. Haven't you noticed that you're fast becoming the minority in your own land, boy? Haven't you seen the vast influx of migrant workers from Eastern Europe?"

Adam's head was pounding. He was being bombarded with facts the way the Voice saw them. Adam didn't know what was real or false any more. The drugs that were being filtered into his system via his food and water made judgement impossible. He thought about not drinking or eating anything, but the rations that his captor supplied him with were all that was available, and they were barely enough to keep him alive as it was.

"I don't understand any of this, sir," Adam said, resting his head in his dirty hands.

The Voice sighed. "Now is the time to listen and learn, Adam. I'm going to explain to you why you need to fulfil your destiny. Before you leave here, you will understand why there's a need for you to do what you have to do. The fact that you've been bold enough to tell me that you don't understand what's required of you at least shows that you're listening. I shall make you a promise, my disciple. When you leave here to fulfil your patriotic duty, you will be ready and will have no doubts what's required of you. I shall leave you to go back to your studies—"

"I haven't had the questions, sir. I haven't eaten."

"Today there will be no questions, Adam. I'm pleased with your progress. Today you shall have your meal without answering any questions. Today you shall see how benevolent I can be when you show a willingness to learn. Please, carry on watching the film and learning. Shortly, your lunch will be served."

"Thank you, sir," Adam said, then, just in case his tormentor changed his mind, he went back to studying the film.

The loud Brown Shirts' marching music pounded through the speakers as Adam watched yet another Nazi torchlight parade. As his food and drink were slipped through the door bars of his prison, Adam knew that the food and drink were laced with drugs. He looked at them, momentarily wondering whether he should eat and drink them. It was only a brief hesitation. Without them, he was dead, though he also knew that once he'd eaten and drunk what was given him, his captor would have even more control over Adam's life. As he picked up the water bottle and drank, in his head, he could picture his captor smiling at him. As he started to eat the weak soup his captor provided, Adam knew that the drugs would very soon make him lose any will he had of his own. As he sat and pondered his future, he realized that the Voice would soon have complete control over him and from then on the Voice would have his new disciple.

CHAPTER 12

Machin and Roberts sat opposite DCI Asif Khan in his blandly decorated but efficiently organized office. Khan was a straight-talking boss who demanded to be brought up to date on any progress in an investigation. There'd now been fifteen deaths as a result of the bombing, plus a number of walking wounded who'd be permanently disabled. The Brighton bombing was a situation for which the public and press wanted answers. Khan was surrounded by photos of his smiling family, but the general aura of happiness in the pictures wasn't reflected in the scouring look on Khan's lined face as he reviewed their progress report.

"The public wants someone arrested quickly for this, Machin," Khan said, adding, "Nobody believes this boy acted on his own—this boy wasn't capable of planning this without outside help."

"We brought Ian Bailey, local EPP activist, in for questioning. Unsurprisingly, he denies any involvement," Machin reported. "Since the bombing, we've had him and some of the leading far right activists under surveillance, but so far we've come up with nothing."

"After Brighton, they know they're being watched,

so they're not likely to make any mistakes," Khan reck-oned. He wasn't shocked by the bombing. With Islamic terrorism on the rise and threats from the new IRA al-ways out there, Khan was more surprised by the direction that the bomb had come from rather than the actual bombing.

"After some threats, Bailey gave us the names of fa-natics on the fringe of the far right. I've got people in the team checking them out, but I get the feeling that Bailey is only trying to tell us what he thinks we want to hear, sir," Machin predicted glumly.

"I still want all the names checked out," Khan said. "With the depth of public outrage surrounding the bomb-ing, we can't afford to be seen to be anything other than proactive on this." Khan had already had the press and the Home Secretary badgering him for answers which he didn't have. "What do you think of Bailey's claims that he's innocent?" he asked her.

"I know he's a piece of filth, sir, but in this case, I tend to believe him. After their recent electoral success, what would the EPP have to gain by becoming involved in terrorism?" Machin concluded.

What would they have to gain? Khan thought. Nothing was the only answer he could come up with. "Maybe one of the names Bailey gave us will know something," Khan said more in hope than in expectation.

"I think we're looking for an independent not a ter-rorist cell, sir," Roberts said. Roberts was confident in his abilities, was never shy about coming forward with an opinion. "I think we're looking for someone that either Bailey or his cronies know. Bailey is an ex-copper, he knows how we operate, he's going to just tell us the min-imum he has to so we back off."

"If he's not involved, it's in his interests to help us find the bastards," Machin remarked. "All the while these nutters are out there it's doing irrevocable damage to his party's chances of future support."

Khan decided that was the only positive to come out of this. The bombing showed the depths of depravity of the far right lunatics, making the EPP unelectable to the British people. "If you're right, Sergeant, then it means only one thing," Khan said, "whoever is doing this has got a taste for it and is likely to strike again."

And from the worried looks on Machin's and Roberts's faces, Khan was sure they agreed with him, and, like him, they knew that the clock was ticking speedily against them if they were going to be able to prevent further atrocities.

CHAPTER 13

It was mid-morning on a warm autumn day. The Folkestone street was busy, a bustling community, a wide diversity of humanity congregating for various purposes. This street was in the heart of bedsit land, a land where all the unfortunate dregs and desperadoes of society came together. Years ago, it would've been filled with single men and young single mothers, who were too far down the council's waiting list to ever aspire to the ultimate goal of a council home. The inhabitants of the street in the twenty-first century were just as desperate. In the twenty-first century, it was full of a new kind of desperation—the desperation of poverty, immigrants who'd flocked to Britain using the last of their meagre resources, hoping that their economic migration to Britain would find them a better life in what everybody told them was the land of milk and honey.

After the Stagecoach bus pulled to a halt at a bus stop in the middle of the street, slowly passengers began to disembark. First, a young mother wrestled her pushchair down from the step, her sleeping baby oblivious to the world around her. Behind her, a hand-holding old couple stepped from the bus and ambled off in the direction of the sea front. The last passenger to exit the bus was a boy with a mesmeric stare. That boy was Adam. Adam was on a mission, a mission that the Voice had been lecturing him about for the last couple of weeks, a mission that the master had said was vital for the saving of Britain.

Once the bus pulled away into the trundling traffic, Adam stopped for a moment to survey his surroundings. The Voice pounding in his head was incessant, uncompromising in the way it was telling him what to do. The Voice was always there, would make sure that no mistakes would be made by him here today. Slowly, Adam walked along the street surveying his surroundings. His probing eyes were immediately drawn to a nearby wall where a group of male Slovakian immigrants sat smoking and talking in the glaring autumn sun. As Adam approached them, they continued talking and ignored him. When Adam suddenly stopped walking and turned to face them, they finally noticed Adam's presence. As he stood at attention in a parade ground military fashion, Adam suddenly had their interest. If any of them had taken the time to look at the boy beforehand, they'd have noticed the glazed look of drug-induced insanity in Adam's eyes. If they'd bothered to examine him more closely, they would have seen that he had the eyes of a disciple, the uncompromising glare of a boy on a mission.

If they hadn't noticed him before, as he pulled out the Beretta 92FS handgun from a shoulder-holster hidden beneath his Fred Perry jacket, he suddenly had their undivided attention. The only thought racing through Adam's mind was to clinically and coldly obey the master's orders. With the precision the master taught him, he opened fire on the men on the wall, each shot killing and maiming, his robotic actions oblivious to the pain and suffering he was causing all around him, unhearing of his victims' screams. As the last bullets in his ammunition clip had almost run out and the bodies lay dead and dying all around him, Adam stood proudly at attention and stopped firing. Staring straight in front of him, he was lost in the drug-induced world of the Voice's creation. As one of his wounded victims edged slowly toward him, and just before the victim was about to jump him, Adam, as instructed by his master, turned the gun on himself and pressed it hard to his temple.

"Britain for the British!" he shouted and then pulled the trigger.

The bullet from his Beretta splattered his blood and brain mucus all over the ground. As his lifeless body fell to the pavement among the dead and wounded, a woman hurried to where her husband's dead body lay. On seeing the lifeless, cold stare in her husband's unflinching eyes, the woman screamed, unleashing all her anguish and pent-up fury. Disbelief and dismay were Adam's legacy, alienation and unrest his weapons, death and disharmony had proved, sadly to all those in this Folkestone street, his gospel, on this now far-from-beautiful autumn day.

CHAPTER 14

Where the Slovakian bodies had recently lain in the now-silent Folkestone street, there was now a hotbed of police activity. The area had been cordoned off, and a police forensic team, wearing white protective suits and latex gloves, were busily at work. Outside the cordon, DI Machin and DS Roberts were trying to talk to a witness. The witness, Mr. Balog, one of the men who'd been sitting on the wall when Adam started shooting, had lost many friends in the atrocity. His hands were shaking, and he was smoking nervously as he vividly relayed the horror of the shootings.

"I know this is traumatic for you, Mr. Balog, but anything you can tell us about the shootings while it's still fresh in your memory could be invaluable to our investigation," Machin prompted.

Mr. Balog was the best English speaker of the witnesses. The others would have to wait for the interview room and the presence of the interpreter.

"The kid was a lunatic," Balog said, his tight-lined nicotine stained face alive with tension. "When he stopped near where my friends were sitting, I knew, by the strange look in his eyes, that something was wrong."

"What kind of look?" Machin asked.

Balog thought carefully. "It wasn't normal, his actions were robotic, as if he was being controlled."

"Could he have been drugged?" Roberts ventured.

"Maybe. It all happened so quickly. After he pulled out the gun and started shooting, everybody panicked and dived for cover. While he was firing the gun, it was chaos," he told them, tears welling in his eyes. "Once he'd killed all those people, he turned the gun on himself, shouting something about Britain, and then committed suicide."

Balog stood in a moment's silent reflection then stubbed his cigarette out on the wall. He told Machin that his cousin had been wounded and taken to the hospital, and he needed to go and see him. Machin let him go and would take a written statement later. She stared along the street at the tape markings near the wall showing where the bodies had fallen. There were six bodies in total. Six men had been killed in the shooting and two wounded. Machin thought about the lives of these men and their families being wiped out by this lunacy. The way the boy had attacked, similar to the style of the attack of the Brighton bombing, had left her in no doubt that the teenage boy who'd committed this atrocity was part of the same brand of insanity.

"It all happened so quickly, ma'am, nobody could've stopped him," Roberts said.

Machin walked to the bus stop where Adam had alighted from the bus a few hours earlier. She studied the bus timetable affixed to the bus stop. Roberts joined her.

"The woman we spoke to earlier said that the boy got off the bus about eleven o'clock," Machin reaffirmed, studying the bus timetable which showed that a Dover to Folkestone bus arrived at the bus stop around that time.

"According to the timetable, he must've gotten off the Dover bus."

Roberts took out his mobile phone. "I'll get onto the local bus company."

"If you're quick, we might get the driver before he finishes his shift. We need to speak to him while everything is fresh in his memory. Some buses have got cameras, or maybe he'll remember where the boy got on the bus," Machin thought aloud.

Roberts went and sat on a nearby wall to make some calls. Machin looked at the street that would now be forever etched in the minds of the locals as the street where brutal murder had taken place. The bodies were now starting to stack up. Witnesses confirmed that the shooter had a strange mesmerized look on his face as he'd started shooting. With the evidence that Machin and her team had now accumulated from both crime scenes, she had no doubt that the two attacks were connected. It showed that the loonies carrying out these terror attacks weren't going to stop. Time was racing against her, but then again, hadn't it always in all her past cases? In any terrorist investigation, the main goal was to stop the perpetrators from carrying out their attacks. Unless Machin and her Counter Terror colleagues stopped them soon, then the ethnic tolerance that had bound Britain together for the past fifty years was about to fall apart.

Then there was always the possibility of a vigilante, unimpressed by the police's efforts, on the lookout for vengeance. What would the targets of the attacks do in retaliation if the police didn't stop these senseless murders? If there was retaliation from the victims and if the terrorist attacks continued, then it was a recipe for anarchy and mayhem. It was a world that Machin tried not to think about, a world of dark and menace, a world that the Britain of the twenty-first century wasn't ready for. The terrorists had to be stopped, Machin concluded, for if they weren't, then she and her colleagues would be facing many sleepless nights thinking about the evil about to happen.

CHAPTER 15

ailey hated coming to London. London was an ecliptic mix of multi-cultures and diversity, and, therefore, in Bailey's eyes, a cesspit. The EPP headquarters were the upstairs offices of an old plumbing firm in Camden Town. The offices were regularly targeted by anti-Nazi demonstrators, trying to bully the EPP into inactivity. For those that worked for the party in London, the threats were a constant. It meant that security at the offices was tight. As well as CCTV cameras everywhere, there were also three heavily locked doors to bypass, and a security guard post permanently maintained at the headquarters' entrance.

After the recent terrorist attacks which were now being linked to a far right terrorist group, most of the public looked at the EPP as a legitimate target on which to vent their fury.

As Bailey entered party leader, Toby Henson's office, he could see by the tense lines and sweat on Henson's nervous face that he was not managing the current situation very well. Once Bailey was seated opposite him, Henson stated the obvious. "This is a bloody mess, Bailey."

Henson had a penchant for stating the blindingly obvious, Bailey thought. It was only the fact that he had a lot of connections that had secured him the party's leadership, that and the fact that his inherited wealth bankrolled the party. "Not a mess of our causing," Bailey tactfully reminded him.

"Two terrorist attacks linked to the far right within a few weeks. If this nutcase carries on with these meaningless attacks it'll destroy our support base forever," Henson predicted pessimistically.

Bailey had news for Henson—now after the second attack, their support had probably already gone. He decided it was time that Henson faced up to reality. "After these last shootings, our chances of getting any votes in the local elections is virtually nil, Toby."

"Which is why we need to do something," Henson suggested.

"And what are we supposed to do? Counter Terrorism Command and the police are going at this full throttle. What could we possibly do that they're not already doing?"

"You were a police detective for five years, Bailey, maybe you should look into it."

At last, they were getting to the real reason for his summons, Bailey thought. He didn't like where Henson was going with this. "I can't get involved in police matters, Toby."

"For the good of the party you have to," Henson insisted.

Bailey couldn't mask his irritation. "And what am I supposed to do?"

"Just spend some time looking into it. You must have some connections from your time with the force. Ask around, just see where it leads."

"I've got connections, but whether they want anything to do with me after these terrorist attacks, I've got no idea."

"We need to do something—at least try to find out who's behind it," Henson pressed.

Bailey could see there was going to be no way out of it. The party's needs and his now-fledgling political career had to be accommodated. If there was ever going to be a chance of any future support from the voters, then the maniacs who were doing this had to be found and stopped. "I'll look into it for the party," Bailey promised.

"Good man," Henson said.

Bailey stared out the tinted glass window in a moment's reflection. "Don't you find all this suspicious?"

In Henson's eyes, it looked like a lunatic fringe terrorist organization loosely attached to the far right. He didn't understand Bailey's point. "How is this suspicious, Bailey?"

"The EPP has suddenly become a prominent force in the South of England, and, just before campaigning starts for the local elections, these random acts of supposed far right terrorism occur, destroying any support that we might have."

"Who knows the mind of a lunatic?" Henson said.

"That's just my point, the clever way these kids seem to have been kidnapped and brainwashed is not the work of a lunatic. The way they're used in these suicide attacks doesn't strike me as the unintelligent workings of an insane person. Whoever is doing this is a person of extreme intelligence, the work of someone who's clearheaded and methodical in all they do."

"Brainwashing kids and sending them out as suicide bombers, isn't intelligent, Bailey. Sending out a kid as a gun-toting assassin—how can you not see that as anything other than lunacy?" Henson pressed.

"Think about it, Henson, who's got the most to gain

from all this terrorism linked to the far right?"

"The only people who gain from this are our enemies," Henson concluded.

"Exactly, so maybe I won't just limit my investigation to far right loonies," Bailey stated. In all his years on the force, two as a detective, he'd learned that you should never take anything for granted, and people's duplicity meant that things weren't always what they seemed.

"So you're saying it could be our enemies making it look as if we're the culprits," Henson summarized. "Do you really think any of our enemies are capable of this?"

"I've seen the hatred in their eyes as they shout at us when we have a parade. If they could frame the far right for these atrocities, then they know it would finish the far right in Britain for good."

The more he said it, the more Bailey thought it made sense. A lot of the leftie loonies would love to see support for the far right, after the recent resurgence, waver. Were they evil enough to murder innocents for their cause? Bailey didn't know, but one thing he was certain of, when he left a worried-looking Henson's office a couple of hours later, he was determined to put all his efforts into finding out.

CHAPTER 16

Any town or city in England on a Friday or Saturday night would do, the Voice thought as he trawled the streets of Margate in his car in the early hours of a Saturday morning in late September. He'd long ago realized that the young were like a rudderless ship without any destination. Alcohol was the escape valve for the terminally weak. The brewers were willing to supply that weakness with their constant new inventions of ever more trendy ways of weaning the young off fizzy drinks and onto booze. As the nightclubs were chucking patrons out, the Voice's eyes were waiting and watching in his bogus taxi parked in the shadows. The perfect specimen could only be obtained through careful observation and selection, he'd once thought. Now he believed, after his two successes, that any teenage boy could be brainwashed, using his superior brainwashing techniques.

Along the street from where he waited and watched, a group of teenagers stumbled out of a nightclub door, laughing and joking and looking decidedly the worse for wear. A boy in the group tripped over a loose paving slab and drunkenly fell to the ground. The girl and the other boy slowly picked the fallen boy up. As they walked off up the street, a drink-fueled argument was breaking out among the group as drunken accusations started to fly. The Voice was always alert to trouble, always ready at the right moment to make his move. Just when the argument reached its zenith, the taxi that the Voice was driving slowly pulled up alongside the teenagers. The Voice slowly stopped and wound down his window.

"Did you wave me down?" the Voice asked.

The teenagers' argument stopped. Chelsea, the girl in the group, was about to say no, then she suddenly changed her mind. She turned to her boyfriend, Brad. "The only way we're going to go to this party is to send Craig home."

Brad, who'd been trying to get Chelsea alone all evening, quickly decided that the taxi was the answer to his prayers. Craig started to protest, but Chelsea and Brad finally persuaded him that he was too drunk to party and then bundled Craig in the back of the cab. Chelsea handed the Voice Craig's home address and a tenner, and then the Voice drove off into the night. When the cab had gone, Brad immediately moved closer to Chelsea and put his arm around her. Now that his loser mate had gone and Brad was off to the party alone with Chelsea, he realized how things had suddenly picked up for the better. Abandoning your best mate in times of trouble on a night on the raz' so you could get closer to a girl—now that, Brad quickly decided, was what the true spirit of being a best mate was all about.

CHAPTER 17

The café was in a quiet Brighton side street in the Lanes. When he was a cop, Bailey had often used it as a place to go to get a break from the daily grind. After his meeting with Jimmy Clayton the day before, and Clayton telling him that, as far as he could see, there was no link with any extremist element of the far right in the terrorist attacks, Bailey had nowhere to turn. He trusted what Clayton told him—Clayton knew everybody inside or on the edge of neo-Nazism in Britain—and if he couldn't find a link, then Bailey decided there wasn't one. He was now desperate. To make headway, he needed to explore other avenues.

As he sipped his coffee and stared out the steamed-up window at the misty rain, he saw her appear furtively from out of an alley and hurry across the pavement to the café doors. DS Jacobs had a nervous look up and down the street then decided it was safe to enter. Inside, she got herself a steaming mug of tea from the counter and then came and sat opposite him.

"I didn't think you'd come," Bailey said. He looked into Jacobs's tired gray-brown eyes and could see that the years on the force were starting to have an alarming effect on a face that was once so alert and vibrant.

"I nearly didn't," Jacobs admitted.

Bailey remembered the good and bad times of the spell when they'd been partners. There'd always been a mutual sexual attraction between them, but neither had ever done anything about it. "After what we went through together, I'm pleased you found it in your heart to help me."

Jacobs laughed. "Don't start all that old comrade twaddle, Ian. When you left the police and joined the EPP, you forfeited all rights to be treated with anything other than contempt."

"The fact that you came shows that you must still have a soft spot for me," Bailey said, holding her stare.

"Since you joined them, you're out of bounds as far as the detective division is concerned," Jacobs stated coldly.

Bailey glared at her. "I've just as much right as anybody else to pursue a career in politics."

"Maybe you've got every right to go into politics, but going into politics doesn't mean getting mixed up with fascist loonies like the EPP."

"They're not loonies!" Bailey snapped.

"Of course not, Ian, they're just misunderstood patriots," Jacobs quipped sarcastically. She had seen the bodies piled up on Brighton sea front, murdered in cold blood by these lunatic fascist terrorist killers, now she was starting to have second thoughts about agreeing to meet Bailey.

"In the English council elections, we got one hundred twenty-three seats," Bailey told her in a bold attempt to stamp a badge of legitimacy on the proceedings.

"A pinprick in the political process," Jacobs said.

"We're the up and coming force in British politics," he stressed.

She laughed. "After the recent terror attacks attributed to the far right, your support is going to dwindle. I presume that the terrorist attacks are the reason why you asked me to come here."

"The EPP has got nothing to do with those attacks," Bailey promised. "Why would we do anything like that and risk what we've gained?"

Jacobs sighed. "I hope for the sake of our past relationship, as ex-colleagues, that you aren't lying, Ian. Something deep inside me tells me that the loyal, caring partner I once worked with could never be capable of such evil."

"We're not terrorists, Ellen, we're elected politicians who believe in the democratic process," he emphasized.

"That's not what the task force investigating the Brighton bombing and the Folkestone shootings think."

"I'm going to say this to you once, Ellen. I was your colleague for two years, and, in that time, you came to know what I'm capable of. Do you really think that I, or anybody that I would choose to become associated with, could be capable of committing such atrocities?"

On the table, Bailey tried to rest his chunky fingers on her slender hand, but Jacobs quickly pulled her hand away.

"Even if I believe you, it still doesn't change the fact that you're tainted by all this," she said.

"I couldn't kill anybody, Ellen," he pressed.

There was a moment's uncomfortable silence—since his affiliation with the far right EPP, Jacobs didn't know what to believe about her former colleague anymore.

"And the belief that you couldn't be a part of this horror is the only reason why I'm here."

"DI Machin wants me to come up with a name of someone I think might be doing this," Bailey imparted.

"You move in those circles, I can understand why

Machin would think you might be able to come up with a name," Jacobs said.

Bailey was irritated by the way his ex-colleagues seemed to casually think he could be involved with terrorists. It was time they got their facts straight. "It's not the far right the police should be looking at. The EPP has had electoral success, a success that has probably pissed off a lot of people. With the recent success we've had at local elections, why would we upset the apple-cart by getting involved in terrorist actions?"

Jacobs sipped her tea a moment, while she thought about it, and finally offered, "After these recent atrocities, the press and the public want a witch-hunt. The bomb and the shooting changed everything, Ian. After those attacks, you and your party are not going to be viewed in the same light by the electorate as you were before."

Bailey could see things weren't going as well as expected and decided it was time to bring up the subject of past-owed favors. "Remember Webster."

"I knew you'd bring up Webster," she moaned.

Webster was the reason Jacobs was here. She owed Bailey for Webster. Webster, the brutal drug dealer they were close to collaring, had come after Jacobs, and Bailey had been waiting to cover her back.

"I saved your life, Ellen," he said, though he took no pleasure in bringing the matter up as he'd hoped that Jacobs would help him because of their former friendship rather than because she felt she owed him a debt.

"And I'll be forever grateful to you for saving my life," Jacobs said, adding, "Too many people are waiting and watching over this. I can't help you with this, Ian."

"You help me with this, Ellen, and I promise you that I won't ask you for anything ever again," Bailey vowed.

Jacobs didn't want to get involved in any of it. She

didn't want to, she shouldn't have to. She recalled the Webster incident, and the fact that she'd be dead now if Bailey hadn't intervened. "If the task force finds out about this, my career could be over," she warned him.

"They won't find out."

"They'd better not," Jacobs told him.

"You have my oath, Ellen. You help me with this, and nobody will ever know where the help came from."

Jacobs had always found that, in her time working with Bailey, he was someone to be trusted. Could he be trusted now? Were the EPP involved in this? If they were, giving him information could only make matters worse. Jacobs had spent her whole career in the detective division, going with her gut feelings on things. In this case, she was sure Bailey would never do anything to hurt her. She took a chance. "And what exactly am I looking for?"

"I want you to take a look at the files for left wing extremists, people capable of direct action."

"And you really think that some anarchist is capable of killing all these people to set up the EPP?"

"Nobody on the far right would do this—the EPP are winning votes in elections. I've had a person who knows everything about the far right looking into this, and he's confirmed that the far right is not involved in this," Bailey stated, adding, "Nobody on the far right scene would ruin their recent electoral success by committing these atrocities."

Clayton knew almost everybody on the far right of politics and had told Bailey that the days of the direct action of the 1970s and 1980s were long behind them. Bailey believed him.

Jacobs shook her head. "You frighten me sometimes, Ian. No, let's make that, these days, you frighten me all the time."

"Get me some names, and I'll look into it. Anything I find I'll make sure I tell the police," Bailey swore.

"Don't do anything stupid," Jacobs said.

"I won't, Ellen, I just don't like the fact that our party is being set up."

Jacobs came to a decision. "I get you those names, then I never want to hear from you again."

"I thought we were friends, Ellen?"

"The moment you got involved with the EPP, we ceased to be friends, Ian."

It was a sad, brutal fact, Jacobs thought. Since his association with the EPP, Bailey had made himself untouchable for anybody within the police.

"Ignoring a friend because of his politics, that's harsh, Ellen."

"When they're the wrong kind of politics, that's how it has to be," Jacobs stated coldly.

"We're an elected party," Bailey declared.

Jacobs stared at him, deciding that a few meaningless seats in local council elections didn't give a party any power base. "It's all a facade, Ian. If I looked into the EPP, I'm sure I'd find many skeletons in their cupboard."

"Let's not argue, Ellen. We both believe in different things. You just get me some names, something to work with. After you get me those names, I promise you you'll never hear from me again."

"Because of Webster, I'll get you those names," Jacobs decided, "but after you've got them, I never want to hear from you again. Is that clear, Ian?"

"Painfully so," Bailey said reluctantly.

"Give me a disposable mobile number. Once we're finished, I want that phone destroyed."

Bailey wrote down a mobile number and promised, "The moment you've given me what I want, then I'll ditch the phone."

"This is the last time we ever meet like this, Ian." Jacobs stood up. "Don't try and contact me again."

With that, Jacobs left. Bailey watched her go. They'd been close, very close. The debt she'd owed Bailey for blocking Webster's lunging knife thrust was shortly to be repaid. Webster was dead, and, somehow, Bailey had summoned the strength to turn the knife back on Webster and pierce it through his heart. Bailey had spent a month in the hospital. It had been touch and go if he survived the severe internal knife wound. Bailey had survived. He was stronger and harder as a man for the experience. It was during his time in the hospital that he'd had time to think—it had given him the chance to recharge his mind and formulate his plans. The world of the Websters and their malignancy had to be changed if ever Britain was going to be a better place.

The EPP was the party that was going to give Bailey the launch pad to make a better world. That was until the Brighton bombing. The Brighton bombing had changed everything. The Brighton bombing meant that Bailey's dream seemed to be becoming an ever more distant chance of reality. Bailey needed to change his destiny. Hopefully, Jacobs would give him a means whereby he could make that change. Bailey drank the dregs of his coffee and quietly left.

CHAPTER 18

DI Machin's office wasn't as homely as some DS Roberts had visited during his career. Machin had been the same in her time at the Twickenham nick. Machin wasn't a woman who liked anything getting in the way of an investigation. Roberts had come to her office to tell her some important news. It was news he was sure that Machin would want to hear. She'd be irritated. "Bailey's tail came up with something, ma'am," he said.

"Good, that's what tails are for," Machin said.

Roberts decided his boss wouldn't find it so good when he told her what it was. "The tail followed him to a discreet café in the Brighton Lanes, and, in that café, he met his old partner, DS Ellen Jacobs."

"Jacobs knows we're investigating Bailey. What the hell is she doing talking to him?" Machin snapped.

"I don't know, ma'am," Roberts said, and he truly didn't know. Bailey was an ex-colleague that no detective should've been talking to.

"Jacobs talking to Bailey undermines everything." Machin was nonplussed, she knew that Bailey and Jacobs had been partners when Bailey was on the force. Whatever they were, Jacobs shouldn't have been talking to him outside of task force channels.

"They met for about fifteen minutes. They probably both took action to lose any tails and thought it was safe to meet there."

"We need to find out what they met about, Roberts." This was where an investigation got messy, Machin thought. When ex-police were involved, there was always a chance of an investigation being compromised.

"Only Jacobs and Bailey know what was said in their meeting, ma'am," Roberts informed her.

"We need to talk to Jacobs," Machin concluded.

"I've arranged a meeting in Interview Room Three in an hour. Jacobs thinks it's case-related," Roberts said.

It was case-related, Machin thought. Jacobs had put their whole investigation at risk by talking to her ex-colleague. Machin didn't understand what was going on here. Why would someone who'd recently been promoted to sergeant risk her career for a creature like Bailey? The moment he left the force and became involved with the EPP, they should've had no further contact between them. Machin needed to know why Jacobs had met Bailey, and there was only one place they were going to find those answers, and that was in Interview Room Three in an hour.

CHAPTER 19

When Jacobs was seated, she was conveying all the wrong messages with her body language. If Machin wasn't sure that Jacobs was doing something she shouldn't be doing, one look at her cautious colleague made her convinced now she was. Jacobs fidgeted nervously in her seat. "You said this was important, ma'am," Jacobs said.

"Very, sergeant," Machin said, "You were seen in a café off the Brighton Lanes with Ian Bailey."

There was an uncomfortable silence. Finally, Jacobs said, "he's my old partner, he just wanted to talk about the old days."

"He's a possible suspect in a major terrorist investigation, sergeant, you shouldn't be going anywhere near him," Machin fumed.

"I'm sorry, I didn't think - we often meet to talk and see how we both are," Jacobs apologized. "I've been doing this ever since he left the force, ma'am."

"He's got a police tail on him," Roberts told Jacobs.

"When you've worked with someone for a couple of years you can't just ignore them," Jacobs insisted.

"You can when they're a terrorist suspect," Machin said.

"I was only meeting an old colleague for tea and a chat," Jacobs stressed.

"So you're saying that the meeting was just socializing?" Machin pressed.

"No, Ian rang me and asked me to meet. He told me that he had nothing to do with the attacks and was just as horrified by the murders as we are."

Machin laughed sarcastically, "Well, he's not going to admit it, is he, sergeant?"

"I worked with him for two years," Jacobs stated, "and he's not capable of murdering people like this."

Machin was irritated by Jacobs's attitude. "You've heard some of the far right's rhetoric—their hate and intolerance—so don't try and tell me that none of these loonies are capable of this."

"I didn't say none of them, ma'am, I said Ian Bailey isn't," Jacobs reiterated.

"He's a far right fanatic, knows people that have previously been involved in far right violence, maybe it's you who needs to understand that Ian Bailey isn't the man he once was when he worked with you."

"I was his partner and got to know his personality inside out, Ian Bailey isn't capable of murder."

Machin was angry. Jacobs's stupid meeting was in danger of compromising the whole operation. "What I don't understand is that you knew he was a terrorist suspect," she said, "and yet you still went ahead with the meeting."

"There were things between us when we were partners—he once saved my life," Jacobs told her. "When someone saves your life, you don't discard them that easily," she admitted in all honesty.

"Has it ever entered your head, Sergeant, that he's

playing on past allegiances and using you to cover up his terrorist activities?”

“If I thought he was involved I wouldn't have talked to him, ma'am,” Jacobs said.

Machin had seen detectives' blind belief in a partner's infallibility before. Sometimes it was misguided. “Whether he's done anything or not is still open to debate. What exactly did you talk about in your meeting?”

“He told me that he's being set up,” Jacobs said.

“I bet he did,” Machin remarked, her voice laced with sarcasm.

“He reckons that left wing extremists are trying to implicate the far right by committing these awful atrocities,” Jacobs stated.

“Well, he would say that, wouldn't he, sergeant?”

“Like I told you, I worked with him for two years - Ian Bailey isn't capable of this,” Jacobs said. She didn't say he wasn't capable of killing someone. Machin had read the report about Webster's death, of the way Bailey had turned the knife on Webster and run him through. That action alone showed he was capable of killing in a bid to protect.

“So, in this meeting, what did he ask you to do?” Machin asked.

“He didn't ask me to do anything, ma'am.”

Jacobs had denied too quickly, Machin was convinced the meeting had been arranged by Bailey so he could enlist her help for something. “You're involvement with a terrorist suspect like Bailey means that you could be very close to suspension,” Machin threatened.

“You can't suspend me for this, ma'am,” an irritated Jacobs argued. “When I agreed to meet him it could've been for anything. Maybe I thought he was going to give me information about the terrorists, confide in me because I was an ex-partner rather than through the usual channels."

"You should've come straight to me after the meeting," Machin stated.

"He was my partner…"

"This is not a man you want to associate with, Jacobs."

Jacobs lapsed into a moment of reflective silence. "I understand, ma'am, I won't see him again," she finally promised.

"If you see him again, I'll make sure that you're suspended," Machin said. "Do I make myself clear?"

"Yes, ma'am."

Machin decided to leave it at that. There was only so far you could push this. If something underhand had taken place in that café between Bailey and Jacobs, one thing was certain, Jacobs wasn't going to tell Machin about it. A ruffled-looking Jacobs went back to work.

Later, Roberts asked, "Do you think she'll see him again, ma'am?"

"I hope not," Machin said, though she wasn't sure. With the bad judgement that Jacobs had shown by meeting Bailey in the first place, there were no guarantees. "I want Jacobs followed, sergeant, if she goes anywhere near Bailey again I want to know about it."

"After your interview, she'll be expecting it, ma'am," Roberts reasoned.

Machin knew she'd now alerted Jacobs to the fact that they knew about her meeting with Bailey. Jacobs had seen Bailey over some misguided sense of loyalty. Machin prayed that any loyalty she felt for Bailey wouldn't cloud her judgement. If it did, Machin would make sure that one of her team was there to see it, because if Bailey was involved in any of these heinous acts of terrorism, then Machin was going to make sure that he didn't get away with it.

CHAPTER 20

In his claustrophobic cell, on a cold, damp night, Craig lay asleep on his lumpy bed. Suddenly, Nazi marching music boomed through the cell's speakers. On the wall, a film of a Nazi Nuremburg rally flickered to life. Craig slowly awoke as the violent assault on his eardrums made sleep impossible. His tired eyes tried to take in his surroundings. At first, his mind played tricks on him when he thought he was at home in his bedroom. As his eyes cleared and his senses clarified, Craig could see he wasn't at home, and this bland concrete cell had none of the adornments of home. The plain austerity of his situation bewildered him. He sat on the edge of the bed and tried to clear his head. His thoughts were locked in drink-fueled memory. He remembered being with Chelsea, he had visions of drinking too many alcopops. Vague images of a drunken night of revelry skipped through his head in a series of alarming flashbacks. As his eyes finally focused on the Nazi film being projected on the cell's wall, his mind was in complete turmoil. None of this made any sense, and he wondered if this was his friends playing some kind of sick joke or whether it was a nightmare he was shortly going to awake from.

Just as his mind was totally lost in incomprehension, he heard a voice.

"Good, I'm glad you're awake, I was getting worried about you," the Voice crackled through the speakers.

Craig didn't say anything, Craig had no idea what was going on here.

"You'll never know how relieved I am that your alcohol binge hasn't caused you too much damage, my disciple."

The Voice from the speakers had called Craig his disciple. Craig had no idea why he'd been bestowed such a title. He tried to remember back to what had happened on the previous night. He could remember being in some pubs. He'd been pissed up in a nightclub and had fallen over. He looked at his grazed knee beneath his jeans that was starting to scab over. He could remember his friends, Chelsea and Brad, bundling him in a taxi. It was shortly after he was in the taxi that events became weird and disjointed. He could vaguely remember the taxi stopping. After it stopped, the driver had come to the rear of the car and opened the back door. Craig had been too inebriated to fight him as the taxi driver thrust a chloroform rag over Craig's face. That was the last image that Craig could remember before lapsing into unconsciousness. Although the Voice was distorted by the crackling microphone, Craig could still tell it was the voice of the taxi driver.

"Who are you?" Craig shouted. "Why have you brought me here?"

The Voice laughed. "Everything will soon become clear to you, my disciple."

"Why do you keep calling me your disciple?" Craig asked then gingerly stood and walked around his cell, studying his prison. After a brief study of the thick concrete walls and the solid steel bars of the door, he quickly decided there was no escape from his cage.

"I call you my disciple because that's what you now are," the Voice explained.

Craig couldn't take the pounding in his head of the marching band music. He sat back down on the corner of his bed and rested his weary hung-over head in his hands. "Why am I here?" The fact that he was locked in a cell by some weirdo probably told him all he needed to know about the situation. People only locked you in cells for sinister reasons. Whatever was going to happen to him here, it was going to be something bad.

"Maybe you should ask yourself that question, my disciple?"

"None of this makes any sense. I was on my way home—"

"You're here to serve your country. You've found a new home," the Voice interrupted, turning the music down. "Look at yourself, Craig. A strong boy like yourself lost in a world of booze, so drunk on a night out that you allow yourself to be taken prisoner by a nutcase. Because of your actions, you've allowed yourself to be forced into a position whereby you could be used and abused by all and sundry."

"Why do you talk about me serving my country?" Craig asked. "I'm not in the army, I'm not a soldier."

"That's where you're wrong, my disciple. From this moment forward you've become a soldier in the army of Britain. If you're confused, don't worry. Soon I will explain everything to you, soon you'll have a purpose."

"My parents haven't got any money."

The Voice laughed. "How quaint, my disciple, after all I've just said to you, still you're unaware of what's going on here. Misguidedly, you think this is a kidnapping."

"Dad lost his job last year, so my parents can't afford a ransom—"

"Don't concern yourself," the Voice interrupted. "I'm not going to extort money from your parents. This isn't about your family—this is about your duty to this country. Have you noticed how the white indigenous people of Britain are fast becoming the minority, my boy?"

"Why would I?" Craig snapped.

The Voice wasn't impressed. "I'd like to say that I'm shocked, but I'm not. Your apathy is the reason why this country is the shit hole it is today. Maybe if your generation looked at politics now and again, instead of playing Playstation games, you'd realize this is your generation's last chance."

"Last chance for what?"

"To save this island."

"Save it from what?" Craig asked, not understanding any of his captor's rantings.

"Are you blind, Craig, can't you see what's going on around you?"

"If I could see, I wouldn't be asking," Craig grumbled.

"Muslims, Craig, Muslims have big families, big families grow into bigger families, and very soon Britain is swamped. Have you noticed your streets being swamped, Craig?"

"What are you fucking talking about?" Craig shouted, angry and confused.

"That's the last swear-word you will utter in here, Craig. Any further swearing, and you'll be severely punished."

"You're a loony," Craig retorted.

"That outburst means that you'll be going without food for twelve hours," the Voice threatened.

"Fuck off!"

"One more outburst and you won't be given any food

or water for twenty-four hours," the Voice threatened him.

"Starving teenagers, is that how you get your kicks?" Craig demanded.

The Voice laughed. His laugh seemed to be louder and more threatening over the sound system, its echo menacingly reverberating around the cell walls. "I'm pleased with you, Craig. Rather than being angry at your newfound passion, I'm pleased your passion shows you've got spirit. Having spirit is a good thing, but the only problem with spirit is you have to learn how to channel it in the right direction."

"You do talk a lot of bollocks, mate," Craig said defiantly.

"A couple of weeks from now, I'll remember that you said that. For the moment, you need to watch the movie and learn."

"I'm not watching the film," Craig told his captor.

"Don't be stupid, Craig, this isn't something you've got a choice in," the Voice warned.

"You can't make me watch the film. If I don't want to watch the film, I'm not going to," Craig stated in defiance.

"I'm afraid that's where you're wrong, my disciple. In the next few weeks, you're going to find I can make you do anything I want you to. Whether you get sustenance depends on your ability to answer questions about the film. You need to understand this, Craig, you need to understand that if you don't answer these questions, then you aren't going to eat or drink again."

"You can't be serious!" Craig shouted.

"I'm deadly serious."

"You can't expect me to remember any of this old historical crap," Craig said irritably, his mind racked with horror as he looked at the images on the wall.

"Well, that's a pity, my disciple, because you'll either remember it, or you'll starve to death in your cell. Do you want to starve to death cold and alone in your cell, Craig?" the Voice asked, letting his words hang in the air. "Look at the film, Craig," the Voice ordered when it was clear that Craig wasn't studying the film.

"This is madness," Craig finally commented, completely stunned.

"No, Craig, this is your chance to do something positive in your so far worthless young life. What you learn from me in this cell gives you a chance to do something worthwhile, a chance to serve your country."

Craig was agitated, didn't know what to say or do. His captor was so crazy he wouldn't listen to any of Craig's protestations. Craig could not fathom any of this madness, he simply had no clue what his captor wanted from him. "What do you want from me?" he asked in desperation, in a feeble attempt to understand what was going on.

"What I want will be made plain to you over the passage of time." With that, the static died on the speaker system, and the Voice was gone.

Suddenly, the music was turned up louder. Booming Nazi marching songs bounced off the cell walls. The silence from his captor left Craig in no doubt that their conversation was over. Craig wanted to shout and protest, kick and scream, to grab this lunatic's attention. Instead, he covered his face with his hands to cut out the pounding in his head. Craig had never felt so helpless in his life, and one thing seemed definite. Trapped in this prison at the mercy of this lunatic, he was living his own personal version of hell.

CHAPTER 21

DS Jacobs, dressed in a tracksuit, folded up some paper and put it into her back pocket. She looked out of her window at the street below her apartment. It was still dark, but in the glow of the orange streetlight, she could see the faint outline of the bored-looking cop, who had been tailing her, sitting in his car. She glanced at her watch, it was six a.m., the usual time for her early morning run. Outside, she jogged up the street past her tail's car, smiling to herself as her tail ducked low beneath his dashboard as she ran past.

She ran at a sedate pace toward the park, making sure she did nothing unusual to alarm her tail. As she ran into the park, the first purple-gray flickers of the rising sun started to brighten the horizon. In the middle of the dewy park, she jogged alongside a mildew-coated pond toward a tree-lined path. The path passed through a cluster of dark secluded trees. In the middle of the damp trees, Ian Bailey stepped out from behind a brown-leafed bush to confront her.

"Have you got it?" he asked desperately.

"I've got it," she said. She'd rung Bailey on his mobile, warned him that the police had observed their meeting, and told him that they were both being tailed. She took out the sheet of printout from her tracksuit pocket and handed it to Bailey. "That's everything I could find out on active left-wing activists."

Bailey quickly looked at the printout. It was a selection of militant workers, anarchists, Communist agitators. "Thank you," Bailey said as he slipped the printout sheet into his jacket pocket.

"You're too dangerous to be around, Ian, I never want to hear from you again," Jacobs told him.

"You won't," Bailey promised, and then Jacobs ran off up the path that led back out the trees.

Bailey stepped back into the damp, dewy, spider-web-encrusted bushes. He stood and waited silently—he would wait at least an hour until Jacobs was well clear of the area.

Bailey had lost his tail last night after he left the Italian restaurant, decided a tail was only any good if you didn't know it was there. Bailey knew it was there. He would, therefore, use it for his own devices. When you were being hounded by the police, when they were trying to stitch you up for a crime you hadn't committed, then it could be no other way.

CHAPTER 22

In his flat, Bailey slumped on his sofa, studying the names on the printout Jacobs had given him. As he looked at the list, nothing became clear in his head. Could any of these lefty loonies really be capable of these atrocities? he wondered. He wanted to believe it was one of them, he needed it to be one of them. If it wasn't, then, for the world, it left a far right fanatic out there completely undermining everything that British democracy believed in. Bailey wasn't a fanatic, or that's what he would have liked the world to believe. He believed in a strong Britain in charge of its own destiny. He believed in the repatriation of immigrants and in having armed forces that were strong. Officially, what his party didn't believe in was mass murder and the slaughter of innocents, but since World War II, for any far right party, that had to be the standard party line.

He knew there were people from the far right who wanted more direct action, but even they had to see that the recent bombing and shootings were complete madness. The terrorist attacks were playing into the hands of the lefties who wanted to see the EPP banned. The British people would never tolerate an attack on the democratic process, something that none of the fanatics ever seemed to understand. Bailey understood, he understood, as an ex-copper, that you always had to remain within the boundaries of the law, either that, or you had to find ways around such barriers.

The first name on the list was a woman called Susana Reece-Smith. Reece-Smith had been arrested on many occasions for militant activity at demonstrations against capitalism in the City. She'd been involved in scuffles in anti-Nazi demonstrations at EPP marches. She'd taken part in plenty of criminal activities, had a charge sheet that showed her as extremely active in recent years. Whether such activity meant she was capable of mass-murder, Bailey didn't know. There were so many names on the list and so many possibilities. He wasn't a fool and realized that, on his own, he had no chance of quickly unraveling any web of deceit among so many names. If there was anything to be found out, he needed to find it out quickly, before what little chance there was of saving the EPP as an electoral force was gone.

From his time as a copper, Bailey knew people. He had always been one of those reprobates who realized that some crimes couldn't be solved by strict adherence to what rules society placed on their law enforcement. Bailey had learned in his early days that some crimes only ever got solved if you crossed over that line. One woman he'd used frequently to cross over that line was Mori Kemp. Mori Kemp was an elite computer hacker, not just a normal hacker. If there were chess rankings in the hacker community, Kemp would be ranked as a grand master. Bailey selected a new mobile phone from his drawer. He had a selection of phones that he never used more than once before he ditched them. Bailey, as a former detective, knew the pitfalls, what mistakes not to make if you wanted to keep your activities clandestine.

When it was dark, he turned on the TV and some lights and then left discreetly via a garden alley adjoining his property. This was one meeting he definitely didn't want his tail to be aware of. Mori Kemp had spent eighteen months in prison for hacking, but since those days she had channeled her efforts into good, and now worked for major companies as an advisor with reference to weaknesses in their computer safeguards. She didn't come cheap, but what she saved companies, by preventing clients' files from being hacked, made employing her services worth every penny. Kemp was a woman who knew the value of the service she provided. Bailey didn't care what it cost—she was the only hope he had of finding what he needed. One thing he was certain of, as he got in his car he'd deliberately parked a few streets from his house, and that was time was running out for him and his party, time was running out fast.

CHAPTER 23

Machin met Thompson for a coffee in a trendy Brighton coffee bar just off the Lanes. Machin was temporarily based in Brighton while involved in the counter terrorism investigation. Thompson had just finished his latest movie—a heist thriller, starring the actress, Debbie Duncan, as a slick jewel thief. Machin and Duncan knew each other before the film. They'd met on the set of *The Valley of Dreams* in Wales. Duncan had been raped during the filming by the serial killer, Peter Rivers, who'd subsequently been killed by Machin. It was complicated, and Machin still couldn't get straight mentally what had happened that night at the Duncan household. She'd ambushed Rivers and killed him at Duncan's home after Rivers had turned up to complete unfinished business connected to his obsession with Duncan. The fact that she was making movies again showed Machin that, at least, Duncan was getting her life back together.

"Is the movie any good?" Machin asked Thompson as she sipped her cappuccino.

"It's okay. If it wasn't for Debbie Duncan, the script would be barely adequate. Debbie is a superb actress—

with her as the star, she can turn mediocrity into a gem."

Thompson hadn't wanted to make the movie but had been pressured by the studio to make it as Regal wanted a movie out at Easter to cash in on the holidays.

"You admire Debbie, don't you, Clay?" Machin said. To her, it was plainly obvious from the way in which her boyfriend always raved about Debbie Duncan.

"She's a great actress," Thompson said confidently.

That wasn't all she was to Clay Thompson. He was a reformed alcoholic, and Debbie was his support partner. She'd saved him from several wrong moves in his life, especially after his wife, Jodie, had been killed by a mugger. When Jodie was murdered, Thompson had been particularly vulnerable. Much of this Machin had no idea about, and as Debbie would never tell, Thompson intended to keep it quiet.

"Making movies with nice people like Debbie Duncan must be a joy compared to the scum I have to deal with every day," she reflected.

"How's the hunt going?" Thompson asked. He rarely asked her about her work—he had quickly learned in his time with Machin that she didn't like to divulge too much about the cases she was working on.

"It's not going well, I'm looking into far right extremists, and, so far, we've come up with nothing."

Thompson stroked his partner's soft hand across the table, realizing from the tired look in Machin's stunning eyes, that the strain in the hunt for these terrorist maniacs was starting to show. "If anybody can find them, it's you," he quietly reassured her.

For a big man, Thompson could be delicate in understanding Machin's feelings. It was the main quality she loved about him, a quality that made them much stronger as a couple.

"I'm having my doubts," she confided. "The boys

seem to be being kidnapped at random. Nobody sees anything, we've no idea what happens to the boys after they're kidnapped. The only time we see them after the kidnapping is when they suddenly appear as drugged zombies about to commit horrendous atrocities."

Thompson lapsed into silence, remembering back to the night that the serial killer, Peter Rivers, had come for Debbie Duncan. Thompson had been there to protect Debbie. Machin's brutal slaying of Rivers had insured that Rivers didn't escape to kill again. Yes, Thompson knew all about death. "They'll make a mistake," he confidently predicted.

Machin wasn't so sure. At the moment, the police had nothing. The assassins were silent and deadly, both of them had committed suicide either during, or straight after their attack. Machin wanted to believe that the assassins would make a mistake, but, so far, they hadn't made a single one. She was about to suggest that they go back to their hotel room to make love to briefly take her mind off the hunt. As she was about to propose it, her mobile phone rang. It was DCI Khan. He wanted to see her for an update. Sex would have to wait. Lately, it always seemed to be put on the backburner. Counter terrorism was the vanguard in the defense of the nation, and, at this moment, that defense, with the recent suicide attacks, was crumbling all around them.

Thompson told her that he understood, but the lost expression on his face as she rushed off to meet Khan made Machin realize that her lover, like all her lovers in the past, would never understand the all-consuming nature of her work. This was always going to be the obstacle that they'd have to get over if they were going to make their relationship a success, and, with what she felt for this cuddly, wonderful man, she really hoped it was a hurdle they could overcome.

CHAPTER 24

When Machin entered the incident room DCI Khan was standing talking to DS Roberts, they were both attentively studying the information board. As Machin reached them, Khan received a call on his mobile. He answered. After a brief discussion, he became agitated. "You were meant to be following Bailey, Andrews. When you tail someone, you don't lose them," Khan said, giving Andrews a loud ticking off. Khan, who was being hounded by the press and his seniors about the lack of progress in the terrorist hunt, was in no mood for the incompetence of underlings.

Andrews promised Khan that he'd quickly pick the tail back up.

As Khan hung up, his sour-faced expression showed to everybody in the room that he was pissed off.

"Bailey's a slippery bastard, sir," Machin said, "being an ex-cop, he knows all our tricks."

"All the more reason to be careful when you're tailing him," Khan snapped.

"We haven't got the manpower to tail Bailey properly, sir," Roberts retorted, showing his usual balls to senior officers when defending a colleague.

Machin had long ago decided that Roberts was a good man to have in your corner.

"The modern police force is all about budget restrictions. If you can't work within that mandate, you're in the wrong profession, Sergeant," Khan countered deftly.

"If Bailey knows he's being tailed, then he knows all the tricks to lose us," Machin remarked. "Bearing that in mind, sir, surely any tail on him now will be worthless."

There was a moment's careful reflection. Khan wasn't a man to make rash decisions. "The way he lost Andrews shows he's never going to let us tail him," Khan concluded. "Call the tail off Bailey."

Machin got out her mobile phone and phoned Andrews.

Roberts handed Khan a file he'd been holding. "You wanted details of all the missing teenagers in Britain, I had the computer printout all of them. This file contains all the ones that have been reported."

Khan looked through the file. The further he looked through it, the more ruffled he became. "There's more than I expected," he confided.

"Most of them are runaways," Roberts stated. "Some went missing under suspicious circumstances, showing no signs in their previous behavior that they were going to go on the run."

Machin finished her call. "Any one of them could be involved in a new terror attack," she warned, not liking her role as a prophet of doom.

"I've had a detailed look at them," Roberts confirmed. "At the back of the folder, I've listed the five locally that I think are most likely to have been abducted by the terrorists. So far both attacks have been in the South East of England, sir. Until he steps outside that zone, that's the area I'm concentrating all my efforts on."

"This is like a time bomb waiting to go off," Khan grumbled. "Any one of these kids could've been kidnapped for the purpose of being brainwashed and used as a weapon."

Khan handed Machin the file, and she looked through it. Machin quickly realized, by the amount of names in the file, how difficult their task was going to be. There'd been CCTV footage in Brighton and CCTV footage in Folkestone. From that footage, Machin could see that both attacks were well orchestrated. After careful study of the footage, they now realized that both attackers had definitely been drugged and brainwashed into committing their evil acts.

Machin couldn't even begin to understand the depths of depravity at work here. The boys had lived stable, normal lives. Machin had no doubts, after surveying the CCTV footage of the atrocities, that the boys had been kidnapped and forced into committing murder.

"This is an extremely warped terrorist organization, sir," Machin said. "The more success they have, the more confident they're going to become."

"We need to look at where and when these kids went missing. There must be some kind of pattern going on here," Khan suggested, more out of hope than expectation. If there was a pattern, in his experience, there was hope. If there wasn't a pattern, regrettably, they had nothing.

"We'll go through the list, see if we can find something," Machin said.

"We need to stop them before they kill again," Khan said.

"We're doing our best, sir," Machin stressed.

"Maybe we are," Khan said, about to answer his ringing mobile phone. "But is our best going to be good enough?"

As Khan left the room to answer his phone, Machin reflected on what her boss had just said. Was their best going to be good enough in the hunt for these terrorist lunatics that so far had come up with nothing? Would the public be forgiving if they failed to stop this madness? If there were more deaths and a further senseless waste of life, Machin had no doubt that the answer to both her questions was no.

CHAPTER 25

It was night time in the cell, and the only sound to be heard was the inexorable rhythm of snoring from the sleeping prisoner. Suddenly, the darkness was broken by the cell lights unexpectedly being turned on, and the cell was bathed in white light. From the cell's booming sound system, the Voice shouted, "It's time to wake up, Craig!"

Craig didn't move. Instead, he truculently turned on his side so he could no longer see the cell's lights.

"Stop playing possum, Craig," the Voice ordered. "If you don't get up immediately and answer my questions, then the food and drink that you have a chance to earn will be off the table, and it'll be another twenty-four hours before you get the chance to eat or drink again."

Craig reluctantly started to sit up, rubbing his tired eyes and trying to adjust them to the glaring light. In his eyes, the spirit had faded, replaced by a look of hopelessness. "Please, just give me something to eat and drink," he pleaded.

The Voice was oblivious to his pleas and asked methodically, "Are you ready to take your test now, Craig?"

Craig was far from ready. "Do I have a choice?"

"You've always got a choice, Craig. You can choose to kill yourself by refusing to answer my questions. The Britain of today is full of kids who've given up." The Voice let Craig mull over what he'd said. "Just remember that there are always plenty of others to replace you."

"I want to live," Craig begged.

"Good, before we start you need to understand the rules. How much food and drink you get depends on how many answers you get correct. Ten right you get everything, five, half the food and drink. For getting no questions right, you obviously get nothing." The Voice paused so Craig could think about what was required of him. "In the future, I expect you to always address me as sir, Craig, is that clear?"

"So, if I don't get a question right you're going to starve me…sir."

"I'm afraid so. Those are the rules you now live by, my disciple. The sooner you understand those rules, the better off you'll be."

"You have to give me something to eat and drink. Without food, my mind is fuzzy, and I find it hard to concentrate, sir."

The Voice laughed. "Nice try, my disciple. The rules say you have to answer the questions to get sustenance, Craig."

"But you make the rules, sir. You can always change them," Craig ventured. The momentary silence he was greeted with gave him a brief surge of hope.

"Are you ready for the first question?" the Voice asked, leaving Craig now with no doubt that the matter was no longer up for discussion.

Craig gave up, concluding if he was ever going to eat and drink again, he needed to answer his captor's questions. "Give me the questions, sir."

"Question one, what does *Ein Reich, Ein Volk, Ein Fuhrer*, mean in English?"

Craig was mystified. He'd heard Hitler shout it, the inscription of what it meant had been in the subtitles when the Fuhrer had spoken. Craig hadn't read them, the information he was meant to study was bombarded at him at such a rate that he found it hard to take it all in.

"I think *Ein* means one, sir," Craig finally mustered.

The Voice sighed heavily. "All the information required to answer the question has been shown to you, my disciple."

"I never saw it," Craig protested.

"Just because you never saw it doesn't mean it wasn't there," the Voice pointed out. "The information was there if you'd studied the film correctly."

Craig didn't argue. If it was there, he hadn't seen it. "The question's too hard, sir."

"No, Craig, the question isn't too hard—it's your concentration that's poor."

"I don't know the answer to the question, sir," Craig finally admitted.

The Voice laughed. "This is a very bad start, my disciple."

Craig was angry. His IQ wasn't high, and his captor was trying to force him into studying boring history, a subject his mind was naturally averse to. "This test isn't fair, sir."

"Enough!" the Voice shouted. "From the day you became my disciple, you were part of the new order. As a member of that new order, you have to harden yourself to your responsibilities to the Motherland. Now is the time to shed your soft, decadent, Western skin. With the way Britain is today, the time for hardened realism is upon us. If you want food and drink, you have to rid yourself of mental weakness, force yourself to study the films that I show you. Intense study is the only way you will learn the necessary facts to be able to answer my questions, boy."

"I'm sorry, sir, I haven't been feeling very well—"

"In this cell, there's no time for excuses, boy. If you're useless at history, maybe you can understand simple maths, Craig. The simple maths of this situation means answering questions, and that equals food, Craig. If you don't answer questions, you die."

"Why are you doing this? I've done nothing to yo—"

"Your generation has given me no choice but to do this," the Voice interrupted him angrily. "If your generation isn't prepared to fight for their homeland, then it's up to me to teach you how to. I will give you the tools to take that fight to this country's oppressors, but first, before I give you those tools, you have to show me that you're worthy to receive them. Are you worthy of being given those tools, Craig?"

"I don't want to die here," Craig said.

"And, if you do everything I say then you won't, boy," the Voice promised. "If you're not prepared to do battle for your race, then you might as well lie down and die in this cell. Do you want to die in this cell, boy?"

"No, sir."

"Good, then let's get on with the quiz. Question Two, what is the name of the Nazi Party Propaganda Minister?"

"I know this one!" Craig desperately said. "It's Joseph, something…"

"Come on, Craig!" the Voice encouraged. "That sip of water is almost on the tip of your tongue, dancing down your throat."

Craig was desperately trying to think. He remembered the small weasely man standing on the podium speaking. He'd tried to take note, had decided it might be one of the questions that his captor asked him. "It began with a G!"

"That's it, my disciple, you can do this!" the Voice encouraged.

Craig remembered. "It's Joseph Goebbels, sir!"

The Voice cheered. "Finally!"

"Is it right, sir?" Craig asked in desperation.

"It's right, my boy," the Voice said happily.

The Voice decided this was the moment when his disciple suddenly rose up from being a useless excrement to society and became a useful hammer to forge out a brave new world. Answering this question correctly meant his disciple had shown the first makings of a modern Viking warrior. The Voice was more pleased than he'd been in a long time. In the brainwashing process, he'd discovered that his disciples had the ability to learn—once they got over the initial hostility after the capture, he found all his disciples became extremely malleable. "Well done, Craig, by summoning up the knowledge from the back of your mind to answer that question you chose life, my boy. It's only a small step, but by getting that question right, you've proved to yourself that you have the ability to study and retain facts. Now we need to move on. From today, my disciple, the real work begins."

With that, the Voice asked Craig a new question, but this time, when the Voice studied Craig on the CCTV monitor, he smiled as he saw that the boy's face was now locked in concentration.

CHAPTER 26

Bailey parked his car two streets from Mori Kemp's flat and walked the remaining mile to it across a stretch of overgrown common. When he was sure that he wasn't being tailed, he jogged up the three flights of the graffiti-ridden stairwell—past discarded drug needles and crumpled rusting coke cans—arriving at Kemp's door just after seven. He hadn't told Kemp he was coming. With his current pariah status, Bailey had concluded that the less people knew about his movements, the better.

His first knock was ignored. His second, much louder, produced a faint twitch of a curtain, something that at least confirmed Kemp was home. After the insistent thump of the third knock, at last, the door opened on the security chain a fraction, and through the crack, Bailey could see Kemp's dark-brown eyes intensely studying him. "Open up, Mori," he said.

Kemp sighed on seeing it was Bailey. Reluctantly, she opened the door. As Bailey stepped into the lilac carpeted hall, Kemp said, "After you left the police force, I never thought I'd see you again."

"Mutual," Bailey said. "Times and events change

things. Sometimes we don't have a choice what we do in life, Mori."

Kemp laughed, showing the wrinkles on her face, "You were always a deep one, Bailey. I read about you winning that Council seat for that Nazi party you joined—"

"The EPP isn't a Nazi party," Bailey said irritably.

"That's not what the press says," Kemp countered.

"The press is all bullshit and lies," Bailey responded defensively.

Kemp smiled in a way that said she didn't believe him, "If you say so, Bailey."

Bailey hated the press in Britain. The EPP was a legitimate political party who followed the electoral process, so why did the press always attack them when they were voted in fairly? Bailey didn't understand this sham democracy, why a legally elected councilor like himself was harassed so badly by the press.

"I need your help," Bailey told Kemp. "A problem has occurred, and I need your help in fixing it."

"If you want help, go to the Salvation Army, Bailey. Any work I do for you now that you're not a cop, I want paying for," she said. "Anyway, all of that's irrelevant. You know how much I charge. In that little-league world of politics you now mix in, you know that my fees are way beyond what you tinpot Nazis can afford."

"I need you to find some information for me." Ignoring Kemp's sarcasm, he persisted. Bailey had worked with her on many occasions when he was with the police. Kemp was a talented computer hacker. In the age when computers dominated every facet of life, Kemp's services were in high demand.

"You can't afford me," Kemp decided, immediately concluding that Bailey had come there to try and throw his old police weight around. She decided that he was probably looking for a freebee.

"I'll find a way to pay you. The job I require needs the best—frankly, it needs you, Mori."

"You can stop all the sweet talk," Kemp said. "Sweet talk doesn't get you a discount."

Bailey laughed. "I see you're still the hard-nosed cow who never gives an inch."

"It's a tough world out there, I can't afford to be anything else." Kemp wasn't going to let Bailey intimidate her. He had been out of the force for a few years and had no power to make her life a misery any more.

"Remember that I know things about you, Mori," Bailey threatened. He could see by the alertness that quickly appeared in Kemp's nervous eyes that he finally had her attention.

"You're not a copper any more, Bailey," she pointed out.

"No, I'm not, but if I really want to, I can still hurt you."

Kemp thought back to the past and the illegal things with computers she'd done for Bailey over the years, and yes, Bailey was right, if he told the authorities everything she'd done, then it could hurt her. "If you told the police about your former extracurricular activities, you'd be incriminating yourself."

"I would, but think how satisfied it would make me feel if you didn't help me and what I told the police put you back inside," he said.

Kemp smiled. "Maybe I'll call your bluff."

Bailey smiled back. "The police are trying to claim the EPP was involved in the Brighton bombing They're taking so much flak over the number of lives lost in the bombing that they're desperate to arrest anybody for the crime. They need a scapegoat. I know the EPP had nothing to do with it, and the only way I'm going to get the police off my party's back is by proving that fact."

"Should I get out my hanky?" Kemp asked. "Is this tale going to make the tears flow?"

Bailey didn't comment—he would let her have her moment of humor at his expense. He was focused on finding the terrorist killers and needed to make them pay for their mindless attacks that were ruining the EPP's credibility. "I need you to check out some people for me," he persisted. "I need it done discreetly and quickly."

Kemp thought about the damage Bailey might be able to do to her, concluding that nothing would be served by antagonizing him. "As you know, my skills are well sought after. If I work for you, then you'll pay the going rate, is that clear, Bailey?"

"Of course, I'd expect to do nothing else," Bailey remarked.

"Give me their names," she said, thinking the quicker she got this done, the faster Bailey would be out of her life.

Bailey took from his pocket the computer printout that DS Jacobs had given him. He hadn't checked the names out on his own computer. If there were problems, the police would like nothing better than to trace the meddling back to Bailey's computer. "I'm reliably informed that all of these people are involved in the violent left. I need to know if any of them are lunatic enough to be involved with terrorist murders."

"If they are, they're not going to be open about the fact," Kemp stated.

"Obviously, that's why I came to you."

"I'll do it for you, but if I find out that you're trying to involve me in an attempt to cover up an EPP death squad—"

Bailey laughed sarcastically. "You've been reading

the biased press, Mori, the EPP doesn't do death squads."

"If you did, you're not likely to tell me," Kemp reasoned.

Bailey sighed. "And this is what we're up against. In the local elections last year, we made big inroads, even if any member of my party was lunatic enough to commit such atrocities, they wouldn't do it because it would destroy everything we've worked for."

Kemp didn't comment. She had her own thoughts on the matter. That mad Norwegian who'd killed all those people on that island was another far right nut. Kemp decided to do the work for Bailey, but she'd do it as quickly as possible and cover her tracks completely throughout the whole process. "I need half the money up front before I do any of the work."

"How much is half?"

"Two and a half grand."

Bailey baulked at the figure. Kemp was the top of the tree in the local hacking community and obviously knew how to charge for her talents. He needed to find the bastards who were ruining his life. Therefore, he couldn't afford to quibble about cost. "I'll get the money to you by tomorrow."

Kemp usually insisted on the money up front before she started any work. In Bailey's case, she'd make an exception. He always gave her an uneasy feeling. He was a man who trouble always seemed to follow around. Any whisper of her involvement with him would force the police to come down hard on her. Kemp couldn't afford the inconvenience of interruptions at this stage of her blossoming career. She was on the brink of a big City share scam that would soon leave her able to retire to Australia. She needed Bailey off her back quickly.

Bailey handed her the printout with the names on. Kemp promised to start work on them that evening. "Nazism is a dead political force," she said calmly.

"We're not Nazis," Bailey corrected her.

"Not in name, but in your deeds—in your deeds, you're everything that those vile creatures espoused to."

Bailey wanted to lash out and defend his party's position, concluding that Kemp believed what the press reported about the EPP and would never view the EPP as anything other than Nazis. "The left-wing press would love to fit us up with this, prove the EPP were terrorist murderers."

They probably were, Kemp thought. "Anything I get for you, I don't want any comeback from."

Bailey was upset with her. "Mori, what do you take me for?"

"I take you for a desperate man who will do anything to deflect these terrorist atrocities away from the EPP. In my experience, desperate men are dangerous. They don't play by the rules, Bailey."

"Just do what you have to do," Bailey told her. When he thought about the five grand he was paying for her services, he wondered how much Kemp was making. People working outside the law came to her. Criminals, who wanted any connection with skullduggery erased and were willing to pay for the privilege, used her. Five grand for a couple of days' work on the computer—Bailey reckoned it was best not to think about it. "The prices you charge, I'm surprised that you don't live in a Beverly Hills mansion, Mori."

"This flat gives me anonymity to do my work," Kemp explained. "Anyway, Bailey, if you can find anybody as equally skilled in their art as I am for cheaper, then you're welcome to use them."

Kemp was good, and she knew it. Her arrogance was sometimes her weak link, the fact that she thought she couldn't be caught had led to her downfall once before when Bailey had arrested her for credit card fraud. He knew Kemp wouldn't make the same mistakes again. In his time as a copper, he'd successfully utilized her services in previous investigations. Jacobs had always been uncomfortable about Bailey's association with Kemp, so uncomfortable that when they were partners, they'd had words about Kemp on many occasions.

"Okay, Mori, we've established that you're the best in the business, now get on with the work."

"I've every intention of doing so. You being with the EPP, there's every chance you might be arrested before you pay me if I don't."

"The EPP is a law-abiding democratic party," Bailey reiterated irritably.

"So you keep saying. When you keep saying this, Bailey, please remember that I'm a computer wizard who can thoroughly research your members. If there's any anomalies in any of your members' pasts, you can be certain I'll be able to find them."

Kemp seemed to have a particularly smug look on her face when she said it. People like Kemp were the new gangsters who could be more intimidating with one little press of a button on their keyboards than the Krays ever were with their threats of torture and murder.

Bailey smiled. "I know you could, Mori."

Kemp decided that was what she liked about Bailey, the fact that he understood how limited dinosaurs like him were in this computer-generated world. Detective work would soon become unnecessary in the autocratic world that the Kemps of this world were slowly creating. The police would still have their uses, Kemp thought, but only as pawns in the computer wizards' games. There were still manual tasks that would need to be undertaken by the police, but the actual business of investigation would be taken over by machines. Some would call the world that Kemp envisaged sterile—she looked at it more as utopia.

"I want the money in the morning," Kemp insisted.

"I'll courier you it by lunchtime," Bailey promised.

"And I'll get the data to you by Wednesday," she told him, and he had no doubts that she would.

As he started down the landing steps, he was eyed up by a bunch of beer swigging teenagers who suddenly went silent as he walked past them. Bailey started walking faster—he couldn't afford to get involved in a scuffle with them and possibly draw the police's attention to the fact he was at Kemp's flat. After a nervous journey across the dew-soaked common to his car, he arrived there minutes later. A quick examination around the door handle showed scratch marks where somebody had been trying to force the door open. Rough housing estates were the breeding ground for theft and vandalism. He thought about the money. He would have to ask the party for it, as he didn't have five grand lying around. If they wanted results, then they had to learn quickly that they had to pay, and if they didn't pay, then there was every chance that very soon the party would be finished, and then none of it would matter anymore.

As he started his engine, he considered it was a sobering thought, and when he drove off, he knew that, unless the EPP got a result through Kemp, then, in the public's eyes, they'd be permanently linked with terrorism, and that would make them completely unelectable.

CHAPTER 27

Roberts was hot on her tail. He'd followed her to a secluded side street, where she'd hurriedly changed from dowdy jeans and T-shirt to a party frock and stockings. Shortly after changing, she'd driven straight to a restaurant, where she'd met a handsome dark-skinned younger man who was all hair and teeth. Roberts parked the car on the other side of the street just past the restaurant. He made sure he was in a position where he could view the dimly lit restaurant from out of the shadows. A good surveillance officer instinctively knew how to blend into the background without being noticed.

Inside the restaurant, lit by electric candlelight, he could see the couple dinning. They were laughing and joking, quite at ease with each other. It was obvious to a professional like Roberts that the couple had known each other intimately for quite a while. He thought about checking in with Machin but decided against it. Machin was eating out with her live-in lover Clay Thompson, the movie director, and their friend, the Hollywood actress Debbie Duncan. It was Machin's first evening off from the terrorist investigation in a week, and Roberts had no intention of being a party pooper and spoiling it for her.

Instead, he checked in with the incident room, who told him they had nothing to report. The same couldn't be said of Roberts, who had plenty to report. The woman and man were kissing across the table, furtively touching and stroking the way lovers did before they booked a room for the evening. After they left the restaurant, Roberts tailed the couple to a motel, where they did book a room. From across the street, Roberts observed them enter their room and shut the door, making it plain that they were going to be there for a while.

This was the third time he'd tailed the woman, and each time he'd tailed her, she'd followed the same elaborate routine. There was nothing more to see here. The couple would be making love for hours, and Roberts quickly concluded that he didn't want to waste any more time on what was plainly a regular routine between the man and his lover.

Roberts would go home for supper and have a few hours' sleep, so he was bright and fresh in the morning. It was essential to prioritize when on a case. A tired, lethargic Roberts would be no good to the investigation, he quickly surmised, as he drove home.

When he reached home, the house was in darkness, and there was a note on the breakfast bar in their retro kitchen, saying that his wife, Jill, was at her friend, Marcia's, for the evening. With the chaotic nature of his job, it meant Roberts wasn't there for days at a time, and these days, he could sense a distance developing between himself and his wife. That distance was fast becoming a problem in their marriage, and there was no quick solution with him working all hours of the day and night. His promotion to Counter Terrorism Command and the work outside of normal office hours that entailed had only made matters worse between them, leaving a bitterness that never used to be there early on in their marriage.

Roberts made himself a sandwich and opened a beer then sat watching TV for a while. After he'd eaten the sandwich, his eyelids suddenly became heavy, and, half a can of beer later, he was asleep on the sofa. He didn't know how long he dozed for, but long enough for him to be still lying on the sofa asleep when his wife, Jill, arrived home from her friend's. From Jill, there was no tender peck on the cheek or a "Let's get you to bed, darling." If it wasn't for the gentle thump of the kitchen door closing as she entered the house via the backdoor—which woke him—he was convinced that his wife would've left him on the sofa for the night.

"How's Marcia?" a sleepy Roberts asked.

"She's a bit down. She's just split up with her boyfriend," Jill lied.

The lies from his wife were the things he hated most. Roberts noted the way Jill's face twitched when she spoke to him these days. There was a nervous look in his wife's eyes in the rare moments that Roberts was able to engage her stare. All these were sure signs she was up to no good. But all of those signs were insignificant, compared to the surest sign of all that she was a cheat—the discovery of her infidelity when he'd tailed her to the restaurant and motel this evening. At that moment, seeing her with that lounge lizard, all thoughts of love for his wife were at an end. Love had now been replaced by thoughts of loathing and hate. Roberts felt the intense hatred that only a cheated spouse could summon for an errant partner. It was a hatred that would never go away, a hatred that could eat away a man's soul. Roberts decided, as he lay next to his cold-hearted wife in their sexless marriage bed, that it was a hatred he'd have to do something about.

CHAPTER 28

I don't know how you do what you do," Debbie Duncan said to Machin, crossing her long stockinged legs as she sat drinking coffee and liqueurs with Machin and Thompson after their wonderful meal.

"Somebody has to do it," Machin said matter-of-factly, adding "If we didn't have someone chasing these psychos, what a terrible world it would be."

Debbie Duncan knew all about psychos. Her life had been chaos after her rape by a serial killer, Peter Rivers. Slowly she'd managed, through psychiatric counseling, to rebuild her life and go back to making movies. It hadn't been easy, and the mental scars would always be there. But she was a fighter and would never let the memories of Rivers's evil ruin her life. "I couldn't do it," she admitted.

"Well, I couldn't do what you do," Machin confessed. "I once had a small part in a school play, standing in front of an audience and talking. I've never been so scared in my life."

Duncan was amazed that a woman who could gun down a serial killer in a shootout could be nervous of a little thing like going on stage in front of an audience.

Duncan was starting to realize that Sarah Machin was a much more complex character than she'd at first thought. The beaming smile that always seemed to be on Thompson's face these days showed that Machin was good for him, and that she was the perfect tonic for her friend, Thompson, and had helped him get over his wife, Jodie's murder.

"Acting's not for everyone," Thompson interjected. "There's a reason why I've never done a walk on part in any of my movies."

"We should all stick with what we're good at," Duncan remarked.

With that, Machin took out her mobile phone and went outside to check in on the incident room. They were working their way through the missing teenagers, searching for a link, a possibility, anything that could make sense of this mess. And what a mess it was. This case was eating her up inside. It involved teenage kids and indiscriminate murder. It showed all the loathsome attributes of mankind. Although there was nothing she could do for the investigation tonight, she made a vow to herself that she'd be up early and back at work by seven the next morning.

She looked at Thompson and Duncan through the window. They seemed so suited to each other. There was a bond between them that was obvious to all who knew them. Duncan had helped Thompson work through his drinking problems after his wife had been killed. Sometimes, when Machin saw the two of them together, she wondered whether their world was the same as her world. When they got home later, she spoke about it.

"Did you and Debbie ever do anything together?" she asked when they were lying in bed, cuddling after sex.

"We're just good friends, we've never been a couple," Thompson said. There was a time before Duncan had seen Peter Rivers, and after Thompson's wife, Jodie's death, where Thompson thought that he and Debbie Duncan were going to be lovers. Rivers changed everything.

After the horror of Peter Rivers, Duncan had made it plain that she'd never go out with movie people again. It meant that Thompson was only ever going to be just a friend.

"The way you talk with each other, you talk like ex-lovers," Machin pressed.

Thompson held Machin close. "We're not ex-lovers," he clarified, "and I don't want Debbie because I love you."

His hand crept between her legs the way she liked it, his fingers' rhythmic movement removing all her inhibitions. As she mounted his phallus and got lost in the frenzy of love, Machin had no doubts that Thompson was telling her the truth. When she felt his hard manliness inside her, she was a hundred percent certain that, for the first time in her life, she was experiencing true love. It was a love that was all-encompassing, a love that made you sometimes feel jealousy when you shouldn't. As Thompson came inside her, it was the ultimate act of coupling, an act that told Machin that whatever horrors she encountered in her world, she couldn't live without this man in her life.

CHAPTER 29

Craig was lying on the bed, and his stomach was churning. It was crying out for food, food he didn't have. His lips were also parched and dry. It had been hours since he'd had a drink, hours locked in the oppressive heat of his clammy cell. There was some kind of generator heating the place.

What would, at first, appear to an observer to be a comfortable living environment became uncomfortable and claustrophobic with the absence of drinking water. He had no idea what the time was, what day it was. His captor had made sure that Craig's grip on reality was limited. As he lay, unable to sleep, he thought about the construction of his cell. It was made of ancient brickwork, all of which had been reinforced with concrete, making the walls more solid. The bars of the door were also made of solid steel and, therefore, impregnable. The fact that there was no rust on them showed that they'd been specially built in a foundry somewhere recently.

He studied the CCTV camera outside the cell's bars, giving a full view of the inside of the cell. Where the computer monitor for the camera was, he had no idea, but not being able to see it meant that he couldn't tell if his captor was outside in the rest of the complex watching him. The not knowing was what he hated the most. Any thoughts of trying to escape had to be put on hold. From what he'd seen of his captor since he'd been taken, there was no doubt that if he was caught trying to escape, then he would be killed.

He could hear something outside the cell. In the shadows, he sensed movement. There was a scraping sound near the door and, by the time he looked up, he could just see a shadow departing around the corner. Where the shadow had been, by the cell door, there now sat a metal plate with a sandwich on it. Next to it was a plastic water bottle. Craig rushed over and grabbed the food and drink before it was snatched away. He hurriedly opened the water bottle and guzzled the contents down. As he was ravenously devouring the sandwich, the cell's speaker suddenly crackled to life, signaling his tormentor was about to speak.

"As you can see, Craig, I'm a man of my word. You answered eight out of twenty questions correctly—for showing your ability to learn, you deserve something," the Voice said.

"Thank you, sir," Craig said, savoring every mouthful of his meal.

"There's no need for thanks, my disciple. Any food or drink you get from me, you'll have earned. You sit there and enjoy your meal, very soon your education continues, and I'll be showing you a new film."

Craig was tired of trying to concentrate when he always felt tired and hungry. Why he felt so tired, he had no idea. "I can't wait, sir," he said sarcastically, unable to mask the irony in his voice.

As usual, his captor showed that he didn't miss anything. "No more sarcasm, Craig. If you show any more acts of defiance like this, then I'm afraid that you'll have to be punished."

Craig suddenly didn't feel right. His head was fuzzy, and his sense of balance had suddenly gone. If he wasn't sitting on the bed, he was sure he would've collapsed to the floor. He'd been okay until he'd drunk the water and eaten the food. "You put something in my food!".

"It's nothing harmful, my disciple, just something to help you relax and enable you to take in the information you're trying to learn more easily."

"You've poisoned me!" Craig snapped.

The Voice sighed. "Don't be a drama queen, Craig. You're my disciple—a boy I'm trying to show a way forward to a brighter future. There's no way I'd ever poison you, when I've got so much work for you to do."

Craig wasn't convinced. Whatever was in his food was making his legs decidedly wobbly. He tried to get up from his bed and found he couldn't. "What have you done to me?" he asked in desperation.

"All I've done is given you a helping hand on the road to enlightenment. The road to enlightenment is no easy path, and the more aids you get to help you along that path, the quicker you'll learn what's required of you," the Voice explained.

"I need to lie down." Craig lay on the bed and was surprised that his captor hadn't immediately ordered him to stand, like he had on previous occasions.

"You lie there and get yourself together a moment, my disciple. I shall play your next film on a loop, so you don't miss anything."

The film started. On the wall, an image of Oswald Mosley speaking at a fascist rally at the Royal Albert Hall in the 1930s suddenly appeared.

"Listen to what this man says, Craig, Mosley was the leader that this country was crying out for. He could have been the man to save us from becoming this horrible mish-mash of ethnic diversity."

After his brief message, the Voice went silent. Craig was lost in a hazy world of ranting fascist ideologues. He was now in the moment of his greatest fear since his capture. Up until now, he'd been in complete control of his thoughts and feelings. Now he'd been drugged, and he had no idea what he was doing or where he was going. But one thing was for sure. Wherever he was going, from what he'd seen of his captor's actions to date, it wasn't going to be to a good place.

CHAPTER 30

Bailey was sitting outside a new build block of flats along Folkestone's rundown sea front. The flats were called Trenton Villas and were about as soulless and blandly functioning as a new build could be. In the old days, they'd have been called cheap and cheerful. In the modern world of slippery estate agents, they were probably being marketed as compact and bijou. It hardly looked the likely breeding ground of a Marxist revolutionary, the hotbed of anarchy and rebellion, but, as Bailey had found with the lefty loonies over the years, they seldom followed the creed of what they preached.

He took out the printout that Kemp had given him and read the details on Fiona Tredwell. It said she was self-employed, that she worked for a left wing newspaper called the *Invicta Star*. The *Invicta Star* was a digital paper only accessible over the internet. In the couple of hours Bailey had been parked across the street, Tredwell hadn't so far left her apartment. He could see it was going to be a long waiting game. He had a picture of Tredwell he'd procured off the internet. Pictures of extreme fanatics were always out there if you knew where to look. Bailey, in his time as a policeman, had quickly learned to look. He had been a detective who'd been willing to use any tool at his disposal that would help him get the job done. It led to a high arrest success rate.

After his third lukewarm coffee from the thermos flask he'd wisely brought with him, he was starting to get bored and was bursting for a piss. Just as he was thinking of giving it up for an hour while he went to the toilet and found somewhere to eat, a scruffy bohemian-looking woman suddenly stepped out of the apartment block's main entrance. Bailey looked at his grainy photo for confirmation. Although the photo was from a demonstration a few years ago, the creature who was now getting into an ancient-looking Volkswagen Polo was definitely Tredwell. When she had driven off in a black cloud of exhaust fumes, Bailey left his car. He had no idea how long Tredwell was going to be gone, but one thing he definitely knew, however long she was gone, it was now a race against time to get in and out of her apartment before she returned.

Bailey rushed across the road and entered the hallway of the apartment. He jogged up the clean concrete stairwell. Tredwell's apartment was on the second floor. At her door Bailey rang the doorbell three times, making sure that nobody was at home. In his pocket, he had a selection of forged IDs, ranging from cop to local government building inspector.

When nobody answered the door, Bailey took out his selection of skeleton keys and found one that was similar to the lock. After a quick jiggle around of the key in the lock, the door sprang open. Inside, the flat was cramped and pokey.

Wafting in the air was the clawing smell of cigarette smoke. The yellow nicotine stains on the white ceiling showed the sure signs that Tredwell was a heavy smoker. Bailey's detective brain carefully studied and noted everything around him. On finding nothing of note in the hall, he went to the living room.

The open laptop on a table in the corner of the living room, combined with the anarchist literature lying around, showed this was Tredwell's workspace. Bailey turned the computer on, hoping it had been left lying dormant while Tredwell popped out. After finding it password protected, he turned it off and began searching the book-laden living room for anything that might tell him what Tredwell had been up to. After thumbing through books and drawers with his gloved hands, he found nothing of interest. He looked at his watch. He'd been in the flat five minutes. He hurried along the soft, carpeted hall to the bedrooms. The first bedroom was full of dusty old books, reams of writing paper, and old copies of the *Militant Worker* magazine. Bailey thumbed through them but found nothing hidden amongst the pages. On finding nothing, he moved on to the main bedroom. The main bedroom showed more promise. The messy unmade bed with a scattering of dirty underwear on the floor meant the room was disheveled and unkempt, but at least it showed it was in active use.

Bailey meticulously searched through the drawers of a bedside cabinet. The top three drawers had a selection of T-shirts and underwear, the bottom drawer sweaters and jeans. He fumbled through the sweaters and found a notebook buried among them. He quickly opened it. Inside the notebook, Tredwell had foolishly written down all her bank codes and computer passwords. Among the passwords was a password for something called, "Red Vengeance." He hurriedly jotted down everything he thought might be relevant from Tredwell's notebook into his own, then put Tredwell's notebook back where he found it.

Bailey smiled to himself in relief that, at last, he was

making progress. Tredwell had made a big mistake, a mistake that was going to be very costly to her and her anarchist friends. As he walked over to the window and looked out at the front of the building, his feeling of elation quickly turned to one of horror as he saw Tredwell's Polo parked in her parking space. Thoughts of a rapid escape quickly ended as he heard the sound of a key being inserted in the front door lock. His senses suddenly became alive with the tension that only the fear of discovery during a wrongdoing can bring. As Bailey frantically looked around for a hiding place, the realization that discovery could mean that all his plans could soon be in tatters was reverberating in his head. When he heard the front door shut and could hear movement in the hallway, there was now only one thought in his head, and that was that the horror of Tredwell finding him in her flat was only moments away.

CHAPTER 31

Tredwell was cold. She'd stepped out of her apartment, expecting the recent flourish of heat from the last vestiges of summer. Instead, she'd been greeted by the first icy blast of autumn. After a brief trip to a nearby post box to post a letter, she'd decided it was too cold to walk around in just a jumper and jeans, so she went back to her apartment to get her coat. Inside her apartment, she rushed to her bedroom, opened the first door of her two-doored wardrobe, and grabbed a coat off the rail. As she put it on, she felt a shiver run down her spine. She attributed her momentary feeling to the cold air, but, just in case it was a premonition of imminent disaster, she quickly went to the drawer housing her notebook and put it in her coat pocket. The *Invicta Star* had many enemies, with most of the hatred aimed at the paper being fueled by Tredwell's inflammatory articles about banking and big business.

Tredwell wasn't naïve and knew that, over the years, she'd made some pretty powerful enemies, enemies who wouldn't think twice at stooping to any level to stop her articles.

In the living room, she turned on the computer and

checked her mail inbox. Her mail was full of a mixture of support from friends and virulent attacks from her enemies. As she read some of the poorly worded insults from some of her opponents, she decided that if this was the literary level of the opposition, then the militant left had already won. A few minutes after she'd left the apartment again, a nervous Bailey stepped out of the wardrobe in the bedroom from the other side of the rail from where Tredwell had taken her coat. He rushed over to the window and was relieved to see Tredwell's car pulling out of her parking space and trundling off into traffic.

Bailey hurried into the living room, took Tredwell's laptop over to the window ledge, and placed it on the ledge in a position from where he could see the front of the building. Now he'd know immediately if Tredwell returned. Using her access codes, he looked at the "RED VENGEANCE" files. The files contained a list of all members of British far right parties and members of various fascist organizations. Tredwell and her friends had been compiling a dossier on everybody involved in the far right in Britain. The files showed right wing activists' personal details. When he found the files on the EPP and his name and personal details on that file, Bailey had all the confirmation that he needed that Tredwell and her friends were fanatics hell-bent on his party's destruction.

It suited his purpose that they were. It meant that Tredwell and her friends were capable of mass murder, that they could easily kill in their misguided crusade. It now meant that Bailey could provide the police with further suspects other than the EPP, and those suspects were going to be more valuable to him than anybody could ever imagine.

CHAPTER 32

Roberts needed time to sort the mess out that was rapidly becoming his life. Jill was indifferent to him and was going out on a more and more regular basis. She said it was to comfort Marcia after Marcia's recent split from her boyfriend, Roberts knew it was nothing of the sort and that she was sneaking out to be with her lover. He could have forgiven his wife almost anything but this. If it had been a one off, a brief meaningless fling that quickly ended, then Roberts might've been tempted to just let the matter run its course and then somehow try and resurrect his marriage. The level of intimacy between his wife and her lover that he'd personally witnessed in their regular meetings meant such a course of action was impossible. His wife's attachment to her lover was permanent, and he knew it was just a matter of time before she left him.

Roberts watched them one last time, as they enter the motel room that they'd entered on many previous occasions, and he decided that enough was enough. As he drove home, he was already finalizing his plan. The difficulty was finding a way to cover everything. Now that he was with Counter Terrorism Command, a means to an end was available. It was dangerous work, work where you could encounter the wrath of the terrorist every day of your working life. Roberts reckoned it was time he felt the wrath of the terrorists, and maybe it was time they struck a target close to his home.

As he reached home, an angry Machin called him on his mobile, wanting him back at the incident room immediately. Machin was taking the fact that they were making little progress in the hunt for the killers personally and was trying to force greater efforts from those around her so she could stem the wrath of DCI Khan. Roberts would do as the inspector wanted. He knew the politics of command, knew when to suck up and when to bow down. When Roberts returned to the incident room, a furious Machin was waiting.

She ordered him to her office, and, after the door was shut, she said, "I told you to stop tailing Bailey."

Roberts lapsed into silence.

"Palmer told me that you told him to continue tailing Bailey. Is this true, Sergeant?"

Roberts suddenly looked guilty. "It's true, ma'am, Palmer is very good at tailing. I thought he'd be able to tail Bailey unobserved."

"I told you to take the tail off him," Machin fumed.

"I'm sorry, ma'am," Roberts apologized.

Machin decided that the-less-than-contrary look in his eyes said he didn't mean it. "It's only the fact that Palmer came up with something while tailing Bailey that's stopped me from reprimanding you over this, Sergeant. Palmer told me Bailey went to see a convicted computer hacker called Mori Kemp. She's still suspected of being involved in major computer fraud."

"Why would he go to Kemp, ma'am?" Roberts asked tentatively.

"That's what we're going to get her in to find out,"

Machin told him. "I want her brought in discreetly. Bailey's not to get a whiff of this."

"Yes, ma'am," Roberts said and then was dismissed.

After Roberts left Machin stood for a moment staring out of the window. She found Roberts hard to understand nowadays. Disobeying orders like that could've been catastrophic for the operation. Something was wrong with him, but, at the moment, she didn't have the time or the inclination to find out what it was. At the moment, she had to concentrate on the manhunt for the terrorists and everything else would be banished to the background.

When Mori Kemp arrived in the interview room, she was extremely anxious about being forced to come there. Machin and Roberts sat opposite her. Machin had considered going in with someone else other than Roberts but decided she'd give Roberts a chance to redeem himself. This was one interview Machin wouldn't record. "Ian Bailey came to see you on Monday," she stated.

Kemp was fuming. She had expected Bailey to at least be professional enough not to be followed to her flat. "And what's that got to do with anything?"

"The EPP is part of an ongoing investigation we're involved in, concerning the recent terrorist attacks in Southern England," Machin told her.

It was best that Kemp realized from the start how potentially dangerous to her liberty such an association to Bailey could be.

"I don't know what you're talking about, Inspector. I worked for Bailey when he was a copper on a couple of cases. He's an old associate of mine from his police days. He was just having a catch up," Kemp said.

Machin laughed. "And you expect me to believe that?

"Why wouldn't you? It's the truth."

"Don't try and be clever with me, Miss Kemp. We're

talking major terrorism here. One whiff of any involvement on your part, and you'll be facing twenty years in the slammer," Machin warned.

"It was just a catch up," Kemp reiterated.

"You spent five years in Rochester prison for computer fraud. If you carry on with this tone, you'll be catching up with all your old cronies there," Machin promised.

"If Bailey knows anything about the recent terrorist attacks, he's not going to tell someone like me," Kemp said.

"You make a lot of money," Roberts said.

"I barely get by," Kemp snapped.

"I've got contacts," Roberts told Kemp. "I know what goes on in your world."

"What goes on is that I try to find private work to pay the rent. Being a con who's been convicted of computer hacking means that companies don't want to employ me, are scared of what I'm going to do to their computer system." Kemp laughed, adding, "What most of the stupid twats don't realize is, that if I wanted to access their stupid company files, I could do it easily from the outside."

"What did Bailey ask you to do?" Machin asked.

"He was having some technical problems with his computer. He just dropped by with his laptop to see if I could fix it for him."

"You paid five thousand pounds into your overseas bank account the day after his last visit—you're not the only computer wizard out there, Miss Kemp. In modern policing, we all have to be adept in such matters." Machin savored the puzzled look on Kemp's face as she tried to work out how her supposedly fool-proof banking system had been compromised. "Before you say another word, Miss Kemp, I'd like you to consider very carefully what you say next. You've been reported by the officer tailing Bailey to have been visited by him twice in the last week. You've taken a large sum of money off a man that's an ongoing terrorist suspect. You can understand, in light of your various computer convictions, that we want to know what he asked you to do for that money." Machin paused to let Kemp consider the vulnerability of her position. "If you're not careful, you're going to be drawn ever further into a major terrorist investigation, could be implicated as part of a terrorist cell involved in mass murder." She paused again for effect. "There is always another scenario. You could always talk to me about an alternative path."

"You mean the alternative where I don't say another word until I'm all lawyered up."

"No, I mean the alternative where you tell us what you gave him, and then I promise you that your part in all this goes away."

Kemp was momentarily lost in thought, weighing up all the complications of this and where it could lead. The fact that Machin's computer specialist had managed to find her secret account that she'd put Bailey's money in was the most worrying aspect of everything DI Machin had so far told her. It meant that Kemp would have to review all her security codes before the city shares scam she had planned next month could be carried out. None of that work could be completed with the police hovering over her shoulder, watching her every move.

"Bailey's not involved in terrorism, Inspector," Kemp stated confidently.

"That's really not for you to decide, Miss Kemp," Machin pointed out.

"A terrorist suspect has paid you money to get information for him," Roberts reminded Kemp.

"I can't tell you anything. If I tell you what I've been

doing, we both know that I'm putting myself in a compromising position," Kemp said.

"I've deliberately not gone down official lines with this interview. The interview isn't being recorded. At the moment this is off the record and, on this occasion, I'm prepared to turn a blind eye to your hacking activities, providing you tell me what you did for him." Machin could see that Kemp was on the brink of caving in. "Bailey will never learn that we found out about it through you," she promised.

Roberts was angry, masking that fury under a blank expression. The way Machin was caving in to Kemp infuriated him. If Roberts had been in charge, he'd have threatened Kemp with dire retribution, if she hadn't immediately cooperated. He decided his boss was too soft.

"So, if I tell you what he's got, you'll leave me alone?" Kemp probed tentatively.

"We'll leave you alone for this," Machin assured her, "other things you're involved in, now that's another matter."

"I'm not involved in anything," Kemp lied.

"All I want to know about is what you gave Bailey," Machin stated.

"Okay, he asked me to get him details of people from a list of left-wing lunatics who were capable of terrorist attacks. He reckons that some left-wing fanatic is committing these horrendous attacks and is trying to set up the EPP for them."

"I want that list," Machin pressed.

"I obtained most of the information off the list through illegal access—"

"Just give me the damn list, Miss Kemp!" Machin demanded.

"Bailey knows some dangerous people, Inspector, I need to be careful—"

"You're hardly in a position to make demands, Miss Kemp. I promise you that whatever you tell me here won't get back to Bailey, and you won't be prosecuted for it."

Kemp decided she had no alternative but to trust her. "I haven't got it with me."

"That's okay, Sergeant Roberts can go back with you to your flat, and you can print him out a copy," Machin said.

"Maybe I haven't got a copy," Kemp said.

"A sleaze ball like you has always got a copy," Roberts said.

"Come on, Miss Kemp, the sooner you give us that list, the quicker you can go back to your sad little world of ripping off the general public," Machin stood, letting Kemp know that the interview was over.

Kemp stood. "It looks like you've given me no choice, Inspector."

"You've always got a choice, Miss Kemp, for once in your life, you could employ your skills working inside the law."

"Since I came out of prison, I usually work inside the law. Bailey, because he was an ex-copper I've worked with in the past, was a momentary aberration."

Machin was being bullshitted, but she wasn't bothered. For the moment, her sole task was to obtain the list of names that Kemp had given Bailey. If Bailey was involved in terrorism then what better way of shifting attention away from himself than by setting up his political opponents to take the fall. As Roberts left with Kemp, Machin reckoned they were much closer to finding evidence as to what Bailey was involved in. If they could catch Bailey in the act of setting up an opponent for the recent vile terrorist acts, then they'd have him.

Machin had a good feeling about this. Bailey was

starting to make mistakes, and Machin was convinced those mistakes would lead to his downfall.

CHAPTER 33

As he stood leaning against the bars of the cold metal cell door, Craig felt decidedly groggy. While he stood and regained his balance, a film of an anti-capitalist riot from a few years ago in the city was being projected onto the wall. Craig was trying to focus on the images the Voice recently implanted in his head and was demanding that he study. It was stern and harsh, a voice that he seemed unable to disobey. Slowly he made his way across the hard concrete floor until he arrived at the bed, gingerly sitting down on the bed's lumpy corner while he tried to watch the film.

From the cell's speakers, he heard the usual crackle signaling that his jailer was back. Craig had been unconscious for hours. How long his captor had been watching him lying on the bed, he had no idea.

Finally, the Voice spoke. "Good evening, my disciple, how are you feeling?"

"My head is a muddle, sir," Craig admitted.

With all the scopolamine the Voice had put inside Craig's food and drink to get him to the required state where he was susceptible to suggestion and make him subservient, the Voice wasn't surprised that the boy couldn't think straight.

"I want you to look at the images in front of you, Craig, look at the hatred in the eyes of the vile demonstrators." The Voice paused a moment, so his disciple had time to take in the images of the demonstrators on the screen. "These people are prepared to tear down the fabric of our society with their violent acts of social unrest. We need to act, boy, do something to stop them. If we don't stop their evil, Craig, then Britain is heading for years of chaos."

"We must defend our country, sir," Craig said as the voice inside his head erupted in all its verbal fury.

The Voice was pleased. "That's right, my boy, we have to fight for our country. At last, you're truly worthy of being my disciple. What you will soon learn is that sometimes the best method of defense is to attack. The mission I have planned for you is the most important mission that I've ever had one of my disciples embark upon. Your mission will decide the future of this country, my boy; the success of your mission will ensure that this country is steered in the right direction."

The Voice paused to let Craig take in what he said. The boy was drugged heavily, making him completely susceptible to brainwashing. The Voice had learned with the other disciples he'd recently trained that these things couldn't be rushed, and that to create the perfect terror weapon took time and patience.

"I'm ready to do what's expected of me, sir," Craig said blankly.

The Voice would check that the syringe was ready. The moment that Craig went back to sleep, the Voice would give him another dose of drugs to make his disciple more susceptible to the Voice's commands. There were still a couple of weeks until it was time for Craig's mission. The Voice looked at Craig's young, unlined face staring at the film of the riots. Craig's eyes were glazed, had the dreamy quality of the almost converted. It was now just a matter of time and patience, and then, in two weeks, his latest disciple would be ready to be unleashed on an unsuspecting world.

CHAPTER 34

Machin had been summoned to DCI Khan's office. Khan looked far from pleased when Machin sat down opposite him. She had always found Khan's studious, uncompromising-looking face hard to read. Khan had the sharp eyes of a grand-master chess player, eyes that told you this man was very intelligent, didn't take fools lightly, wasn't a man to be trifled with. Machin had handed Khan the list that Kemp had given them. As Khan, who was wearing thick-rimmed reading glasses, studied it, a disgusted look quickly appeared on his face.

"What a bunch of misfits and losers, Sarah," Khan observed as he put the list down on his gleaming, polished mahogany desk.

On her first visit to Khan's office, Machin had noted that the furniture was stylish and a cut above the standard police office furniture.

"Kemp claims that Bailey reckons that one of these misfits is trying to set the EPP up, that they, and not the EPP, are responsible for the recent terror attacks."

"And what about the far right activists Bailey gave you?" Khan asked.

"None of them seem capable of this, sir. All these terror attacks have been elaborately planned, have involved a high degree of brainwashing. It's clear from the CCTV images we have of the boys just before the attacks that their minds are not their own."

"So Bailey has given you nothing," Khan said.

"I'm afraid not," Machin reluctantly admitted. "The fact that he's trying to connect militant worker and anarchist fanatics with the murders shows me he's doing everything he can to divert attention away from the far right and on to the militant left."

"I've seen the leftist loonies at the anti-capitalist marches, some of them are mad enough to kill," Khan reflected as he looked again at the names on the list, wondering if any of them was the one responsible.

"Surely, none of them are capable of this kind of mass murder," Machin said.

"Who knows, but one thing is certain, Sarah, with the death toll mounting, someone is. The EPP got fifteen percent of the vote in last year's local council elections. If the EPP's enemies could manage to link them to this, then all the EPP's support would be gone." Khan would like nothing better than, with all the hatred they propounded, to see these neo-Nazis wiped off the face of the earth. He had a problem, though. With the EPP's recent electoral success, he couldn't see any party that had made such a breakthrough being stupid enough to get involved in violent terrorism.

"I can't believe any of the leftie loonies on Kemp's list could be that sick," Machin offered. "I think this is an independent, someone nobody knows about acting out there on his own."

Khan stared out the window in a moment's reflection. He was meant to attend a press conference later that day to keep everyone informed on how the investigation was progressing, and, at the moment, he had nothing to tell them. "In all my years in Counter Terrorism Command, Sarah, I've learned a lot of things. One thing I've certainly learned when dealing with extremists is that extremists are called that name for a reason, and most of them are capable of anything."

Machin didn't argue. After the aftermath following the mayhem caused by serial killer, Peter Rivers, she knew, from personal experience, how evil people could be. "I suppose you're right, sir."

"There's no suppose, I am right, Sarah. Bailey's visit to Kemp and this list show that we need to check these names out. If Bailey's trying to set them up, we need to know everything about them. With the intrusive press coverage, we can't afford to make mistakes."

And, with that, Machin was dismissed. *Dismissed to do what?* She really didn't know. The more she saw of Bailey's actions, the less she thought he was involved. She had spoken to Bailey's former colleagues, and they all said he'd been an excellent detective. If the EPP were being set up, Machin could understand how Bailey was angry enough to do something about it. Back in her office, she stared at Roberts outside sitting at his desk working quietly on his computer. Something was going on with her trusted sergeant.

Roberts had never disobeyed orders before, and, although on this occasion, it had achieved results, it was still, as far as Machin was concerned, a worrying new trend in her sergeant that she wasn't going to tolerate.

Within a couple of minutes, Roberts knocked on her door and entered. "Palmer just rang in. He followed Bailey to some apartments, called Trenton Villas, in Folkestone. Trenton Villas is the home of Fiona Tredwell, a Marxist revolutionary, who works for an internet newspaper, called the *Invicta Star*." Roberts had a smug look on his face, his expression suggesting to Machin that he thought the results that Palmer was getting justified him disobeying orders. "Apparently, Bailey broke into Tredwell's apartment with a set of skeleton keys."

"I want you to get everything you can on this Tredwell. If Bailey's interested in her, then so are we," Machin stated.

Roberts went back to his desk to do some research.

Machin used to be very close to her sergeant, but, lately, they'd been drifting ever further apart. She vowed to arrange a night out with Roberts and his lovely wife, Jill, when this was all over, and try to resurrect some of the old camaraderie. But all that would have to wait until the terrorists were caught, because, after their recent attack's success, Machin concluded that it was only a matter of time before the terrorists, fueled by the adrenalin of triumph, struck again.

CHAPTER 35

His name was Sunil Patel. Roberts had found out everything he could about his love rival, and what he found out he didn't like. Patel was wealthy, ran a successful furniture importing business on a local industrial estate. Patel was making a fortune from selling furniture he imported from China. He drove an E Series Mercedes with a personalized number plate, was a two year divorcee who was therefore unmarried and available. The bastard with his good looks and money could've had the pick of all the single women out there. Instead, he'd chosen Roberts's wife, Jill, to lavish his attentions on. That was what Roberts would like to have believed, but knowing his wife, he decided that, maybe, by the way Jill was all over Patel every time she met him, that probably Jill was the one who had instigated the affair.

At home, there were no signs of Jill's treachery. So much so that Roberts was even thinking of having a word with Machin. Jill was becoming such a good actress these days, maybe Clay Thompson could put her in one of his movies. Roberts was finding it hard to mask his anger when he was in the same room as his wife. Anger was something he had to put on the backburner until he was ready. With work and the rest of his problems he was overstretched, these days he seemed to be constantly on the move in his car from one destination to another. He now had the Semtex he'd procured from an underworld contact.

Everything was in place and ready, it was now a question of choosing the right moment to do the dirty deed.

While Jill was having a bath, he slipped out the front and had a look at her car parked on their drive. Tonight she was supposedly going to see Marcia. Roberts wasn't sure whether he hated Jill or Marcia the most. Marcia had helped to perpetuate the lie, so much so that whenever Roberts asked Marcia about Jill's visits, she always lied and said how much they enjoyed their girly nights in.

It was a shame that he couldn't catch Marcia in the car with Jill, now that would be justice. Alas, it was only going to be Jill. Tonight was the night. Roberts took the hunting knife from his coat pocket and punctured Jill's rear tire with it. As he watched the worn tire slowly deflating in front of him, it reminded him of the way his life had also deflated in recent years.

Over a year of discreetly following his wife, he'd never once given her the slightest hint that he knew she was cheating. It had been hard, and he couldn't have done it without help from an old friend, but, after tonight, it was all going to prove worth it. Roberts put the knife in the garage. He would discard it later after his wife had left.

He hung his coat up and went up to the bedroom where Jill was standing there in black bra and panties. He moved up close behind her and gently cupped her breasts with his hands. As usual, she made an excuse about having to put on her makeup and quickly pulled away. Sex between them was rare these days, and if she did ever give in, then Roberts surmised she only gave in so it would avert his suspicions.

"I love you, darling," Roberts said as Jill sat at the dressing table carefully putting on her makeup.

"And I love you, too," Jill lied. It was a lie she'd told on many occasions in recent months, a lie she decided that her husband was too stupid to notice.

Seeing the bulge appearing at the front of her husband's trousers was all the sign that Jill needed to tell her it was time to quickly leave. She couldn't stand the thought of her husband's sweaty body all over her. Compared to Sunil's solid abs and beautifully shaped arse, Morgan's body was a mess. She wanted a life with Sunil, but Sunil wasn't having it.

Sunil was happy the way things were, he'd made it plain on many occasions that he wasn't a man to commit long term. It left Jill's life in disarray, had made her wary about making a decision. Once she'd left her husband that was it. Her husband wasn't the forgiving kind, expecting the same fidelity from his wife as he'd shown throughout their marriage.

After she'd changed, she hurriedly pecked her husband on the cheek and was out the door. He followed her out to the car.

Just as she was going to get in the car, Roberts said, "Hold on, darling, you appear to have a flat."

Jill looked at the left rear tire where Roberts was pointing. She glanced at her watch, she was already late for her rendezvous with Sunil at the quiet hotel bar out in the country. If she had to wait around while Roberts changed the tire, she would be even later.

"You're not going out tonight, can't I borrow your car, darling?" Jill asked.

Inside, Roberts's heart leapt for joy. This was going

better than expected. Jill was pressing toward her own destruction. "I don't know, I might have to go in to work," Roberts protested feebly. He gave Jill a lecherous look, adding, "Why don't you call Marcia and cancel? I'm sure we can find something else to do."

The momentary look of horror that briefly appeared on Jill's face when she thought of a night at home having sex with her husband confirmed to Roberts her loathing for him. Any doubts about the course of action that Roberts was about to embark upon ended with the hurt of that look.

"I promised Marcia I'd be 'round," Jill quickly said. "You know I don't like to let people down, darling."

And she was right. She didn't let anybody down, apart from him, Roberts thought. "I suppose I could change the tire after you've gone. I could always use your car if the office needs me."

Sucker, Jill thought. "That's wonderful, darling," she said.

They exchanged keys, and Jill was quickly on her way. As Roberts's car disappeared around the corner, he was lost in acrimonious thoughts as he realized he'd probably see neither his wife or his car again. It made him sad. They'd had some good times together, Boy, was he going to miss that car, he thought, and then he went to the garage to get the spare tire.

CHAPTER 36

Jill kept glancing at her watch as she was now nearly an hour late. She'd met Sunil at the hotel long ago when her husband had been away in Wales with DI Machin, following up on a murder suspect. That had been over a year ago. It had been lunchtime in early October, and it had been light when she drove there. Under cover of evening darkness, even with the aid of her satnav, finding the hotel was proving difficult. In these winding country lanes, there were so many tracks and offshoots with no streetlights, she was finding following the satnav's directions harder than she expected.

She stopped at a junction, took out her mobile phone, and hastily dialed Sunil's mobile number. As the dreaded no signal sign came up on her phone screen, she swore loudly.

With no way of contacting her lover, she had no choice but to push on to where the satnav said that the hotel was. Above her, at the next left turn, there was, at last, a signpost for Wetherly Grange. When she was minutes away, all kinds of thoughts were racing through her head. Thoughts like, how long could she keep a hunk like Sunil in her life if she proved unreliable and turned up for her dates with him an hour late? Jill wasn't stupid. She could see the way that other women looked at Sunil when they were out together. Sunil was a good-looking man, and he made no effort to hide the fact that he knew it.

In the distance, she, at last, could see the glow of the orange-yellow hotel lights. She turned the satnav off and erased its memory, so there'd be no record of her hotel visit when her husband used the car in the morning. Jill smiled as she thought how clever she was. Regrettably, her smile lasted barely a moment, for it was at that moment that the bomb that Roberts had planted underneath her seat exploded as the electric timer attached reached the designated witching hour, and electrical energy was routed from batteries to an initiator, causing detonation and hurtling millions of her body parts into the stratosphere.

CHAPTER 37

As Roberts got back from his brief visit to Patel's penthouse apartment to plant incriminating evidence relating to the bomb there, he looked at his watch, he'd timed the bomb to go off at twenty-fifteen hours, fifteen minutes after his wife left the house. It was now twenty-twenty hours, and Jill Roberts was hopefully now waiting outside St Peter's gate to meet her maker. Roberts smiled at the pleasing thought, but he didn't smile for long, as now was a time for a clear head and cool reflection.

Because he didn't know where his wife was going tonight to meet her lover, he had no idea where the bomb had exploded. Jill was predictable. In any of the bars and restaurants near to their house, there was a chance of recognition by a neighbor, so she wouldn't meet Patel in any of those. It meant that Jill would've gone farther afield, a minimum of half an hour to make sure. Roberts decided that the extra distance guaranteed that she would be driving when the bomb exploded and meant it would be her death knell.

Jill had thought she'd known her husband, but she had never really known Roberts. When you wanted to kill someone, you had to think with the mind of a detective. A detective always looked for flaws, probable mistakes that became improbable. The change of cars was a probable, due to the flat tire. Roberts was going to pick up the phone to call Marcia, but it was too soon, too close to the bomb's detonation. He'd leave it a bit longer, it would take them a couple of hours to trace the car back to him. Marcia would lie like she always did.

Poor, gullible Marcia would have no idea what the perfect dupe she'd been in Roberts's plan. He'd call, and she'd make an excuse why Jill couldn't come to the phone. When she made that excuse, as far as the police were concerned, it meant that Roberts thought his wife was at Marcia's house.

The investigation would unwind complex layers of duplicity. Roberts would have to summon all his strength to look suitably shocked when he was told his wife was dead. As he sat and reflected on his evening's work, a feeling of elation pumped through his veins. After another twenty minutes had passed, he decided it was long enough and made the call. Marcia, as expected, told him that Jill was sitting on the toilet, and she'd take a message. Roberts told her he'd changed the tire on Jill's car and that he'd use Jill's car in the morning, so there was no need for her to hurry back tonight. As he hung up, in his head, Roberts could picture the smug smile on Marcia's face as she thought that she and Jill had yet again easily fooled gullible Morgan Roberts.

Roberts decided there was nothing else he could do now but to go to bed and wait. In his head, he mulled over the workings of the crime scene. It would take at least two hours for enough of a crime scene team to arrive to determine some cold hard facts. If enough of the number-plate survived the explosion, they'd quickly determine that the owner of the car was their colleague.

With the bomb planted beneath the driver's seat and the damage that would cause to Jill's torso, identification was going to take quite a few hours. Roberts estimated at least six. He went to bed, needed to be asleep in bed and to, thus, be suitably sleepy when his colleagues came knocking on his door with the grim news of Jill's murder.

In his head, he went over and over his story. His wife had gone to Marcia's, she'd used his car because her car had a flat. Roberts had changed the tire and ditched the hunting knife he'd used to puncture it. When his colleagues knocked on his door, he'd claim that the bomb victim couldn't be his wife as she was staying at Marcia's. Those wise old sages that told you that if you told lies, then those lies would come back to haunt you were being proved right. In Jill's case, that was exactly what was about to happen.

As Roberts calmly brushed his teeth, he thought about mistakes he might've made and couldn't think of any. Then he remembered, there had been one, and that was on his wedding day to Jill Dodd when the priest asked him to take Jill as his lawful wedded wife, and he'd said, "I do."

CHAPTER 38

At just after ten o'clock, Machin had been called from her warm bed, where she lay with her hunky boyfriend, to answer a call on her mobile from a very perturbed sounding DCI Khan. He frantically told her that, at around eight o'clock in the evening, a car had been blown up by a bomb near a hotel in the Sussex countryside. Khan was worried that the terrorists had struck again and wanted Machin at the bombsite with him to determine whether this atrocity had been committed by the same terrorists who had carried out the Brighton carnival bombing. As she stepped from her car into the floodlit area created by the forensic team along the country lane close to the hotel, forensic officers in their white suits wearing latex gloves were busily examining the crime scene.

An agitated Khan rapidly approached her. "We've got a big problem," he solemnly stated, adding, "We've identified who the car belonged to."

"To find that out so quickly, that's a positive, sir."

Khan suddenly became pensive, but the soft, genuinely disturbed expression on his face instantly told

Machin that this was something bad. "The car belonged to DS Roberts," he said.

Machin was stunned. Khan had said Roberts. How could the car belong to Roberts? This was one of the many questions racing through her head. Roberts had taken the night off, was supposed to be at home relaxing. It looked like he'd gone out for a meal at a country hotel. Machin concluded that Roberts was probably taking his wife out for a meal when the bomb had ripped his car apart.

"How many people were in the car?" Machin asked tentatively, knowing that if there were two, then her initial guess was probably going to prove right.

"There's just one body, the forensic team are looking at what's left of the body now," Khan said.

Machin thought of her colleague, of how close she'd worked with Roberts on cases in recent years. The police had rung Roberts's home, and the phone had immediately gone to voicemail. Khan had tried Roberts's mobile phone, and it was turned off. He was wondering if the bomb blast had caused it to be turned off permanently.

"I know his wife, Jill, sir, I'd better go and see her," Machin suggested.

Khan didn't argue. If Machin wanted to relay the grisly news of Roberts's death to the distraught wife, then who was Khan to stop her? Machin hurriedly drove to Roberts's house, trying to work out in her head what she was going to say to the poor hysterical widow. It wouldn't be easy. No colleague's death on the job was ever easy to explain to their loved ones. When Machin pulled up outside the Roberts's household, the house was bathed in darkness. Jill Roberts's car was on the drive. At least it showed she was probably at home. It was almost one o'clock in the morning. Being a policeman's wife, the moment Jill Roberts heard the late night knock on the door, she was immediately going to sense something was wrong.

After Machin rang the doorbell several times, a light suddenly appeared in the hallway, and through the frosted front door glass, Machin could see a dressing-gowned figure slowly ambling toward her. As the door opened, Machin stepped back in shock at the sight of Roberts standing before her. She surprised Roberts by grabbing his arm to check that he was real.

"What's wrong, ma'am?" Roberts managed to ask, trying to summon up a baffled expression on his face.

"We need to step inside," Machin said, desperate to get out of the street and into the relative privacy of the house.

They stepped into the house. "Has there been another terrorist attack—"

"You need to sit down, Morgan," Machin told him.

Machin was tenderly using his first name rather than being official. Roberts had no doubt that they'd discovered Jill's body. "What's wrong, ma'am?" he pressed.

"Your car was blown up in a bomb blast this evening—"

Horror quickly registered on Roberts's face. "Jill borrowed it. Her car had a flat!"

"The driver of the car is dead, Morgan," Machin said, now in no doubt that the driver of the car was Jill Roberts.

"It can't be Jill," Roberts quickly informed Machin, "Jill's staying at her friend, Marcia's house tonight." He hurriedly took out his mobile phone and turned it on.

Machin should've reprimanded him for being out of contact, not leaving his mobile on at all times. She wisely decided that now wasn't the time or the place for petty reprimands.

Roberts dialed his wife's mobile phone and got a

dead signal. "I can't raise Jill on her mobile," he said, swallowing hard. "I'll ring Marcia's land line number."

At first, Marcia didn't answer, but Roberts kept trying. Finally, a sleepy Marcia reluctantly answered the phone.

"Hello, who is it?" a tired-sounding Marcia asked grumpily.

"It's, Morgan, Marcia, I need to speak to Jill urgently."

"Do you know what time it is?"

"Of course, I bloody do! Please, be a dear and get Jill for me!"

"She's asleep," Marcia lied.

"Are you sure?" Roberts asked.

"Of course, I'm sure. She's asleep in the other room."

Roberts smiled with relief. "Okay, Marcia, would you take a look outside and see if my car's there."

"If Jill's here, your car must be here—"

Roberts made himself sound irritated. "Please, just take a look for me, darling."

There was a silence for a few moments while Marcia was supposed to be checking that the car was outside on her drive.

Marcia returned a few minutes later. "It's out there," she told Roberts.

He made sure that Machin had heard the conversation. There could now be no doubt that Roberts thought that his wife was staying with Marcia.

With that one statement—the lies about Robert's car still being on her drive—it had been confirmed to Machin what Roberts had known for a long time, and that was the fact that Marcia Bradley, long-time friend of Morgan and Jill Roberts, was a liar.

CHAPTER 39

Machin and a furious-looking Roberts were seated in the interview room across the table from a very nervous-looking Marcia Bradley.

"You've got a lot of explaining to do, Miss Bradley," Machin said.

"I'm sorry, Morgan," Marcia said to Roberts.

"Why did you lie?" Roberts asked her angrily.

"This isn't easy," Marcia replied rather timidly.

"It's going to get a lot harder if you don't tell us what the hell is going on here," Machin told her.

After Roberts had called Marcia, and they knew that she was lying, they'd gone to Marcia's house to confront her. The moment they'd pressed her about the car and where Jill was, Marcia had become evasive in her answers. They'd brought her in for an interview.

"Jill rang me early in the evening. She told me if Morgan rang and asked for her, I was to tell him that she was at my house," Marcia explained.

"I don't believe this!" Roberts snapped, an agitated expression firmly locked on his face.

"I was only doing what she told me," Marcia repeated nervously.

"My wife is dead!" Roberts shouted at her. "She's dead, and you've been lying to me about what she's been doing."

Marcia shifted uncomfortably in her chair. She'd been good friends with Jill Roberts for years and had lied for her with the ease that only a best friend and confidante could. If she'd known her lies were going to lead to this, she'd never have agreed to lie in the first place. She didn't know what to say.

Machin sensed her apprehensive mood. "If you tell us everything you know, then there's a chance you won't be charged with anything."

Charged? Marcia thought. How could she be charged when she hadn't committed a crime? The police had told her that Jill had been murdered in a bomb blast, but none of it made any sense. "Look, none of this is my fault. I was just trying to help out a friend in an unhappy marriage."

Roberts looked suitably shocked. "What are you talking about? Jill loved me."

Marcia lapsed into a painful silence.

That silence told Machin everything. It told her that Jill Roberts had been having an affair with someone for a long time and her friend had been covering for her. "So, Jill was having an affair?" Machin pushed.

Marcia saw little point in denial now that Jill was dead. After someone died, it gave a blunt finality to things, and she concluded none of it mattered anymore. "She was involved with a guy. It's been going on for about a year."

"Jesus!" Roberts snapped, fixing Marcia with an angry glare.

"I really am sorry, Morgan," Marcia offered weakly.

"How could you?" Roberts asked, but the fact that Jill and Marcia had been friends since they were at school together, and also the fact that Marcia had never really liked him, convinced Roberts that she could quite easily, and she had.

"Someone planted a bomb in Detective Sergeant Roberts's car. It was a bomb that was put there to kill Morgan." Machin waited to allow what she'd told Marcia to sink in. "If it wasn't for Jill's car having a puncture, then Morgan would've been driving that car."

Marcia's face reddened as she thought about the mess she was now left with. "I'm guilty about lying to Morgan about Jill's visits here, but that's all I'm guilty of."

"Who was she seeing?" Roberts asked angrily.

His question was greeted by silence.

"You really need to work with us here," Machin told Marcia.

Marcia decided there was nothing left for her here now but to cooperate. Whatever cesspit of lies and deceit it uncovered, one thing was certain, it couldn't hurt Jill any more. "His name's Sunil Patel. He owns a furniture factory up on the Brompton Industrial Estate."

As Marcia spoke, Machin wrote notes. Roberts stood and started pacing the room. Marcia could see he was fuming. She couldn't hold his angry gaze and had to look away. Every time Roberts looked at her, she looked at Machin.

"Is that why she was out in the country heading toward Weatherly Grange?" Machin asked.

Marcia nodded. "She was meeting him there at seven-fifteen, and she was running late because of the flat tire."

"So, this Patel fellow was waiting for her at Weatherly Grange," Machin confirmed.

"That's what she told me," Marcia said.

"All those times you've told me that Jill was with

you when I've called! All those times, and she was really with him!" Roberts raged angrily as he pretended to finally comprehend Jill and Marcia's treachery. Marcia's silence confirmed everything. "You really are a piece of work, Marcia Bradley!" he shouted.

Marcia didn't bother saying she was sorry again. She wasn't sorry about all the lies she'd told Roberts in the last year, all she was really sorry about was the fact that her deceit had been found out. Tears started running down her face as she thought about Jill's body being ripped to pieces by the bomb. Machin handed Marcia some tissues from a box in the corner and Marcia slowly dried her eyes.

"I need some air," Roberts suddenly said and left the room.

Machin didn't go after him. Sometimes you had to give colleagues some space, especially when they'd suffered the body blows that Roberts had suffered tonight.

"What a mess, Miss Bradley," Machin remarked when they were alone.

"Why would anybody plant a bomb in Morgan's car?" Marcia asked.

Why, indeed? Machin thought. Roberts had gone off on a tangent with this investigation, disobeying orders. She was beginning to wonder if, during his investigation, he'd found something important about the terrorists, and they were trying to silence him.

Khan was always warning them about personal security, checking for tails, looking for anything unusual. Everybody who worked for Counter Terrorism Command was a prime target for the extremists. Then there was this Patel fellow. Could he be mental enough to try and kill his love rival so he could make a life with Jill Roberts?

"Have you ever met Patel?" Machin asked.

"Once. He's an extremely good-looking man. We

met him when we were out one night at a wine bar. There was an instant attraction between them."

"Is he married?"

"Jill told me he was divorced."

"So the only thing stopping the two of them becoming a couple was Roberts," Machin said.

She could see by the startled look in Marcia's gray-green eyes that she'd finally realized where Machin's chain of thought was leading. Marcia didn't like where it was going. It was going to a dark place of hate and murder where someone like Marcia Bradley had never gone before, and she had to admit, it wasn't a place she felt comfortable in.

CHAPTER 40

DCI Khan made Roberts sit down opposite him. Roberts looked a wreck. His wife was dead. She'd been murdered by a bomb probably meant for him. "I'm sorry for your loss, Morgan," Khan said. "Be reassured that we won't rest until we've got the bastards who did this," he promised.

Roberts sat and stared blankly out the window at the view, trying to act out the dazed persona of a grieving widower. "I keep thinking about the car. If I hadn't let her use my car, then she'd still be alive."

"Some things are out of our control in life," Khan said feebly. After finding out about Patel, Khan was starting to think that there might be more to the bombing than terrorism. Khan had sent Machin and a Crime Scene Investigator team to Patel's house and Patel's office at his factory. If there was anything to find they'd find it. "Take as much time off as you need to sort out the funeral and get yourself together, Morgan."

The funeral, Roberts thought, the funeral was going to be like something out of the *Twilight Zone*. It would be the funeral of a cheating wife, attended by Marcia Bradley, the lying friend. The ringmaster of the whole event

would be Detective Sergeant Morgan Roberts, the grieving husband, a man who'd murdered his wife. Not to
mention, Jill's vast assortment of relatives, who were
now going to blame him and his wretched job for Jill's
death—all because the bomb had been placed in Roberts's car. Their blame wasn't misplaced, Roberts
thought, as Khan rattled on about bereavement and the
availability of a police counselor if Roberts needed to talk
to someone.

During Khan's speech, his mobile phone rang. He
answered it. It was Machin. During the phone conversation, Khan smiled, commended her on her good work,
then after writing down all the detailed information she
had given him, he hung up.

"Did DI Machin find anything, sir?" Roberts asked.

"It's good news. There was some residue from the
Semtex in the kitchen of Patel's apartment. CSI is in no
doubt that it was Patel who planted the bomb in your
car," Khan explained. "DI Machin's just arrested him for
your wife's murder."

Roberts, who wanted to scream with delight, contented himself with, "I thought the bomb had been planted by terrorists, sir."

"So did I, but it looks like it was Patel. He knew you
worked for Counter Terrorism Command and obviously
thought that if he planted a bomb in your car, we'd think
it was the work of terrorists," Khan said. "He wanted you
dead, Morgan, he wanted you dead so he could start a
new life with your wife."

How naive, Roberts thought. Khan seemed to have
decided that everything had been tidied up in a nice easy
package. "Instead, he bungled it and killed Jill," Roberts
reflected.

There was a moment's reverential silence. Even
though they'd managed to quickly solve the crime, nei-

ther man felt elated. With his sergeant's current state of mind, Khan didn't think that it was a good idea for Roberts to be working on any cases. He'd like him to take a few weeks off away from things. "Maybe you should take some leave," Khan suggested.

Roberts's expression was filled with horror. "I'd sooner work," he said.

"Have some time off until after the funeral," Khan insisted, and Roberts could see by the steely look on his commander's face that this time there'd be no shifting him.

"Just a few days," Roberts reluctantly agreed.

"I don't want you in on the interview with Patel—"

"But, sir—"

"There's no but, sir, about it. You're not going to sit in on the interview, and that's my final decision."

Any court case would be in tatters if Roberts was involved in the interview, Khan thought. At any future trial, Patel's defense barrister would tear apart any confession obtained by Roberts as he was directly connected to the case. To his credit, Roberts realized this and didn't argue.

As he quietly left the building, he thought about the murder of his wife. Now that she was dead, the house would be empty. Everywhere he looked around the place, he would find her things. He'd already made the decision to move, but that would be in the future, not until this chaos had died down. At the moment, he needed to remain unhinged, a man destroyed by his loss. It would be a long time before Roberts could openly show joy as an emotion. Though he couldn't show any joy on the outside, inside was another matter.

The satisfaction he derived, knowing that he'd made his wife pay for her treachery, meant that Roberts would be dancing a jig for all eternity.

CHAPTER 41

The Voice knew how to maneuver people into places, how to choose the right moment to make his move while also working within the tight constraints of time. It was an acquired art that not many people in this fast-paced, computer generated society were capable of. The Voice knew he had exceptional abilities. The way his disciples had weaved their path of death and destruction across a swath of southeast England without leaving any clues was truly a mighty feat of planning and preparation on the Voice's part. You only made mistakes if you were reckless. The Voice wasn't reckless, the Voice would never let any of his disciples leave the lair until they were fully prepared for battle.

The Voice stood along the street outside Tredwell's Trenton Towers apartment block. He noted that Tredwell's beat up Volkswagen Polo was parked outside, so he knew that she was home. He took out his mobile phone and called her private number that he'd obtained from his sources. As it was her private line, she answered quickly. On discovering it was a stranger calling, she was surprised. The Voice told her he was a freelance reporter, and he had information regarding the recent far right terror attacks in Brighton and Folkestone.

"Why are you calling me?" Tredwell asked warily.

"You work for an anarchist internet paper, you're a journalist, I thought you might be prepared to pay me a fee for a scoop like this." The Voice could tell, by the fact that she hadn't hung up and she was still on the line, that she was interested.

"What kind of information are we talking about?"

"The right kind, Miss Tredwell—the kind that exposes these evil killers." The Voice could tell by her momentary lapse into silence that she was now attentive.

"And how do I know what you're selling me is legitimate info?" she asked suspiciously, wondering if this was a clever scam by one of her many enemies to set her up.

"Don't worry, everything I'm going to sell you will be invaluable and categorically proves who the killers are," the Voice promised. "I'll contact you in two days, and we'll conclude the deal."

"But you—"

The Voice hung up before Tredwell could finish her sentence.

She was left baffled by the call. She should've called the police and told them about it, but, through her beliefs, she viewed the police as Fascists who couldn't be trusted. Ringing the police wasn't an option until she had undisputable proof of who the killers were.

Tredwell didn't trust anybody. Because she was always ranting about corruption in government and the media, the *Invicta Star* had many enemies. She was sure they'd try and cover it up, that they'd somehow put the blame for the recent atrocities at the feet of the militant left. She wasn't going to give them that opportunity. This time, the Fascists weren't going to escape retribution for their sins. If the reporter wanted to make a deal, then she would make it. She knew, with the Fascists' recent support in the local elections, that the militant left needed to knock down their house of cards and knock it down quickly. If this information for sale was for real, then this was the chance to do so, or so she hoped, because if they didn't stop the Fascists soon, then there was a real danger that their success would destroy everything she believed in.

CHAPTER 42

In the cell, Craig sat up, quite alert, watching the movie about the Mosley march and the battle between the British Union of Fascists and anti-Fascist demonstrators at Cable Street in 1936. As the fighting between the British Union of Fascists' supporters and their opponents erupted into running street battles, the Voice said, "Take a look at the film, Craig, and see how true patriots battle to protect their homeland."

Craig avidly watched the battle. The Voice could see on the monitor screen that his youthful unlined face was twitching intently as he watched the drama unfold. He had now been drugged and brainwashed for three weeks. The boy no longer had a will of his own. The Voice decided he was almost ready for the sacred task which had befallen him.

As the battle of Cable Street finally ended, the Voice slipped Craig's drugged drink and sandwiches through bars of the cell door. There was no need for the Voice to set his disciple further questions. The glazed look on Craig's face was a look that the Voice had encountered twice previously. It was a look that told the Voice that his disciple was almost ready.

"After your meal, I want you to lie on the bed and sleep for a few hours," the Voice ordered.

"Yes, sir," Craig said, collecting his meal off the floor and then taking it back to the bed to sit and eat it.

Once his disciple was asleep, the Voice would enter the cell and administer further drugs by means of a needle. The hour was now rapidly approaching whereby the biggest act of retribution for the ineptitude of crown and government was about to occur. The other attacks had been minor warnings for those who had infiltrated and destroyed British culture.

The next attack the Voice perpetrated was going to be the culmination of everything he'd been working for. To have a lasting effect on the hearts and minds of a populace, you had to strike right at the heart of its institutions. In a few days' time, the Voice was going to strike at a target finally worthy of his efforts, a target that, in the Voice's eyes, would make a difference to the whole direction in which Britain was heading. As he watched Craig eating his meal on the monitor, he wondered if there was any inkling in the boy's head of what awaited him. He was going to make history, and even if his death didn't make his parents proud, it would make the Voice proud, because after his time in the cell and at the end of his life, the Voice was the only true family that Craig would ever have.

CHAPTER 43

Machin and Khan sat opposite Patel and his solicitor, Mrs. Indra Kholi. Kholi was a dusky mid-forties stunner whose brains matched her beauty, the police officers quickly found out. Khan was insistent about sitting in on the interview. He owed it to DS Roberts to personally make sure that they nailed this bastard who'd murdered his wife. So far, Patel denied everything, and his complete denial was proving an irritant.

"How long have you been seeing Jill Roberts, Mr. Patel?" Machin asked.

"It's been over a year. I haven't really been counting the days," Patel answered matter-of-factly.

Khan had already taken an extreme dislike to the murdering businessman. "According to Marcia Bradley, you met Jill Roberts in a Worthing wine bar last October when Miss Bradley and Mrs. Roberts were on a night out."

"That's right," Patel agreed.

"And you've been seeing Jill Roberts behind her husband's back ever since," Machin stated.

"I'm not proud of the fact that she was married.

There was an attraction between us that meant that we couldn't give up seeing each other," Patel explained. "In life, a man can't always choose the person he falls in love with, Inspector."

"I agree, which is why you had to remove all obstacles from out of the way that could interfere with your happiness." Machin paused to let her comments sink in. "Roberts was the obstacle stopping you from making a life together with Jill—removing that obstacle is the reason you planted the bomb in DS Roberts's car."

"My client has already told you he had nothing to do with Mrs. Roberts's murder," Kholi interjected.

"Then, how do you explain the traces of Semtex explosives that the CSI team found in your client's apartment, Mrs. Kholi?" Machin asked.

"I can't explain it," Patel cut in, and Khan could see Patel's eyes were slightly red where he'd been crying. Whether it was tears of upset that the love of his life was dead or tears because the police had caught him after committing murder, Khan had no idea.

"Now, isn't that a surprise," Khan said in a voice laced with sarcasm.

"My client has no idea how the traces of Semtex explosives got into his kitchen, my client didn't have Semtex in his home, and has never dealt with explosives in his life," Kholi emphasized.

"Yet, we still found traces of explosives in his home," Machin said.

"I've no idea how they got there," Patel reiterated.

"We will be charging you with murder," Khan told Patel.

"But I didn't kill her—"

"That's just the point. You did not intend to kill *her*. When you planted the bomb in Roberts's car, you were trying to murder Roberts. With Roberts being a member of Counter Terrorism Command, you knew we'd think he'd been killed by terrorists," Machin explained calmly. For the sake of her colleague, she had to make sure that this interview was calm and structured, and that they made no mistakes in getting their man.

"I didn't plant the bomb," Patel said defiantly.

"My client isn't involved in this murder. The fact that you found the traces of Semtex in his kitchen surely shows that someone is trying to set him up," Kholi interjected coolly.

"We're confident that the court will see it the way we see it, Mrs. Kholi," Khan declared. "If the car had blown up with DS Roberts in it, we'd never have had any idea that Jill Roberts was having an affair. It was only because the tire on her car was flat, and that she'd had to switch to her husband's car, that we found out through Jill Roberts's friend, Marcia Bradley, that Jill was having an affair with your client."

The room lapsed into silence as Kholi realized that this was going to trial, and there was nothing she could say or do that was going to change that fact. "How do I know that DS Roberts didn't know about his wife's affair beforehand?" she pushed.

"I know he didn't because I was with DS Roberts when he called Marcia Bradley to talk to his wife. Miss Bradley lied and told DS Roberts that Jill Roberts was there, and it was only after we went to her house and confronted her that we found out that Jill Roberts was having an affair with Mr. Patel," Machin confirmed.

"That still doesn't prove anything. None of that proves for certain that DS Roberts didn't know about his wife's affair before you confronted Miss Bradley," Kholi pressed.

"Marcia Bradley admitted she'd lied to DS Roberts every time he rang there on her make-believe girly nights with Jill Roberts—nights when Jill Roberts lied to her husband and told him she was staying at Miss Bradley's. If Marcia Bradley and Jill Roberts consistently lied to him, how could he have known?" Machin asked.

Kholi didn't know, but it would give her another angle of attack in the courtroom. That and a possible terrorist bombing of DS Roberts's car would at least give her something to work on. Kholi decided all that could wait. She waited until the officers had formerly made the charges and then asked to speak to her client alone.

As Machin stepped out of the interview room, all sorts of thoughts were racing through her head. She tried to remember back to the night of the bombing and when she'd had to tell Roberts the grim news of his wife's death. Roberts had reacted with shock and uncertainty, exactly how Machin had expected him to react. Machin tried to think. Could it have been too much as expected? Was Roberts playing her?

Machin cleared her head of doubts, deciding that the fact that Mrs. Kholi, who was used to working on juries and creating doubt, was playing mind games with her. She had worked with Roberts for a long time and had always found him straight and above board. She had no doubts about her colleague—he had covered her back on many occasions in the past. He wasn't a killer, and, in court, she'd make sure that the arguments for the police's case were strong enough to prove that Patel was the guilty one.

CHAPTER 44

The funeral parlor was cold and lifeless. Sweet smelling flowers were scattered liberally around the room in ornate vases to try and lessen the decay of death for the distraught relatives. This was the moment put aside by the funeral director for the bereaved relatives to pay their last respects to the deceased, in this case, Jill Roberts. Roberts sat on his own, staring at the gleaming mahogany coffin with his treacherous wife lying inside. Because of the state of Jill's body after the bomb blast, the coffin advisably remained shut—as the funeral director had solemnly explained when he'd spoken to a distraught Roberts about it—in this case, it was surely better to remember a loved one the way she was before the blast.

News of Jill's affair had slowly filtered out to her angry family. The fact that she'd been killed by a bomb, in her husband's car, and that he happened to work for Counter Terrorist Command, meant that most of Jill's side of the family blamed Roberts and the profession he'd chosen in life for the demise of their dearly beloved. It meant that, in his hour of grief, Roberts was alone. Alone was how Roberts liked it. With his wife's coldness in recent months, he'd been alone mentally and physically for a long time. At least with the bitch now dead, he had the chance to start a new life without his anger at her treachery constantly niggling at him.

He'd so wanted to be included in the interview team that interviewed Patel. To experience the joy of seeing the man that had destroyed his marriage sitting there squirming in front of Machin's grilling would have been the ultimate revenge. Alas, it was a pleasure he'd been denied. As he thought of his wife lying inside the coffin, he tried to think of the good times, but all he could think of in recent times were the bad. They'd never been as close as they should have been. At first, in the marriage, the sex had been rampant. Soon the excessive frequency had been replaced by once a week if he was lucky. In the end, after Jill had hooked up with Patel, it had come down to virtually never.

The irony of Jill being killed in a quiet country lane while sneaking off to a lover's tryst at a country hotel wasn't lost on Roberts. At least she'd had the decency, in the end, to die on her own and not kill innocent bystanders. Khan had rung Roberts, just before he left home to come to the funeral parlor, to inform Roberts that Patel had officially been charged with murder. Machin was the one that bothered Roberts. She knew Roberts better than anybody on the force. If there was anyone who could see any flaws in his story, it would be her.

As Roberts sat in a moment's quiet reflection in the serene setting, suddenly the chapel of rest door opened, and he was surprised to see Marcia Bradley dressed in black standing there. "I'm sorry, I thought you'd gone," Bradley quickly apologized, then she turned to go.

"It's okay, I'm done here," Roberts said.

As he walked past her to go out the door, Bradley said, "I'm really sorry for lying, Morgan, whatever happened between you and Jill in your marriage, you didn't deserve to be treated the way she treated you."

Roberts paused, looked long and hard into Marcia Bradley's sorrowful eyes. "Your lies now seem irrelevant with Jill lying dead, Marcia darling." Roberts was relieved as somehow he managed a tear. He took out a hanky and wiped his eyes. The expression he saw on Bradley's face showed a level of guilt that Roberts had seldom seen even on the faces of arrested criminals.

It was too much, even for Bradley, already riddled with guilt. Roberts was surprised when the lying bitch grabbed him in a hug and held him tight. She hugged Roberts to her breast and gently offered endless apologies.

They were apologies that meant nothing now. As he held her, the only feelings that Roberts had regarding her was the wish that Marcia Bradley had been in the car with Jill when the bomb had exploded.

As they held each other in this moment of bereaved comfort, Roberts somehow summoned the strength for an anguished bout of tears on Bradley's shoulder. Roberts was playing the distraught, grieving husband, to perfection.

By his grief, he intended banishing any of the suspicions from his doubters that he'd been anything other than destroyed by his wife's murder.

The smell of Bradley's elegant Chanel perfume was making his pretense of grief difficult. Bradley had always had a voluptuous figure and an openly sexual nature that somehow seemed more prominent when she was dressed in black silk stockings under her mourning clothes.

It was at that moment that an unfortunate event occurred, an event that even Roberts found tasteless in light of Jill's shattered body lying in state barely yards away.

The fact that his phallus was quickly hardening and

pressing against Marcia Bradley's leg was, he decided, a fact that even a grief-stricken Marcia Bradley couldn't help but notice.

CHAPTER 45

The Voice returned to his lair at midnight. At midnight, the hills around his lair were quiet and dark. Any stray dog walkers that sometimes walked by on the distant path were long gone by this time of the night. Brainwashing wasn't just about administering the drugs to the victim and wasn't only about showing the films. Although the drugs and films were a main component of the brainwashing process, one component that was also never overlooked by the Voice was the necessity to disorientate the victim.

When the Voice looked at the TV monitors, he could see his charge lying fast asleep on the bed. Quietly, he entered the cell with the syringe and pressed the needle into the vein of the sleeping boy's warm, sweaty arm. Craig stirred momentarily as he felt the jabbing needle prick into his flesh, but didn't stir for long, as once the injection of the will-sucking drugs had been made, Craig soon became acquiescent.

The chance for Craig to prove his worth to the nation was only a few days away. As the Voice stood and looked at the sleeping boy, he wondered if he was ready. By his inability to do anything other than obey the

Voice's commands, he'd shown all the signs of being ready. In the last week, the Voice had easily been able to mold his disciple to his will. Molding a disciple in the controlled confines of the lair was easy. The disciple he sent off on his mission into the outside world, and it was at that moment that the Voice would find out whether the correct training had been administered or not.

D-Day was rapidly approaching. The Voice was nervous, as this was going to be the culmination of all his plans. It had taken a lot of time and careful planning—the main reason why he'd chosen his lair here in the first place. Soon his lair would no longer be needed, and the imprint on society that he'd attempted through his terrorist acts would have been achieved. He looked at the reinforced concrete and the bars with love and affection. His lair had been his special place, somewhere he could work from to right the wrongs of British society and administer his own form of justice.

Tredwell wasn't an easy woman to coax into a trap, but somehow the Voice would manage it. Tomorrow, he'd arrange the meeting. She would come. The chance of proving that the neo-Nazis were behind the terror campaign would be too much of a temptation for her to resist.

The Voice put on thick rubber gloves. Now wasn't the time for making errors. From a leather doctor's bag on the floor, the Voice took out the chemical bottle containing the deadly germ ready for the morning of the mission. The flowers weren't here as they would be purchased fresh and pure nearer the day of the mission. The Voice liked to call it the day of reckoning, the day when the culmination of his plan came together. He switched on the movie projector and started a rerun of a Mosley speech. Even while sleeping, his disciple's intellectual development had to be constantly nurtured.

His disciple was going to have a chance to strike at the top. All his disciples had been given the opportunity to strike back at the people who were to blame for the mess the country was in. If the people at the top in politics had steered this country on a better path, if any of them had understood, like the Voice, the direction this country needed to go in, there would not have been any need for the Voice's actions. They'd ignored the soothsayers, the Mosleys, the Enoch Powells, and the justified protestations of the National Front in the 1970s and 1980s. They'd ignored them, and what were the British people left with? They were left with a weak youth going nowhere, a youth full of get-rich-quick decadence and trashy reality TV fame.

The Voice had shown with his three disciples to date that strength and will did exist among the youth of Britain, but that will needed to be led and channeled in the right direction. Around the entrance to the lair, he carefully set the explosives, making sure that there was not too much to make too loud a bang. All he needed was enough impact to collapse the entrance, enough to set off the necessary chaos and confusion if it ever became necessary for him to do so. So many things had to be taken care of—Tredwell, Bailey, the little matter of the police, and then Mori Kemp. They all thought they were in control of things, though really they were just marionettes in the Voice's puppet show, a show that was soon to reach a dazzling conclusion.

As he surveyed his work around the entrance, he was pleased. Outside, he hid the trigger switch in the bushes near the doorway. He now had the means whereby he could seal his lair at a moment's notice. He made the boy a sandwich, poured him a drink, and left it on the bed next to him for when he awoke. In a short while, Craig would be on his way, for tomorrow was the day when the

Voice's plan would be set into full motion. Although the Voice was a master in setting people up, he wasn't arrogant, always remembering the fact that he couldn't afford to make any mistakes. In the Voice's master plan, there was no room for mistakes as they would mean the end. And mistakes would mean his dream of a new Britain would be over.

CHAPTER 46

The funeral was an unusually openly unsympathetic affair, Machin thought, as she stood near Roberts. Nobody could fail to notice the hostile glares emanating from Jill's parents. They obviously blamed Roberts for their daughter's death, thought Jill had been killed by a terrorist bomb aimed at Roberts. Machin wanted to grab them by the throat and tell them the real story, explain about Jill's treachery and of how she'd, in fact, been accidently killed by her lover trying to murder Morgan Roberts. Wisely, she didn't say anything. A funeral wasn't the time or the place for such outbursts or for people to deal with the harsh reality of the truth.

There would be no wake after the funeral. Roberts had immediately decided that the circumstances surrounding Jill's murder might make it seem hypocritical to have one.

Machin agreed. She stared at Marcia Bradley and decided she couldn't hope to ever understand the depth of hatred Roberts must now feel toward Bradley. Bradley's lies had carried on the duplicity for over a year, a deception that had made Roberts think that he had a happy marriage when, all the while, it had been a sham.

The priest seemed to sense the funeral party's enmity, mumbling his words as they lowered what was left of Jill's body into the grave. It was a relief to everyone when the service was over. As the mourners drifted away, Roberts and Machin stood for a while in the tranquility of the peaceful graveyard.

When they were the only two people remaining, Roberts said, "I want to come back to work."

"After all this, that's not wise," Machin said.

"It's wiser than sitting at home, mulling over all the lies Jill and her friend told me. It's better than staying home and seeing all her possessions around me and wondering who the hell my wife really was."

She understood. By her infidelity, Jill Roberts hadn't been the wife that Roberts thought she was. A wife being murdered by her lover in a bungled attempt to murder you was certainly not a scenario any man could envisage when he agreed to tie the knot. She wondered whether she should mention the fact that by willingly taking Roberts's car, Jill Roberts must've had no notion of Patel's intent to murder her husband. Looking at the desolation on her colleague's pale, lifeless face, she decided it was obviously not the time or place for reaffirming that Jill had not been involved in the plan to kill her husband.

There was nobody left lingering around the church gates when Roberts and DI Machin made their way back to the funeral limo. On the journey back to his house, Roberts tried again. "I need to get back to work, ma'am."

"If I allow you to come back, then you mustn't interfere with the Patel case," she warned him.

"Do you really think I'm that stupid, ma'am?"

Machin knew he wasn't. She also knew DCI Khan would not allow it. Khan liked to do everything by the book and would probably insist that Roberts take part in some kind of psychiatric program to rehabilitate before he returned to work. "No, Sergeant, I know you're not stupid," she said.

They got out the car and, after the limo had departed, they stood on the pavement a moment, staring at the house.

Machin had been through a lot in the company of this man, and before she went back to her car, they hugged briefly, Roberts shedding some tears. Her parting words were, "If you come back in the morning, Morgan, you do everything I say, I don't want you going off on a tangent or disobeying orders as you did with the Bailey tail."

"Keeping the tail on Bailey produced results, ma'am," Roberts said vehemently.

"And that's the only reason why I haven't reprimanded you for disobeying orders." Machin turned to leave, adding, "One word of warning, if you ever disobey any of my orders again, I'll personally finish you, sergeant. Is that clear?"

"Clear, ma'am," Roberts said.

As Machin slowly walked back to her car parked up the street, Roberts was sure that his superior meant what she said. At her car, she opened the boot and checked all around her car for bombs. Since Jill Roberts's death, DCI Khan had made sure that all his Counter Terrorist Command officers were on high alert.

Roberts watched Machin's checks with interest, thinking that, as usual, his colleagues were reacting too late to events. Such searches were too late for Jill, Roberts having already taken care of that problem. He'd also taken care of the Patel problem.

As he stepped into his house and shut the door, he smiled to himself, relieved that, at last, the pretense of the day was over. He got a beer from the fridge and sat on the sofa, thinking of Patel languishing in his jail cell, and then Roberts laughed. It was the first time he'd laughed in a long while, it was the first time he'd laughed since before he found out about Jill's affair, and boy did it feel good!

CHAPTER 47

Mori Kemp sat in her dressing gown, listening to Vancouver punk on You Tube. As she drank her vodka and coke, she thought how wonderful the world was. Today had been an exceptional day. After her talk with the police, and on realizing that her overseas account had been compromised, she'd immediately changed that account to a new account, registered to a bank in Perth, Australia. She'd now installed endless fail-safes surrounding it, and, this time, she was confident that her account could not be compromised. Wise hackers learned from their mistakes, she decided, and, if one wanted to survive in this ever more hostile world, it was necessary to learn quickly.

With the money now safe, she devoted all her attention to the City share scheme con—a con that was only a matter of days away. When the money from this had cleared in her overseas bank, she was gone. Her new identity was already in place, and the documents to give her that new life were safely locked away in the safe-deposit box of a London bank.

The moment she received confirmation that the share con was done, she'd visit the bank and collect her docu-

ments from her safety-deposit box on the way to the air-
port.

Tonight he was coming to pay her. She'd done everything required of her and had acted suitably shocked
when Bailey had turned up at her door, looking for information. It was kinder that way. It would've been a
cruel slight to a man like Bailey—who always wanted to
be in control—to ever let him know that he was completely out of control and that, on this occasion, he'd been
played.

When the doorbell rang, Kemp smiled. The one thing
she'd noticed with her dealings with this man was that he
was always punctual, and someone that you could rely
upon. He was paying her twenty-five grand for her services, money that, along with what Bailey had paid her,
would ensure that when she began her new life in Australia, for the first year, she wouldn't have to touch any of
the share scam money.

As she opened the front door to greet him, Kemp was
relieved to see he was carrying the case containing her
money.

"I'm glad to see you," she said.

Looking at the greed in her eyes, the Voice could see
that it wasn't him but the case she was talking about.

The Voice put the case down on the landing. "It's
nice to see you too," he said and then grabbed her dress-
ing-gown and pulled her out at lightning speed onto the
balcony. He then hurled Kemp over the landing barrier
and out into the abyss. As her horrified screams rent the
air like a banshee wail in the night, the Voice picked up
the case and hurried toward the stairwell.

Before Kemp's body shattered against the hard, un-
forgiving tarmac, the Voice was already hurtling down
the stairs back to the street. As a crowd started to gather
around her body, the Voice slipped away, keeping well

back from the glare of the yellow street lights. By the time an ambulance siren's screech drifted on the air, the Voice had disappeared like a ghost in the night.

CHAPTER 48

They'd stopped at a service station on the way to Folkestone. While Machin was filling up the car at the petrol pumps, Roberts had walked across the road and was sitting on a wall making some calls on his mobile phone. It was private business to do with Jill and her personal belongings, and she could understand why Roberts needed some privacy to make his calls. She was still concerned that, after his recent bereavement, she'd let Roberts come back to work too early. Khan had allowed her to make the call, and, so far, there had been nothing in Roberts's actions throughout the morning that would cause her to think anything other than that he was back on his game.

Machin was trying to digest the news that had just filtered through to her about Mori Kemp. Apparently, she had fallen to her death from the balcony of her flat. It was surely too coincidental that a hacker who was uncovering dark secrets for Bailey about leftist loonies could die of an accident like this. Machin had her own thoughts on the matter, and her thoughts were drifting along the lines of murder.

Foster was keeping an eye on Tredwell's apartment.

He'd followed Bailey there—Bailey was farther up the street outside the apartment block, still spying on Tredwell. If either of them moved, Foster was ready to follow. Bailey's interest in Tredwell meant that Machin was also interested. Either Tredwell was up to something, or Bailey was trying to plant evidence on her that would make it look to the police like she was involved in the terrorist attacks.

When they arrived at where Foster was parked up the road from Tredwell's apartment, they assessed the situation and Bailey's location. Machin now decided to relieve Foster for a few hours. Bailey was ten cars away parked at the curbside, there was no way he could see them. If either Tredwell or Bailey moved, they were ready. She took a look at the recent MI5 picture of Tredwell, a dissident known to the security services. She was a woman who had always been politically active, a fact in these days of rampant terrorism that had quickly drawn her to the security services' attention.

After half an hour, there was movement by the apartment door, swiftly followed by an anxious looking Tredwell rushing to her car. As she drove off, she was quickly followed by Bailey, and, at a distance, Machin. She wondered if Bailey was involved in Kemp's murder. She would like to have arrested him and grilled him about it, but, at the moment, with so much happening now, any thoughts of arresting Bailey would have to be put on hold.

"She looked like she meant business, ma'am," Roberts said as the procession slowly drove off into the busy early afternoon traffic.

They followed the A20 toward Dover, at a roundabout, close to a Megger Group factory, Tredwell suddenly turned left and then started driving up a hill toward the Western Heights. It was too open to tail too close behind,

Machin had no choice but to linger far behind so she wouldn't be spotted by Bailey. It meant they might lose both of them, but that was a better scenario than Bailey realizing he was being followed.

As they reached the top of a road called Military Road, they spotted Tredwell's car parked in a clifftop car park overlooking Dover's bustling harbor. Machin drove on, trying not to draw attention to herself. Rather worryingly, she realized there was no sign of Bailey. She stopped a little way up the road out of sight of the car park. "I can't risk going any closer to her than this," Machin told Roberts. "You'd better get out and work your way back to the car park through the bushes," she ordered.

Roberts slipped out the passenger door and ducked into thick bushes. Machin drove up a road toward the Western Heights citadel, parking just past the shell of a Knights Templar Church. Machin got out of the car and stared through a gap in the brown-leafed trees at Tredwell who was sitting in her car in the car park below. As she watched Tredwell. Machin heard a rustling sound and then saw movement in the nearby clumpy bushes. Suddenly, a smiling Bailey surprisingly stepped out of the bushes in front of Machin. He said, "You wouldn't make a very good Marine Commander, Inspector."

"I've got Roberts with me—don't try anything!" Machin told him nervously.

Bailey sighed. "You still don't get it, do you, Inspector? I'm not involved in any of this."

"The fact that you've been following Tredwell tells me you're involved," Machin retorted angrily.

"I knew Foster was following me, I caught on that you were following me the moment I drove off from outside Tredwell's apartment block," he explained. "If I didn't want you following me, believe me, Machin, you wouldn't be."

Machin edged back toward her car. They were just off the barely used road to the Citadel. If Bailey killed her, nobody was likely to see it. If Bailey had murdered Kemp and was desperate, then what did he have to lose by murdering her? Machin thought. She lunged for the door handle, opened the door, jumped in the car, and shut and locked the door. "Don't try anything,"

Bailey's unshaven face looked genuinely shocked by Machin's behavior. He stepped back a yard to pacify her. "Why would I try anything?" he asked, then he saw the Glock 17 pistol Machin had removed from her shoulder holster pointing at him, and he could see she wasn't in a reasoning mood.

"Kemp is dead," Machin stated, "did you kill her?"

Bailey looked stunned. "I don't know what you're talking about."

"Kemp's dead. She was found in the car park in front of her flat. She'd crashed to her death from the veranda outside her flat—initial reports reckon she might've been pushed."

There was a moment's tense silence.

"Listen, Machin, I didn't kill her. This is the first I've heard about it," Bailey protested. He was lost in thought for a second. "Anyway, hasn't your tail been following me? Wouldn't your tail have seen me go to Kemp's flat if I went there?"

Machin had already checked. Foster had followed Bailey to a Folkestone sea front hotel where he had stayed the night. At night when he was out of Foster's view in his hotel room, Bailey had the opportunity to sneak out of the hotel, kill Kemp, then sneak back to his room. The hotel had two exits and a fire escape. It had been too much ground for Foster to cover on his own,

Foster couldn't guarantee that Bailey hadn't left the hotel the night of Kemp's murder.

"Did it upset you that Kemp talked to us? Did you decide to go to her apartment and silence her?" Machin pressed.

"Of course not, I've been in Folkestone for the last couple of days," Bailey told her angrily.

"You've got a mobile phone, Bailey, there's nothing to stop you from ringing a friend to do the dirty deed." Machin could see that Bailey was rattled. "I suppose, being an elected politician, you didn't want to get your hands dirty. It was better to remain unattached."

"As you say, I'm an elected politician. Why would I get involved with murdering a woman I went to for information?" Bailey calmly pointed out.

"Illegally hacked information."

"I've no idea where Miss Kemp got it from, all I know is, she was an old acquaintance from my days as a police detective and was once a valuable information source. I asked her to make some private enquiries about some things for me, I've no idea to whom she made those enquiries or how she obtained what I wanted," Bailey said.

Bailey was being careful with the wording of everything he said. Machin reasoned, with his guarded attitude to life, Bailey was truly on the road to a bright political future. His problem was, it would only be bright if he could attribute the recent far right terrorist attacks to someone else other than his party.

"Before Kemp died, she told us what she gave you, she gave us the same list she gave you. That's why we knew you were following Tredwell," Machin explained.

Bailey looked furious at Kemp's betrayal, his irritated expression showed his horror that the police knew what he knew. "I think Tredwell is involved in this in some way," he said.

"Although she has a past record as a militant troublemaker, there's no record of her being involved in any terrorist activity," Machin stated. "What you've been doing by spying on her is virtually harassment, Bailey."

"My party isn't involved in this," Bailey declared. "I've made enquiries among friends and colleagues. With the recent gains we made in the local elections, none of them are involved in terrorism, and all are solidly behind the electoral process."

"Nobody is going to admit to this, Bailey. Brainwashing teenage boys to do evil acts of murder, these are the type of cowardly attacks carried out by fiends who always stay in the shadows."

"You've seen Tredwell's file. She fits the pattern of someone loony enough to try and destroy the far right by doing this," Bailey reckoned.

Machin laughed. It was a laugh tinged with sarcasm. "That's right, the imaginary pattern where everybody but far right extremists is responsible for terrorist attacks."

"I've seen her personal files," Bailey reluctantly admitted. "She's in a secret anarchist group, called 'Red Vengeance,' their objective is to smash the EPP. What better way of destroying us than by setting us up for this horror."

"We can't arrest everybody who wants to smash your regressive party, Bailey, if we did that we'd have to arrest most of the population of Britain."

Bailey was irritated by Machin's contemptuous statement, he needed to ignore it and concentrate on getting his point across. "She's in an anarchist terror cell. I've got proof of that fact off her computer files," he confirmed to her, rather unwisely.

"So you've illegally tapped into Tredwell's personal

computer files, at best that's a breach of privacy and makes you liable under all sorts of hacking personal information laws," she informed him.

Bailey tried to change the subject. "Why do you think she's come to the Western Heights fortifications?"

"To look at the boats, meet a friend, maybe she just likes coming up here because it's quiet, and it's a place where she can think," Machin offered. "She's not doing anything illegal here. It's a shame the same can't be said about your actions."

"She was violently active in that riot in the City last year. Kemp showed me several incidences of her and her colleagues involved in vicious assaults on the police and vandalizing private property."

Machin sighed. "You're just digging that hole deeper and deeper, Bailey. Illegally accessing CCTV cameras, breaking into Tredwell's personal computer files, there seems to be no end to your crimes, Mr. Elected Politician."

"Kemp was good at what she did," Bailey said.

"May I remind you that you're not a cop anymore? As a private citizen, you shouldn't be involved in any of this."

"I shouldn't be, but, in your eyes, it seems to be okay for an anarchist terrorist cell like Red Vengeance to operate outside the law."

"Stop trying to twist things, Bailey. You've admitted breaking the law. I'd worry more about defending your own position rather than attacking Tredwell."

"It was stupid of me to expect an unprejudiced approach from the police. The police have always been biased against the EPP."

"We're biased against anybody who incites hatred," Machin told Bailey. "Society wants nothing to do with dinosaurs like you stuck in the past."

"We're patriots, only interested in what's best for Britain."

"A ragtag Nazi mob," she stated.

"I'm a democratically elected politician, Inspector. Since I am a democratically elected politician, you should be accountable to me."

"If your activities were inside the law then maybe I would be," Machin lectured. She thought about what Bailey was doing, adding, "What was the idea of tailing Tredwell? Were you trying to stitch Tredwell and her colleagues up by planting evidence on her?"

"Of course not," he snapped. "From what I've seen of her personal files, the only reason that I've been following her is because I think she might be involved in terrorism."

"Well, you would say that if you've planted evidence to set her up," she said.

"I'm not trying to set her up," Bailey retorted.

"If it wasn't for the fact that I am aware of your deviousness and I wouldn't be able to prove any of this, I'd arrest you for planting evidence on her," Machin threatened.

Bailey ignored her goading remarks. "If the police were doing their job properly, I wouldn't need to follow Tredwell."

"There's no evidence that Tredwell or any of her comrades are involved in these terrorist attacks. I've only got your word for it that this Red Vengeance exists, and that that information you only acquired through illegally accessing Tredwell's private computer files."

"Believe me, the evidence is there," Bailey said, not mentioning that he'd accessed Tredwell's computer by breaking into her flat and stealing her passcodes from a book in the drawer. With the police on an EPP witch hunt, Bailey decided that some things were best left un-said.

"Evidence you can never show me because you obtained it illegally," she mocked.

"I'm just looking for the truth," Bailey offered.

"No, Bailey, you're looking for a scapegoat." Machin's mobile phone rang, she answered, making sure that her gun was trained on Bailey while she talked to an excited sounding Roberts.

"She's walking along the track to the left of the car park, ma'am. She's acting very suspiciously," Roberts reported.

"Keep tailing her. I've found Bailey, I'll be bringing him with me," Machin said surprisingly.

"Is that wise, ma'am?" Roberts asked.

"Probably not, but if I want him where I can see him, then what choice do I have, Sergeant?"

With that, Roberts gave her more detailed directions of where he was located. She confirmed she'd be there shortly and then hung up. She stepped from the car, pointing the gun at Bailey.

"There's no need for the gun," Bailey said.

"I think there's every need," she said as she kept him a few yards in front of her with the gun trained on his back. "Get moving," she ordered and then pointed in the direction of a nearby muddy, overgrown track Roberts had directed her toward.

Bailey reluctantly started walking, didn't like the way any of this was panning out. He looked at Machin's cold eyes and quickly decided that she was a mean fucker and not someone to be trifled with. He started walking slowly in the direction where she had pointed. "And might I ask where we're going?"

Machin wasn't in the explaining mood. "Just shut your trap and go where I tell you," she ordered. "And one word of warning, Bailey, if I get any inkling that you're trying to be clever, then I'll kill you."

Usually, Bailey would protest at such threats, but today he said nothing, for in the brief time that he'd known DI Machin he was sure of one thing, and one thing only, and that was that she was a detective with balls and a woman who didn't make idle threats.

CHAPTER 49

The track was thick with clawing mud from the recent heavy rain. Even in her hiking boots, Tredwell found that her feet could barely grip and that she was slipping all over the place as she walked. The Voice had rung her shortly after she'd arrived at the car park, was giving her directions to a meeting point where they could talk in private, and he could give her full disclosure. Tredwell stopped close to a crumbling stone post, a relic from the derelict Napoleonic fortifications that still littered this fortress escarpment. It was where she'd been ordered to wait for further instructions. She didn't like it. Her eyes were nervously scouring the trees and bushes all around her, looking for movement. Her mobile phone rang, and she answered it immediately.

As expected, it was the Voice.

"I'm where you told me to come to," she stated nervously.

"I know," the Voice replied menacingly, leaving Tredwell in no doubt that even if she couldn't see him, he could see her. "Does the thought of exposing these far right loonies excite you, Miss Tredwell?" the Voice asked. "Does the thought of being an anarchist heroine make the blood rush through your veins?"

"You told me you had information on the recent terrorist killings," Tredwell urged, irritated by this whole charade. She didn't like the loneliness of the escarpment, and, although the hustle and bustle of the busy harbor could be seen below, on this dark, cold autumn afternoon, the atmosphere of these crumbling fortifications was bleak and haunting. She had recently read a ghost book on this part of Kent. The Western Heights were reputed to be haunted by the ghost of a headless drummer boy who'd come to a horrific end at the height of the Napoleonic garrison's occupation. If you let your mind wander, it could make you believe you could hear a rat-tat on the wind.

"That's why I asked you to meet me, Miss Tredwell. You must understand my position. Before I impart any information to you, I have to know that you've come alone, satisfy myself that you're someone I can trust."

"And what exactly is that information?" Tredwell asked.

"I've seen the evil atrocities this man has been carrying out, Miss Tredwell. I think we both agree that he has to be stopped. I intend to give you information about him that you can take to the authorities, I'm going to give you the proof you need to stop these Nazi fanatics from ever posing a threat to this country again."

Tredwell was suspicious, making up her mind to tread carefully. "The only way that you could know about who's doing this is if you're involved."

The Voice sighed. "There needs to be some trust here, Miss Tredwell. I'm not involved, I just know the person who is."

"I should go to the police," Tredwell said.

"And tell them what?"

Tredwell was silent. What could she tell the police?

One thing she'd learned in her dealings with the police was their animosity toward the militant left. If she went to the police with a ridiculous tale of a stranger ringing her and telling her he had information on the recent terrorist attacks, she knew it wouldn't wash. She definitely needed more. "Look, if you want to give me information on the recent terrorist attacks in Brighton and Folkestone, just give it to me."

"Just do exactly as I say, Miss Tredwell, or I'll hang up, and you'll never hear from me again. If that happens, then the killing will go on. Do you want to be responsible for a continuation of these atrocities when shortly I'm going to give you the means to stop them?" the Voice asked.

Tredwell could see that if she wanted to end this crazy terrorist madness and finally expose the Fascists for the evil creatures they were, then she had to go through with this. "What do you want me to do?"

"You follow my instructions, and then, after I've shown you the terrorist's lair, you can go to the police."

"This is getting creepy," Tredwell told the Voice. "How do I know that you're not leading me into a trap?"

"This isn't a trap, Miss Tredwell," the Voice insisted. "Rest assured that I know the man who is doing this. I followed him after I became suspicious. I followed him over this old fortress and found his lair. I've been watching him for a while now. I had to make sure before I told anybody. I called you because, at the moment, I know that he's nowhere around. That's why I rang you this afternoon, the reason I needed you here now."

"And why come to me with this? Why didn't you go to the police or the national dailies?"

"I've read your articles, and I've seen how your paper always comes out against the Fascists, warning the nation of their evil. I wanted someone I could trust to make sure that this is acted upon, someone I could deal with outside of the law."

"So you don't trust the police?" Tredwell said.

"Why would I?"

Tredwell was lost in thought. She'd had many bad dealings with the police over the years, so she fully understood the man's mistrust of them. There were many contradictions in what he was telling her, so many things that needed to be explained. She wished she had had more time to arrange for some of her colleagues to come along as back up. On these open heights, she felt too exposed and alone. "So far, all you've given me is the possibility that I'm being set up. I've made a lot of enemies with my exposé stories, there are many people who would like to see me dead." She paused so the Voice could fully understand she had doubts, adding, "What's to stop me from going back to my car, driving off, and telling the police everything you've told me?"

The Voice laughed. "You won't do that."

"How can you be so sure?"

"You're a militant left zealot. There's no way that you're going to pass up this opportunity to finally prove the Fascists are mass murderers. You know that such a disclosure would wipe out their support among the electorate overnight."

"That's if what you give me proves the far right are behind this," she said.

"I can prove it, just remember that. If you drive away from this, then you're always going to wonder if what I've been telling you was true," the Voice told her.

"Or maybe just before you kill me, I'm going to wonder how on earth I got suckered into such a vulnerable position."

"Either way, there's only one way you're going to find out," the Voice urged. He sensed her hesitancy. "If I wanted to kill you, I could've ambushed you from the bushes as you made your way along the track. I'm ex-army. I'm judged to be an excellent marksman. I could pick you off with a sniper's rifle from two hundred feet away. You wouldn't get a chance to move before the bullet ripped the life from you."

Tredwell nervously looked at the hills around her, realizing it would soon be dark. If the Voice shot her up here away from her car, there'd be no chance of survival. If he wanted to kill her, she'd already be dead. She made a decision. "Where do you want me to go?"

The Voice directed her farther along the slippery track to the places in the shadows of the Drop Redoubt where the sun seldom reached. "The lair that I want to show you is only a few minutes away."

"And what happens when I get there?" she asked nervously.

"Simple, we agree on a price, then I show you everything you need to see, and then I'll leave you, and then it's up to you to do what you want with it."

"I'm armed," Tredwell lied.

The Voice laughed, totally unintimidated by her threat. "No, you're not, Miss Tredwell. You're a well-known militant left political activist, in these days of terrorist high alerts you can't afford to be caught by the police carrying a gun."

She could see she wasn't going to get the drop on the Voice in any way. Every move she tried to make, he seemed to counter. "I've got the camera on my phone linked to a friend in case you try anything," she lied. She'd rung Karla, an associate at the paper and a fellow revolutionary, but Karla hadn't answered. Karla was a scatty woman who was always late for appointments and who never seemed to be around when Tredwell needed her.

"You do what you think you need to do to make yourself feel comfortable, Miss Tredwell. Like I said, all I'm trying to do is stop this madman." The Voice had kept her continuously talking on the phone, making sure she had no opportunity to call anybody. There was no way she'd rung her friend. He hadn't given her a chance to. He was slowly reeling her in with his neo-Nazi bait. It was just a matter of time.

"You're the terrorist, aren't you?" Tredwell asked, a question she needed to ask before she went another step closer.

"Of course I'm not, I'm trying to stop this madman," the Voice lied.

"Or this is all a clever set up, and you're trying to set me up, so the militant left takes the blame for these murders."

"I take it by the militant left you mean Red Vengeance, Miss Tredwell," the Voice said, surprising her.

Tredwell could see that their security had been totally compromised. There'd been a leak from someone on the inside. Wherever the leak came from, it now exposed the Red Vengeance members to all kinds of danger. "So you know enough about us to make a set up plausible," she remarked weakly, now totally unsure about everything.

"I know enough to know that you're not involved in this. To turn teenagers into bombers and killers is not something that can be done overnight. To make a brainwashed zombie who's prepared to do anything for a lunatic cause takes time, drugs, and superior brainwashing techniques. Only with drugs and auto-suggestion can a subject be correctly prepared for a mission involving this much violence and mayhem. I know enough about you and your rag tail colleagues to know you're not capable of this," the Voice remarked scathingly.

"If you're not involved in the terrorist campaign, how do you know all this?" she asked, desperately seeking some kind of rhyme and reason as to why she'd been led here.

"I was going to write a book on terrorism, and it was while I was researching that book that I discovered the man behind this terror. He looked me up on the internet, said he could help with my research. We met, and he asked me all kinds of weird questions on my research. There was something strange about the man, so strange that I started to follow him. It was when I followed him that I discovered his lair," the Voice recounted, trying to make everything seem plausible.

"So why didn't you go to the police with this?"

The Voice laughed. "And how would that look? A man writing a book on terrorism knows a man committing terrorist atrocities. I don't think any police interview would bode well for me in these wary times of ever-increasing terrorist suspicion."

"Instead, you're putting me in a compromising position," Tredwell snapped angrily.

"No, Miss Tredwell, I'm giving you a chance to expose this Fascist terrorist plot, I'm giving you a chance to bring an evil fiend to justice."

"This is all a little too convenient," Tredwell said.

"I'm trying to help your organization, plus bring this man to justice. All my days of following him have now led me to a position, where, through you, I can end this nightmare."

"And where exactly is his lair?" Tredwell asked, looking around her and seeing no signs of anything that remotely looked like a terrorist lair among the crumbling concrete fortifications.

"His lair is the place where he takes them—a place where he can work on them. In this lair, he helps the boys develop their full potential as terrorist weapons," the Voice explained. "The Western Heights that you're standing on are dotted with the remnants of the Napoleonic fortifications that were built here to defend the country from Napoleon's failed 1805 French invasion. This place was perfect for this man to adapt a part of the fortifications for his use. As you can see, the area remains relatively undisturbed. Apart from the odd dog walker, who keeps to the path, people hardly ever come here."

Tredwell had seen nobody since she parked her car, so she could see what the Voice meant. She decided, however, that she needed clarification. "So, you're saying that the far right terrorist cell that's caused the recent murders in Folkestone and the carnival bombing in Brighton is based in an old fortification on these heights?"

"That's exactly what I'm saying." The Voice was a good reader of people, concluding that he had Tredwell hooked, and she'd have to take her investigation further. Her hatred of the neo-Nazis was a major weakness. It stopped her from thinking objectively. The chance of proving their guilt overtook the fears for her own safety.

"I could go to the police with what you've told me," Tredwell said.

The Voice sighed. "Yes, you could go to the police, tell them your half-baked theory about how a man rang you claiming the terrorist cell that murdered people recently in Brighton and Folkestone was operating from these hills. You could tell them that, Miss Tredwell. You could risk them thinking you've set it all up to blame the far right by telling them this silly theory. Alternatively, you could expunge all their doubts by letting me show you his lair. When you know where the lair is, you'll have unarguable proof of their guilt."

"And what's this man you say is responsible for all

this going to be doing while you show me his lair?" Tredwell asked.

"Like I said, I've been following him, I know for a fact that he's not there at the moment," the Voice lied.

"Very convenient, wouldn't you say?" Tredwell remarked sarcastically.

"I only called you when I was sure he wasn't there. While he's away, it gave me the chance. Showing you his lair will prove to you this isn't bullshit," the Voice pushed. "His lair is only minutes away from where you're standing, Miss Tredwell. Once we've been inside and I've proved that I'm telling the truth, then I release myself from all responsibility, and it's up to you what you want to do with that knowledge."

Tredwell's head told her she should leave, but being a true believer in revolution, she'd long ago decided that revolution could only be achieved by exposing the neo-Nazis' evil. Exposing them meant proving them culpable for heinous acts like the Brighton bombing, and proving that fact meant following this informer to this hunt's logical conclusion. "Where do you want me to go now?"

"Follow the path for two hundred meters to your left. When you've walked two hundred meters, you'll see an old pillar-box in front of you. At the pillar-box, follow the path directly north until you come to the fort's moat. At the moat, climb down its bank and then await instructions."

Once Tredwell was in the moat, the Voice decided, he had her. He smiled to himself as he thought about the moment when he sprang the trap.

"I'll do as you say, but if you try anything I'll call the police," she warned him.

"I'm not going to try anything," the Voice promised.

"Well, you would say that, wouldn't you?" she said curtly.

"We need to hurry," the Voice pressed. "The terrorist has been gone for a couple of hours. He's usually gone for about four hours at a time."

Tredwell really didn't know what to make of any of this. The Voice on the phone was convincing, seemed to have done a thorough and lengthy surveillance. If this was the terrorist talking to her on the phone, then why would he show her his lair? If he intended to kill her, there had already been plenty of opportunities for him to accomplish her murder away from here. None of it made any sense. "What if he comes back when I'm at his lair? What if you're wrong?"

"I've been watching his movements," the Voice reassured her, "he always keeps to the same pattern."

"If you're wrong, I'm dead," Tredwell said.

"You need to move quickly, Miss Tredwell," the Voice pushed.

"I don't need to do anything."

"If you don't do anything, it won't matter," the Voice said ominously, "if you don't do what I say, then I'll plant evidence in his lair that you've been there. I'll make him angry enough that he'll come after you."

"Don't threaten me!" Tredwell snapped.

"I'm not threatening, Miss Tredwell, I'm making a promise." There was a menacing silence. "You need to start moving, Miss Tredwell. This man is extremely dangerous. He won't hesitate to kill you," the Voice warned. "The worst part of him coming to kill you is because you didn't do what I've asked here, meaning you won't know who he is when he comes." The Voice paused for effect, adding, "One thing is certain, Miss Tredwell, he'll know you, believe me. I'll make sure he knows you."

Tredwell's legs became leaden, and she was finding it hard to make a decision. The danger was real and close, and there was every reason to fear that one false move now could lead to her death. She decided she had no choice but to press on through the sopping mud and damp grass to wherever this was leading.

"This man is extremely dangerous, I strongly advise you to push on, Miss Tredwell."

"I know some dangerous people," Tredwell countered weakly.

The Voice surprised her by laughing again. "Those failed art students and militant anarchists you know aren't dangerous, Miss Tredwell. Those brick-throwing anarchists on those anti-capitalist demonstrations strike fear in the hearts of nobody."

Tredwell was starting to realize by the menacing tone of her caller's voice that she was out of her depth. Her caller had already emphasized the point that he was an expert marksman. It was fair for Tredwell to assume that he was probably armed. He was armed and out there somewhere in the rapidly darkening skyline waiting to kill Tredwell if she didn't do what he asked. "I'll follow your instructions," she reluctantly agreed, deciding cooperation was her safest option.

"When you've seen the lair, you can go," the Voice promised. "Now get to the moat quickly, and please remember, when I hang up, not to use your phone again. If I see you use the phone again, then I'll reluctantly have to kill you."

As she hung up, Tredwell thought about making a dart for some nearby bushes, then using them as a cover to make her escape. She decided that she'd be a sitting duck out here on the hills against a marksman with night vision. Slowly she edged her way along the path. In the distance, in the silhouette of the purple-gray twilight, she could see the steep banks of the moat. She thought about trying to ring for help, but as she studied the dense bushes and trees around her, she concluded that, in such dense foliage, she'd never see her assassin.

When she climbed slowly down the slippery wet grass to the floor of the muddy moat, she now felt exposed and vulnerable. In the next few moments her fate was going to be decided, and as far as Tredwell could see, it was a matter of two simple scenarios—either she was going to live, or she was going to die. It had really come down to mathematics, as simple as that.

CHAPTER 50

Roberts had told Machin that he'd have to hang up. He was too near to Tredwell, and he was worried about being heard or of the blue glowing light from his mobile phone screen being seen in the rapidly descending darkness. It meant that Machin and Bailey had reached a point halfway along the muddy track and couldn't go any farther, until Roberts called them and gave them directions. In the distance, they could see the dark silhouette of a pillar-box, but as twilight rapidly became night, apart from a few nearby wind-rustled bushes, that was all they could see.

Suddenly, Machin's phone rang. She answered immediately.

Roberts was talking in a whisper. "I followed her into the moat, ma'am. She's standing there waiting for something. I'll call you when I know more."

"We'll wait where we are," Machin said.

"Is Bailey causing any trouble?" Roberts asked.

"He's doing as he's told. Don't worry about me," Machin reassured him.

"He's dangerous," Roberts whispered.

"Bailey isn't involved in this, Sergeant."

"He was tailing Tredwell. You can't be sure he's not involved," Roberts protested.

"I'll keep my gun on him at all times, Sergeant. If he tries anything, I'll shoot him," Machin said, making sure Bailey could hear what she said.

Up until the time when she'd gunned down the serial killer, Peter Rivers, Machin had always thought that she'd find it hard to kill. Killing Rivers—because he'd killed Machin's boyfriend, Nick—had proved to her that anybody was capable of murder if they had revenge in their heart.

"I don't trust him, ma'am," Roberts reiterated.

"In command, you sometimes don't have a choice and have to make a snap judgement in the field, Sergeant. I've judged that Bailey isn't involved in this. He is now my responsibility. Call me the moment Tredwell starts moving again," she said, then Roberts hung up.

"You're right, I'm not involved," Bailey told Machin. "I'd like to know what's going on here as much as you would, Inspector."

"I agree with Roberts, I don't trust you, Bailey, but, for the moment, I've got no choice but to bring you along," she stated. "You're either extremely clever, or you're showing the desperation of innocence," she added.

"I'm not involved in this, Machin," he retorted angrily. "Surely, with what you're finding out about Tredwell this evening, you must be suspicious about her motives. What the hell is a woman on her own doing roaming these hills around these old fortifications after dark?"

It was a question that Machin didn't know the answer to, a question she was hopefully going to get the answer to very soon. "I don't know what your game is here, Bailey," she admitted. "All your actions in illegally accessing her computer are outside the law, so I think it's best if you keep quiet."

"I'm not involved in this," Bailey repeated, "but what I've found out about Tredwell and her actions here point to the fact that she could be. I was a detective for five years, Machin. You, of all people, know that, as an ex-detective, I've got a nose for such things."

Machin made a decision. It might be a waste of time, but at least she felt she was covering all bases. She called DCI Khan on his private number and explained all that was happening. She asked him to get on to the locals for backup. Khan and Machin had a mutual respect in their time working together since her transfer, and Khan immediately said he was on it. Machin quickly hung up in order to keep her line clear.

All she could now do was stand, wait for Roberts's call, and hope that Bailey was right and that they were on the brink of discovering Red Vengeance was the driving force behind the terrorist campaign, and that, at last, this nightmare of murder and evil would be over.

CHAPTER 51

At the bottom of the damp moat, a nervous Tredwell stood waiting apprehensively, her senses alert to every sound and movement. The inky-black night was starting to take hold, and soon she wouldn't be able to see a thing. When her mobile phone suddenly rang, she anxiously answered it.

The Voice said, "A hundred yards to the left, you'll see a clump of bushes."

"I can't see anything in this darkness," Tredwell told him.

"I'm looking at you through the night vision sights of a sniper's rifle," the Voice said menacingly. "Keep walking slowly along the floor of the moat to the left, I'll tell you when to stop."

The news that the Voice was staring at her through the night vision sights of a sniper's rifle told Tredwell everything. It told her that her chances of getting out of here alive were rapidly decreasing. If the Voice decided he didn't want her to live, she wasn't going to, she quickly realized. She did as she was told, deciding that now everything was just down to basic survival. Could the Voice afford to let her live once she'd seen him and would be able to identify him? She wasn't sure about his story. The more she analyzed the Voice's story, the more holes she found in it. After a few minutes of slow walking in the direction she'd been instructed to walk, the Voice told her to stop.

"And after I've seen you, what happens then?" Tredwell asked, uneasily voicing her concerns.

"I'm wearing a ski mask. You won't be able to identify me after this is over," the Voice stated.

"You appear to have thought of everything," Tredwell said.

"In my situation, I have to. Do you think I want this maniac coming after me if this all goes wrong?"

"And what if I call the police now and tell them all you've told me?"

"Not a good idea, Miss Tredwell, I've got a sniper's rifle aimed at your heart. With night vision and you being in clear view in the open of the moat, it's impossible for me to miss. Just walk up the opposite side of the moat to the side you came down, and when you reach a cluster of bushes in front of you, stop." The Voice paused and watched her walking slowly toward him. "Just remember, I don't want to kill you, Miss Tredwell, I want the world to know about this."

"Just stay calm!" Tredwell snapped, "I'm almost there."

The Voice would stay calm, now being able to see Tredwell's body getting closer and closer. She was now at the point of no return, almost trapped in the Voice's net. He smiled as he thought about how well he could play people, how quickly he could assess their strengths and weaknesses.

A short distance away, Machin and Bailey anxiously awaited Roberts's call. When he finally rang an impatient Machin chewed him out. "About time!"

"I've been watching Tredwell from a distance away. She's been moving up the slope on the other side of the moat. She's stopped by some bushes a short ways up," Roberts relayed hurriedly. "She's disappeared into some bushes now."

"Don't lose her," Machin ordered.

"I won't, ma'am," Roberts promised and told her he'd call her in a few minutes after investigating further. He gave her general directions to the place where Tredwell had climbed up the moat to the bushes then hung up.

Machin told Bailey to walk in front of her.

He reluctantly did as ordered. "I'm not the enemy here," he protested, irritated.

"With your virulent beliefs, you'll always be the enemy to me," she remarked.

They walked on in an uncomfortable silence, approaching the spot where Roberts said the bushes were. Whatever Tredwell was up to, they were soon going to find out. Could Bailey have been right about this all along? Tredwell had been acting very strange. Her actions were certainly the actions of someone who was up to something, Machin concluded.

"You've got to admit, Inspector, the fact that Tredwell is roaming around this ancient Napoleonic fortress in the dark is strange," Bailey said, adding, "Please admit that you're at least suspicious."

Machin was suspicious. As far as she could see, Tredwell had no reason for her strange actions. When she had parked in the Western Heights car park at the top of Military Hill, Machin had thought she was meeting someone. Her trip into these dark, spooky fortifications after dark suggested that she'd been waiting until she wouldn't be seen because she had something to hide. What was up the side of the moat in the bushes that was so fascinating to this woman? This was something that

Machin needed to find out. She had no idea what all this was about.

At the point where Roberts had advised Machin to walk to in the moat, she ordered Bailey to stop. He looked for Roberts, then turning to Machin he said, "Where is he then, Inspector?"

"Just shut up and stand still," an irritated Machin ordered. She had no idea where Roberts was. The night was cloudy, and there wasn't even the faint twinkle of a welcoming star to dissipate the blackness. Roberts had said something about some bushes. The banks of the moat were dotted with bushes. What would seem like nothing in daylight, now seemed dark and menacing under the cloak of night. Until Roberts felt it was safe to ring her again, there was nothing that Machin could do but stand here in this soggy quagmire and wait.

If it hadn't been for Bailey, she could've caught up with Roberts, and they'd now both be together. Bailey was fast becoming an encumbrance in her life. This was the worst part about police work—in surveillance or when tailing suspects, you were always waiting for something to happen. Machin had given Khan general directions for the backup team, a backup team a nervous Machin hoped would soon arrive. Whatever Tredwell was up to, it was going to end in this moat, and this evil terrorist campaign would come to an end. She would make sure of it.

CHAPTER 52

DCI Khan hadn't made it to the top of his profession without being a dogged policeman and an extremely intelligent man. He'd had further talks with Patel, the bombing suspect, and he was starting to have severe doubts about the guilt of the man. Patel didn't come across as a killer. Patel was a playboy, but, although he'd claimed to love Jill Roberts, Khan got the feeling that he was just stringing her along and that their romance wasn't as heavy from Patel's side as Jill Roberts thought it was.

Khan's conversations with Marcia Bradley had also led him to have more doubts. Marcia Bradley had told him that Roberts had rung her house a lot of times recently during Jill Roberts's visits. Bradley said that DS Roberts always seemed to be checking on his wife. Khan looked back over the phone records and could see that every time Jill Roberts had been staying with Marcia Bradley in recent months, Roberts seemed to have phoned Bradley's land line.

None of it made sense. If Roberts had wanted to speak to his wife, then surely he would've rung Jill Roberts's mobile phone—or that was what Khan would've done—especially if the purpose of Roberts's calls had just been to speak to his wife.

Khan was now starting to suspect a more sinister motive. What better way of proving that Bradley had been lying to him over a period of months than this. It was as if Roberts had already been working on an alibi for the future. Khan was now certain that Roberts had known about his wife's affair long before the night of her murder. The fact that Roberts was checking on his wife showed Khan that Roberts already knew. Roberts was an excellent detective. Was it too farfetched to surmise that he'd discovered that his wife was having an affair long before the night of her murder?

The convenient puncture and the forced swapping of their cars on the evening of the bombing were the things that concerned Khan the most. What could be viewed as a random act of fate became, if Roberts knew about Jill and Patel's affair beforehand, a possible act of sabotage to force Jill to take her husband's car. Khan had to be careful. At the moment, these were baseless allegations. He arrived at Roberts's home with a search warrant, accompanied by a baffled-looking DC Karen Davis.

"What are we looking for, sir?" Davis asked as they stepped through the front door of the silent, eerie house. Knowing the way that Jill Roberts had died, Davis found the house, still full of the murdered woman's possessions, decidedly spooky.

"If I knew what I was looking for, I wouldn't need your help, Detective," Khan said sarcastically, as he started thumbing through some papers on a table.

Roberts was in Folkestone with Machin, so it was the ideal opportunity. They'd work through the house systematically room by room. If there was something to find, Khan would find it.

In the garage, they found the punctured tire. He examined it carefully. The tire looked more like it had been slashed not punctured.

Davis also checked the tire out and agreed with Khan's diagnosis. "This wasn't a random puncture. This tire was deliberately slashed by someone," she stated, voicing her opinion.

Davis used to live on a rough housing estate as a child and had encountered tire slashing at close hand on street gangs cars by rival gangs. The state of crime in her neighborhood had driven Davis into the police force, hoping that working for law enforcement could help her to make a difference. What she found strange was the rabid way that Khan seemed to be going after DS Roberts. Khan, on a hunch, seemed to be going out of his way to find evidence that might point to Roberts being a murderer. Could Roberts, the man who'd always been so courteous and polite to her, be a murderer? She wondered this as she wrapped the tire in an evidence bag.

"If the tire was slashed, then it was probably done by someone who wanted to make sure that Jill Roberts used her husband's car the night of the bombing." DI Khan let his statement hang in the air. The tire wasn't much evidence of wrongdoing, and it was something that Roberts could easily deny. Khan could see in his mind Roberts claiming the tire must've been slashed by kids while his car was parked in his drive.

Khan couldn't get the thought out of his head that if Roberts had planted the bomb, the only way he could have made sure his wife used his car, fitted with explosives, would have been to ensure she couldn't use her own. The tire was something that didn't add up—a factor that needed further investigation. Until he was sure that Roberts hadn't killed his wife, Kahn was not happy with the fact that Roberts was actively involved in a Counter Terrorism Command operation.

After they finished at the house and had found nothing more than the tire, Khan acknowledged the fact that if Roberts had planned this murder, then he'd planned it well. Khan would expect nothing else from his diligent sergeant. One thing was certain, if you wanted to plan the perfect murder then you could do worse than ask a detective—who regularly hunted people and who dealt in deception and murder—to plan it.

Machin had rung Khan for local backup at the Western Heights in Dover where they'd tailed Tredwell, who was acting suspiciously. Khan decided he would drive to Dover himself and see what was going on. He told Davis to carry on looking for anything that could prove that Roberts was involved in his wife's murder. Davis didn't like the fact that she was investigating another officer, but Khan knew she was a good officer and, regardless of her prejudices on the matter, would do as good a job as she could. Yes, Davis was a good officer, but Khan wondered, after the discovery of the slashed tire in the garage, if he could say the same for DS Morgan Roberts. There was a lot he was starting to learn about Roberts, and none of it he liked, he thought, as he rushed to his car to drive to Dover.

CHAPTER 53

Khan had left for Dover. Davis had immediately set to work, doing what Khan ordered. She didn't like having to investigate her colleague, DS Roberts, but if Khan, her boss, wanted Roberts's activities looked into, then that's what she'd do. She'd started with Patel, had asked him to write a list of the places where Jill Roberts and Patel had arranged rendezvous during their affair. Patel had willingly supplied her with all the details of his clandestine meetings, was being as helpful as he could be. This made Davis wonder why he would be so forthcoming if he was guilty of murder. Patel was continually repeating the fact that he hadn't done anything, in the hope that someone would listen to him and believe him.

After discovering the tire on Jill's car with knife puncture marks in it, Davis was suddenly listening.

Patel's list was a weird variety of bars and restaurants, all well away from Roberts's home. The illicit rendezvous had always been arranged out of town, for fear of being discovered. Roberts had claimed that he knew nothing about the fact that his wife was having an affair. The night of his wife's murder, he'd made a big production out of the shock of finding out that his wife wasn't staying at Marcia Bradley's. If he already knew, then he was a good actor, Davis decided, remembering the look of desolation on Roberts's face when he'd arrived at the station with DI Machin shortly after the news of his wife's murder.

Davis knew she'd have to start with the most recent meetings between Jill Roberts and Patel. The affair had been going on for a year, so any of the more distant rendezvous dates would be pointlessly wasting her time. It was the more recent ones that concerned her. The more recent meetings over the last month might give her a chance, she thought, as she contacted the local councils in the areas where the couple's meetings had taken place. It wasn't inside the bars and restaurants that she was looking at. Roberts was too savvy to be stupid enough to ever enter the premises of the meeting places. Roberts was a modern policeman, knew the power of CCTV, and that he couldn't chance leaving a CCTV record of his presence in the restaurants where Jill Roberts and Patel had met in. It was outside these places that Davis needed to look.

While Roberts would have been wary of going inside, outside would have been another matter. She needed to look at the police and council's vast array of CCTV cameras in the streets outside the various meeting points. Looking back at Patel's meeting with Jill Roberts at a Shoreham restaurant two months before Jill's murder, Davis hit the jackpot. From a police traffic camera trained on the street, she could see Jill Roberts's car parked in a spot just along the road from a restaurant. Jill Roberts could then be seen getting out of her car and quickly hurrying along the pavement to the restaurant. It was shortly after she'd entered the restaurant that Davis froze the CCTV image. Just as a car drove up the street, she had noticed something. She zoomed in as far as she could get and then carefully studied the number-plate of the car, illuminated by a nearby yellow streetlight. She was looking at the number-plate of Roberts's dark blue BMW, a number-plate she had written on a notepad on the desk in front of her. She stared blankly at the CCTV image taken weeks before DS Roberts claimed to know about his wife's affair.

She now had CCTV footage two months before the murder, showing that he had tailed his wife to the restaurant and must surely have known she was having an affair with Patel.

Davis went to the toilet and washed her face with cold water. She needed a clear and alert mind for when she rang Khan shortly. She took no pleasure in her discovery about Roberts. He was a popular colleague and had always shown Davis nothing but respect in her time working with him. She now had to tell her boss that Roberts was probably a murderer and that he had lied about recent events concerning his knowledge of his wife's activities. As she dried her face on a hand towel, she thought about what it took for a man to kill a woman whom he had once loved, with whom he had taken the marriage vows. It took a special man, a man without remorse or conscience, and up until a couple of hours ago, Davis had never thought that DS Morgan Roberts was such a man. You lived and learned, she thought, as she got back to her desk and picked up her mobile phone. She knew that DCI Khan would want to learn about this development right away.

CHAPTER 54

Machin was close to the spot now where Roberts had directed her a few moments ago over the phone. As she stood on the muddy, sopping-wet moat floor, looking around her for signs of movement, Roberts rang her. He told her he could see them both below him in the moat.

"I've got the drop on, Tredwell, ma'am," Roberts told her. "Everything is under control."

Control, control of what? Machin wondered. Roberts was talking in riddles. "Just tell me what the hell is going on, Roberts?"

"When you see this place, you're not going to believe it, ma'am," Roberts said excitedly.

"What place, Roberts? So far, in this moat, I've seen nothing but derelict battlements. It would be nice if I knew what you were talking about," Machin pressed.

"I followed her into her lair, ma'am. She's got some kind of prison in these Napoleonic fortifications. In a cell, she's been holding teenage boys as prisoners. You'd better get up here, and I can show you what I mean," Roberts said.

"And where's Tredwell?" a puzzled Bailey asked, wondering where Tredwell had gone.

Roberts laughed. "I followed her into her lair, and she stepped into a cell to look for something. While she was in there, I pulled the cell door shut and locked it."

"Good work, Roberts," Machin said, happy that maybe Roberts was still in control after his recent traumas. She now reckoned that the faith she'd shown in him by letting him come back to work was proving to be justified. "Guide us in."

Roberts told them to climb the grassy slope of the moat directly in front of them. When they started to climb, he instructed them to look for a clump of bushes right in front of them. Hidden behind the bushes was the entrance to the lair. She hung up as they climbed, telling Bailey, "It looks like you were right, Bailey. It appears that this terror group you've been talking about, Red Vengeance, are heavily involved in the kidnappings."

"There's no need to apologize for doubting me, Inspector, I'm just relieved that you now see the EPP had nothing to do with this and you can prove the EPP aren't involved."

Machin had mixed feelings about all of it. Something inside her had hoped that it was the work of the neo-Nazis and the discovery of that fact would be the act that destroyed them. Now it looked like the discovery that it was militant anarchists would only help the EPP gain more support, Machin thought, as she climbed the wet bank's squelchy grass to Tredwell's lair. When she was halfway up the bank, from out of wind rustled bushes, she suddenly saw the black outline of Roberts.

"I'm here, ma'am," an excited Roberts said.

Machin gingerly climbed the last few yards, wary of the steep fall below. Roberts held out his cold hands to guide Machin and Bailey over the parapet. As Machin stepped through the damp saturated bushes, she was greeted by a rusting metal door. She pushed the door open, and the gloom of outside was suddenly replaced by the dazzling, bright, white lights within. On the desk was a camera monitor showing images from CCTV cameras dotted around the rest of the lair. There was an elaborate sound system, and a movie projector in the corner was pointing inside the cell. She was completely astounded.

"This is unbelievable," Bailey said, as he looked at the lair's complex layout.

"This is all the latest hi-tech surveillance equipment," Roberts said. "This stuff costs a fortune. Red Vengeance certainly seems to have a lot of funds for their terror campaign, ma'am."

"They're certainly not cowboys," Machin said, looking at the vast array of technical equipment on the desk.

"The surveillance equipment is linked to a cell around the corner. It seems to be the place where Tredwell and her colleagues must've been holding the boys captive," Roberts told them.

"I can see Tredwell lying on the bed," Machin said, looking at the cell's camera monitor. There was something strange about her, she thought. Tredwell was lying with her back to the camera, facing the wall. Machin had expected her to be ranting and raving like all fanatics did when they were cornered, not this quiet apathy.

"Just follow the path around the corner, and you'll come to the cell," Roberts instructed them and then stood back to let her and Bailey get past.

When they reached the cell door, they were surprised to see it open. Machin stepped inside and carefully approached the bed. As she got close to Tredwell, she could tell by her lack of movement and, by the fact that Tredwell had a large blood-strewn bullet hole in her forehead, that Tredwell was dead. "I thought you told me you'd just locked Tredwell in the cell. You've killed her!" Machin shouted angrily, turning to confront Roberts.

"Very observant, Inspector," Roberts said, and, in a split second, he'd shot her in the leg. She screamed and fell to the floor. As she hit the cold, dank concrete, the Glock 17 pistol she'd been reaching for from her shoulder holster fell from her hand and clattered across the cell floor.

"What the hell are you doing?" a baffled Bailey shouted.

"Just stand against the wall with your hands behind your head!" Roberts ordered him aggressively.

Bailey stared at the Glock 17 in Roberts's hand, and, after seeing how quickly Roberts was prepared to use it, he slowly obeyed Roberts's instructions.

Clutching her wounded leg, Machin shouted. "What the hell are you doing?"

"Sometimes, Sarah, for an inspector, you're not very bright," Roberts said with an evil smile on his face.

She could not understand. None of this made sense. She was desperately hoping this was a nightmare she'd shortly wake up from. The question she couldn't get out of her head was, why had Roberts shot her? "This is madness!"

"No, Sarah, this is someone who's fed up with the state of this country, someone who's tired of immigrants taking everything," Roberts eulogized. "I was never going to let Patel walk away with Jill. It's Patel that led me to my path of true enlightenment. He's the one who made me realize that the time for DS Morgan Roberts being a doormat was over and that now was the time for direct action."

"You can't be…" Machin mumbled as the horrific realization of what Roberts was had finally dawned on her.

"And why can't I be? Don't look so astounded, Inspector. I've known about Patel for nearly a year now. Up until recently, I never bothered to do anything about it because I needed time to perfect my disciples, to give them a chance to wreak their havoc on the world. I needed a period of calm in my personal life."

Bailey was studying the distance to Machin's gun on the cell floor. He concluded there was no way, if he lunged to grab it, that he could reach it before Roberts killed him. "The Inspector's knee is bleeding badly," Bailey said. "She needs a doctor, Roberts."

Roberts laughed. "Neither of you are in a position to make any demands."

"Before we entered the moat, I called Khan to arrange local backup. They'll be here any minute," she desperately told Roberts, in an attempt to try and faze him.

"Don't bother, Sarah. Even if they send lots of numbers, it'll take them a long time to find this place," Roberts said smugly. "That's the reason I chose this place for my lair. Although it's within easy reach of main roads, there's a certain remoteness about it that makes it perfect for my task." He let what he'd said sink in. "It took me weeks of searching this rabbit warren of fortifications until I found this place. This place was perfect for development. It was just far enough away from the road and the car park for secrecy. The bushes helped. The bushes growing across the doorway make it impossible to see the doorway to my lair from the dog walkers' path above the moat. As you can see, I've been very practical. The walls have been soundproofed, the cell strengthened with reinforced concrete. A lot of careful planning has gone into this place. This CCTV equipment took me hours to install, but I think it was worth it, wouldn't you say, Sarah?"

"This is madness," Machin repeated, wincing in pain.

"I'm sure Bailey doesn't think this is madness, I expect he is quietly impressed with what I've achieved here."

"You're a lunatic, Roberts!" Bailey said defiantly. "The EPP don't believe in mass murder."

Roberts shook his head. "What do they believe in, Bailey? Winning a few pathetic seats in council elections. You might've won a few seats on local councils, but you'll never get enough support to gain a seat in Parliament. How much power do you think you're ever likely to achieve through the ballot box?"

"We believe in the electoral process," Bailey retorted, and, even he, had to admit his phrases sounded tired after being repeated many times before for the benefit of the press.

"An electoral process with its first-past-the-post system means that, even if you got twenty percent of the vote, you'd be unlikely to get a seat in Parliament," Roberts predicted.

"And what do you offer apart from death and murder, all you seem to offer as an alternative is hatred and intolerance," Bailey disputed.

"At least I offer something," Roberts said.

Bailey stood listening to this madman. As Roberts spoke, Bailey could see the fury in his eyes. Here was a man who believed in anarchy and murder, that the only way to change things was through violent insurrection. This man, Bailey decided, was never going to let them live. Their only chance was to buy time, and that was exactly what Bailey intended doing. "Why did you kill Tredwell?"

"Tredwell had served her purpose. She was like Kemp, they were both expendable."

The fog suddenly cleared in Machin's head. If Roberts had killed Kemp, then it explained a lot of things. "How many murders are you responsible for?" she asked, terrified at what his answer was going to be.

She stared long and hard at this monster before her. This was Roberts, her trusty sidekick, someone who'd always been there in recent years as a perfect sounding board. It was inconceivable how she hadn't known. How could she not have had any idea? This was the question bugging her, even at this moment of her greatest peril.

"They're not murders, Sarah, they're an attempt by a supreme patriot to reclaim England back for his people," Roberts eulogized, and in his suddenly cold, dark eyes, she could see the glare of inflexibility and the intolerance of a zealot.

Machin didn't understand any of it. Why had Roberts brought them here? Surely it was in his best interests to keep people away from his lair and the evil that frequented it. None of this madness made any sense. Roberts had been clinical and efficient in his terrorist attacks. He'd brainwashed his disciples as the perfect terror weapons, yet he'd willingly led Machin and Bailey to this place he'd been keeping a secret for months.

"I don't understand any of this," she admitted.

She stared at her leg as the blood from her wound seeped across the dirty concrete in what looked like a river of blood.

"You can never understand this, Sarah. If you'd seen your marriage being slowly destroyed by a man with wealth and looks, to whom Britain has given every opportunity so he and his family could forge a life here. All these years, I've worked as a loyal copper, given my all to the cause. Then, after I found out about Patel, I sat back and wondered. Was it to make a better and safer country? Or was it so the Patels of this world could lead a life free of racial intolerance, a life that gave them the opportunity to steal a loyal state servant's wife?"

The cell lapsed into a tense silence. Machin was starting to understand. After listening to his rants, she had begun to understand more about her colleague than she'd ever done before. He was a man without a conscience, a man without feeling. She came to the alarming insight that Roberts was suffering from some form of psychosis. "You need help," she pleaded. "For the sake of what we've been through together, the traumas that have caused you to crack and become this, let me help you, Morgan."

"You are helping me, Sarah, I've lured you here to help me," Roberts said menacingly. "Both of you are going to die, but, first, I wanted you to know why." He made sure his gun was squarely pointed at Bailey's chest. This wasn't the time for mistakes, a time to give a desperate Bailey the chance to jump him. "How do you think this is going to look when the police discover this cell laden with corpses? I'll tell you exactly how it'll look, it'll look like the result of a desperate gun battle between a militant anarchist and the police."

"You'll never get away with it," Machin said.

"Why not? When trailing Bailey, who's following Tredwell, you discover Red Vengeance's lair—the very lair in which they've been brainwashing kids and carrying out horrific terrorist attacks. You'll be pleased to know that I paid Kemp before she died to plant information on Tredwell's computer. When the techies look into her computer's hard drive, they'll find everything Kemp has planted there. It shows purchases of high-tech cameras and a movie projector. On Tredwell's credit card Kemp has placed details of purchases of sand and cement from a builder's merchants. I'm afraid, Sarah, with all my careful planning, I am going to get away with it."

"Nobody will believe it," Machin offered weakly, though from what she'd already heard, she decided there was every chance that they would.

"Once I arrange things in here properly, they'll have no choice but to," Roberts predicted with confidence.

"After all we've been through together, Morgan, how can you do this?" Machin asked, desperately grasping for understanding.

"I did it because it needed to be done. People like Khan have been rapidly pushed up the promotion ladder, more for what they represent than for their ability. When the powers that be decide to hand out the promotions, they now have to be aware of political correctness, and that means that white officers like myself are passed over and that Afro-Caribbeans and Asians are promoted instead."

"Rubbish!" Machin said defiantly, adding, "Khan's a brilliant commander, he got his job through ability alone."

Roberts laughed smugly. "I pity you, Sarah, because I think you really believe all the bullshit they tell you."

"It's the truth, Morgan, not this distorted view your insanity seems to have convinced your mind of."

"Trying to get your country back isn't insanity. It's only viewed as insanity by people, like you, who've been indoctrinated by the system," Roberts lectured.

"You've murdered all those people over this," Bailey stared hard, looking for comprehension in Roberts's cold, hard face. "Nothing can make me understand this lunacy."

"Technically I've killed nobody. I think you'll find it's my disciples who've done the killing, Bailey."

"You're sick, Morgan, you need help," Machin told Roberts. In her head, she was thinking the police would've found her and Tredwell's cars by now. As if to confirm that fact her mobile phone suddenly rang.

"Don't even think about answering it," Roberts warned, turning his gun back on Machin.

Machin's phone rang for a while and then stopped as the caller finally gave up. Moments later, Roberts's phone rang. He took it out, looked at the screen to see who the caller was. It was DCI Khan.

"Our master calls," Roberts said, then answered. He explained that Machin had followed Bailey and that he was following Tredwell into the Napoleonic tunnels around the Drop Redoubt. He shouted that he could hear gun shots and then abruptly hung up.

"Your time is almost up," Roberts told them. "I'm going to take no pleasure in killing you both, especially you, Bailey. The EPP is weak and misguided, but even in your weak, ineffectual way you are at least trying to do something."

"You've murdered women and children, for what, Morgan?" Machin asked, desperately trying to keep Roberts talking.

"It needed to be done, a message needed to be sent out to immigrants who are threatening to come here."

"You're a lunatic," Bailey said bravely. "Just because we want to halt immigration doesn't mean we want to kill immigrants."

"Just remember how well you've been played, Bailey. Think about the way I led you to Tredwell, made you think that Tredwell was actively involved in terrorism. The way I set you all up, maneuvered you here—these clever actions are hardly the acts of a lunatic, Mr. Bailey."

"You evil, sadistic bastard!" Bailey snapped.

"Don't worry. I'll make sure that you come out of this as a patriot, trying to save more innocent children from being killed. As a patriot who's tried to reshape Britain, I owe you that much, Bailey."

"Listen to yourself, Morgan, this isn't you, this isn't Detective Sergeant Roberts, this isn't the caring sergeant I've worked with for five years," Machin reasoned.

"Don't bother, Sarah," Roberts smirked. "I've been to all the seminars about how to talk down gunmen. No matter what you say, you're not going to talk me out of it."

"You must've put those poor kids through hell in this place before you sent them out to commit atrocities," Bailey said. "They were just kids, for God's sake. White, teenage kids. You claim that you're some kind of white supremacist, yet you've been sending the people that you're supposed to be fighting for to their deaths."

"I've given them the opportunity to serve their country, a chance to do something that they were never going to do in their pathetic monochrome lives. The way teenagers lead their lives today, the gloomy future that lies ahead for them the way Britain is now, I was doing them a favor, Bailey."

"Killing the poor sods, some bloody favor," Bailey said angrily.

"You'd never believe how malleable the young mind is, Bailey. With drugs and the right inducements, you can get a young mind to do anything. Maybe this is something your party needs to take note of. My efforts should make you realize what needs to be done to have an effect in this country. These attacks are the kind of thing needed to make the establishment react."

"Nobody wants to have an effect with your methods. Anything we do, we want to do with the backing of the people," Bailey said.

Roberts laughed sarcastically. "You can stop with the political bullshit, I've done more for the far right's cause in this country in a few months than any of you democratic Nazis all these years. It's a shame, all your efforts in the council elections seem pathetic compared to my direct action. Look at the way I've managed to blame the violence on red militants, you should be proud to die for the cause, Bailey."

"And you think this will increase support?" Machin snapped. "By your violence, all you've managed to do is make the public abhor all extremists," she reasoned.

"No, Machin, this is just the start of everything. What I've done is only the beginning of the journey, this is a journey without end," Roberts predicted.

Machin looked hard into Roberts's eyes. There was a depth of hatred she'd never seen there before. "And where is this journey going to end?"

"It ends when I say it ends," Roberts said. "After the way I foiled Red Vengeance, I'm going to be a hero. In the annals of history, I'll always be remembered as the cop who foiled this anarchist plot, the man who stopped the killing," he rambled.

"But if you kill us and claim that Tredwell was behind the attacks, then how can you commit further atrocities?" a baffled Machin asked.

"There's one more disciple," Roberts told her gleefully. "My last disciple is out there now, about to be unleashed on an unsuspecting world."

Bailey gave Machin a wary look. Another brainwashed teenage assassin had been set loose on the world.

"Please don't do this, Morgan," she pleaded, in a last desperate attempt to stop her colleague's madness.

Bailey slipped his hands from the back of his head and let them rest at his side. Roberts was so engrossed with taunting Machin that he didn't notice.

"Someone has to do it for our children," Roberts said. "If we don't do something now, then this country will be lost to the Patels of this world."

"You can't blame the whole immigrant community for Patel shagging your wife!" Machin snapped.

Roberts smiled. "I can and I will, Machin. That's the problem with today's society. Nobody believes in an eye for an eye anymore." Because of his ranting directed at Machin, Roberts failed to notice Bailey slip his right hand inside his coat pocket. "British people just sit back and watch while the immigrants walk all over them—"

"So you're the only one involved in direct action," Machin interrupted, in an attempt to distract Roberts, having noticed Bailey's action.

"Of course, the wankers in the EPP have got no idea of how to take direct action like this," Roberts stated angrily. He suddenly noticed that Bailey's hands were no longer behind his back and that Bailey had his right hand in his pocket. Before Roberts could turn his gun on Bailey, Bailey fired the gun from inside his pocket into Roberts's torso, the bullet ripping away bone and tissue. Roberts stumbled forward onto the floor, and, as his body hit the dirty concrete, his gun dropped from his hand. Bailey rushed across the cell and kicked the gun out of Roberts's reach.

"Is that direct enough action for you, Roberts?" Bailey shouted. He kept his gun trained on Roberts, with his other hand he grabbed his phone from his pocket and frantically called an ambulance. Machin slipped her phone out and slowly rang Khan.

"What's happening?" a tense Khan asked, desperate for news.

"It's a right mess, sir," Machin said.

"I need to talk to Roberts," Khan said.

"Roberts is dead, sir—"

"I'm not dead," Roberts said defiantly. He was lying wounded on the floor, his body splattered with blood.

Bailey hurried over and frisked Roberts, searching for further weapons. When he was sure that Roberts had no other weapons, Bailey retrieved Machin's gun and handed it to her. "I'll have to go outside and direct the police and paramedics to the lair," he explained. "Are you up to guarding him?"

Machin hung up on Khan, then replying in the affirmative, she told Bailey to go, knowing that the emergency services would never be able to locate the lair quickly enough without Bailey's help.

After Bailey had gone, Roberts slowly turned to face Machin. "This isn't over, Sarah."

"Where have you sent the boy?" she asked in desperation.

Roberts laughed. With decent medical attention, he was now convinced he'd survive. His eyes were suddenly heavy and tired, but before drifting into unconsciousness, he said, "I've sent the boy where he can do the most good, Sarah."

After that grim warning, Roberts passed out. Machin stared at the monster that, up till less than an hour ago, she'd called her friend. Her mind couldn't take it in. In her eyes, it was the ultimate in treachery. It explained his long disappearances in recent weeks when he'd claimed he'd been following up leads. The whole messy jigsaw was slowly coming together in her head, and, after hearing Roberts rant, one thing she was now sure of was that Detective Sergeant Morgan Roberts had murdered his wife. Of that fact, Machin now had no doubt.

CHAPTER 55

DCI Khan was seated in an interview room at Dover police station with local Inspector, DI Colin Tonkin, and sitting opposite them was Ian Bailey. DS Roberts was in the hospital on a life support system, and Machin was still recovering after the operation to remove the bullet from her leg at Canterbury hospital. From what Machin had told Khan before she was operated on, he had quickly concluded that this whole business was a disaster. Bailey was the only one from the chaos of the lair episode that was at the moment capable enough to talk to the investigation team.

"What a mess, Bailey," DCI Khan said. "Tredwell dead, Roberts seriously wounded, Machin shot in the leg—it's like the four horsemen of the apocalypse."

"I had to shoot Roberts, he gave me no choice, DCI Khan," Bailey said, reluctantly admitting to having the gun.

"You shot a policeman with an unregistered Smith and Wesson, Model Six-Eighty-Six—"

"Roberts was a fanatical terrorist. When I shot him, he'd already murdered Tredwell and shot DI Machin in the leg. If I hadn't shot him, he'd have murdered me and

Machin in that lair, and you wouldn't have known anything about what he's been up to all this time," Bailey retorted, before Khan could get too heavy about the Smith & Wesson.

"And that's the only reason that I'm not raking you over the coals for this," Khan said. "Machin backs up what you said. She told me that Roberts threatened to kill you both just before you shot him."

"He was trying to start a race war," Bailey stated. "With the assistance of Mori Kemp, Roberts had set the Red Vengeance militant left group up to take the blame for the terrorist acts. If he'd killed us and made it look like we'd died in a gun battle in his lair, then he'd have got away with it," Bailey summarized with great concern.

"You'll be charged with illegal possession of a firearm, but that's all you'll be charged with," Khan promised.

"Thanks. After I saved DI Machin's life and brought this lunatic to justice, your generosity knows no bounds, DCI Khan," Bailey remarked with sarcasm and noted that Khan's face at least had the decency to redden with embarrassment in the light of the police's lack of appreciation for his heroic actions.

Khan let the remark go. In view of the stress of Bailey narrowly escaping death, it wasn't a time for the iron fist. "We're grateful, Bailey, which is why I'm going to talk to the judge and try and make the gun charge go away."

"Thanks," Bailey said reluctantly. "Roberts was trying to set Tredwell up for the terrorist attacks. To make his plan work, he would have had to kill me and Machin."

"We now know that Roberts murdered his wife," Khan said. "We found some evidence that proves he knew his wife was having an affair weeks before the night of her murder."

Bailey tried to take in what Khan said. Roberts had sent two boys to maim and kill in suicide attacks. He'd blown his wife up with a car bomb. Bailey had shot him, yet Roberts wasn't dead but on a life-support machine at Canterbury Hospital. The latest doctor's report said he was going to pull through. "He must've put those poor kids through hell before he sent them out to kill," Bailey reflected, as he thought about the horror Roberts's disciples had suffered imprisoned in that cell.

"Machin said that Roberts has claimed that he's sent another disciple out on a mission of murder," Khan stated.

"The crime scene team examined the cell, sir," Tonkin told Khan, "There's evidence of a recent occupant other than the two boys we know about having been there. Some of the hair fibers that forensics have taken from the bed sheets don't match Roberts's other victims."

"He did claim that he'd sent another disciple out to kill," Bailey reaffirmed. "Looking at the drugs and film equipment Roberts had in his lair, if there is another boy out there, this new lad is a brainwashed ticking time bomb." He paused a moment for thought. "The biggest problem is that nobody knows what he looks like, or the identity of the people Roberts has targeted," he added.

"We need to talk to Roberts," Khan said. "The doctors say that they're confident the operation was a success, and that he is going to fully recover. None of which helps us. Our problem is his recovery from his operation will take time, and time, in light of this new information, is what we haven't got. Even if he's well enough to talk, he probably won't tell us anything."

"Well, why would he? Anything he tells us just condemns him more," Bailey said.

Why would he, indeed? Khan thought. He had his team frantically searching for teenage boys who'd gone missing in the last few months. The first two assassins had been kidnapped boys who Roberts had brainwashed into murder, and Khan had seen nothing so far that would make him think that the pattern would be broken with this new disciple.

"I'm limited in manpower at the moment, sir," Tonkin informed him. "We've had to send extra men to control crowds at the castle. It's Prince Henry's investiture as Lord Warden of the Cinque Ports tomorrow."

Prince Henry, the gentle prince, a man who was always preaching tolerance in today's society. Henry was a man who was always trying to bridge the ethnic divide in Britain—something a white supremacist like Roberts would loathe. In view of the investiture news, Khan was starting to have extreme misgivings about the last disciple's target. "What did Roberts actually say about his last disciple?" he asked Bailey impatiently.

"He said he had one more disciple out there, waiting to be unleashed on the world," Bailey said.

"Did he hint at a specific target?"

"I'm sorry, but I can't remember him saying anything other than what I told you," Bailey said.

Roberts had been rambling on to his captured audience his far right eulogies just before Bailey shot him. He was ranting on about a disciple who was going to be unleashed, that was all Bailey could tell Khan.

Khan sat lost in thought. He was mulling over the fact that the lair had been set up on the Western Heights in Dover opposite Dover Castle. The remnants of the Napoleonic fortifications at the Western Heights were near where the investiture was going to take place.

Was it a coincidence or was there any significance in that fact? Khan wondered. The search of Roberts's lair had come up with nothing concerning the last disciple's target. Roberts had been careful, hadn't left anything of use to the police in his lair. He'd been thinking like a detective would think, covering his tracks. It made discovery of what his plans were almost impossible.

He'd placed explosives around the door of the lair and had booby-trapped the entrance in case his lair was ever breeched when he wasn't there. Any attempted break-in would have caused an explosion that would've killed anybody attempting to force the door. Khan considered the thousands of spectators that would be at the castle to see the investiture. Together with the royal party present, it meant if the target of the attack was Prince Henry, they needed to stop the ceremony.

Khan left the interview room and contacted the royal security team. He spoke to Sir Charles Rutherford, head of royal security. "We need to cancel the ceremony," he told Rutherford, a sense of urgency in his voice.

"The ceremony can't be canceled. Prince Henry views this investiture with immense pride and would never agree to its cancelation, even with a terrorist threat," Rutherford said.

"It needs to be canceled," Khan persisted. "There's a possibility there will be an assassination attempt. If you don't cancel, we can't guarantee Prince Henry's safety."

Rutherford lapsed into an uncomfortable silence and finally said, "I have great sympathy for your position, DCI Khan, but Prince Henry is a brave man, and he'd never agree to call off the ceremony because we were kow-towing to terrorists. I'm sure Prince Henry would sooner die than give in to these people."

Khan sighed—Prince Henry, martyr—not the news he wanted to hear. The ceremony was barely a day away, with a real danger that Roberts had sent one of his teenage assassins out to murder the prince. He decided more details might force Rutherford's team into action. "It concerns the recent terrorist attacks in Brighton and Folkestone. We think the same group who carried out these attacks might be trying to kill Prince Henry," he warned and could tell by the silence on the other end of the line that Rutherford had some severe self-doubts about the wisdom of proceeding with the ceremony.

At last, Rutherford said, "We'll increase security. Anybody entering the castle will be thoroughly searched for weapons. The ceremony will be taking place in the castle's keep, and nobody will be able to get in or out of there without our security team seeing them. Don't worry, Khan, we're professional. We've got it all under control."

"You need to be aware of the threat. We've no idea how this assassin will attempt to kill Prince Henry," Khan pointed out.

The first two attacks had been with a bomb and a gun, only Roberts knew what the assassin's method of attack would be this time.

"Every sniper angle has been covered, so nobody will get past the gates with a weapon. Relax, Khan, the ceremony will be over tomorrow in a couple of hours. My boys will make sure that nothing happens to Prince Henry," Rutherford reassured him confidently.

As Rutherford hung up, Khan wasn't reassured. They needed to know if Roberts had targeted the investiture ceremony or somewhere else. If Prince Henry's life was in danger, then Khan needed to know about it now. Khan's mobile phone rang, he answered—it was a policeman at Canterbury Hospital, one of the guards Khan had posted on Roberts. What he told Khan improved Khan's mood. Roberts had awoken from his post-operation sleep and was now relatively coherent. Khan told Tonkin to keep Bailey at Dover police station until he returned. Even though Bailey had saved Machin's life, Khan was still wary of Bailey's motives.

Khan rushed to his car and sped off up the A2 toward Canterbury. Khan wanted answers, needed them by tomorrow before the investiture ceremony began. It looked like Roberts was the only man who could provide the answers to Khan's many detailed questions. Roberts by now would know that it could easily be proved that he was involved in all the recent terrorist attacks. Would a man who was already facing life in prison for his atrocities be prepared to talk to the police? Did Roberts have anything to gain by talking to them? Khan didn't like the answer his subconscious mind was giving him—and that was a resounding "no." Roberts had nothing to gain by saying anything.

CHAPTER 56

As Khan entered the bland looking private patient's room at Canterbury Hospital, he immediately produced a weak smile from a tired-looking DS Roberts. Khan walked over to a seat by the bedside and sat down. Roberts's eyes never left Khan while he did so. Khan decided he would wipe the smug smile off his now ex-colleague's face. "I know you murdered your wife, Morgan," he said, going straight on the attack.

Roberts's eyes didn't flinch as he stared coldly at Khan. "As far as I'm concerned, Jill has been dead for a long time," Roberts said, not bothering to deny anything as he recognized Khan now knew everything.

The doctor who'd confronted Khan when he'd arrived at the hospital told him that he could only see the patient for a few minutes. If Roberts said nothing, then Khan's visit would be pointless, Khan quickly concluded. With another teenage assassin on the loose, Khan needed to get something out of Roberts fast. "You've killed so many people, Sergeant."

"If it wasn't for Bailey, I would've killed many more," Roberts observed.

One look at the hatred in Roberts's tired-looking

eyes, and Khan had no doubt that Roberts, if he hadn't been stopped, would have fulfilled his morbid prophecy. "You said there was another disciple out there," Khan said. "The doctor has confirmed that now you've had your operation, you're out of danger, and there's every chance that you're going to recover completely from this."

"And what am I surviving for?" Roberts asked.

"You need psychiatric help. Your actions were taken under duress, something cracked inside you when you found out about your wife's affair. Patel made you go over the edge, caused the mental breakdown," Khan suggested, trying to act sympathetic so he could wrench information from Roberts.

"No, Khan, people like you have forced me to take action. Patel stealing my wife just confirmed to me why I hate your kind," Roberts said.

"And what have I ever done to you apart from giving you my support?" Khan asked, incensed, "I've always been fair with my juniors, given them a free hand; I've always treated you right, Roberts."

"That's just the point, the fact that we're your juniors."

"You're not making any sense, Roberts," Khan said, trying to mask the irritation in his voice.

Roberts laughed feebly. "People like you, Khan, you've never really had to do anything to gain promotion. I know how promotion works, how some people jump the queue because politicians want to be seen to be creating an ethnic mix at the top of our profession."

"I gained my promotion on ability alone," Khan responded angrily.

"If you say so," Roberts said in a sarcastically cutting tone.

"People who work for me know I'm good at what I do!" Khan snapped.

Roberts laughed again. "So good that one of your officers is a neo-Nazi terrorist. So good that, if it wasn't for Bailey's intervention, I'd have killed Machin and Bailey in my lair, and you'd have blamed it on Red Vengeance. All of this and without Bailey you'd have known nothing about me being the brain behind the terror campaign."

Khan lapsed into silence. Roberts was right—Khan had had no idea that he was capable of anything like this. Until he had found the slashed tire in his garage and Davis had discovered CCTV footage from outside the restaurant of Roberts tailing his wife—up till that moment, Khan hadn't suspected him of anything other than being blind to his wife's infidelities. "Let's stop the misery, Roberts, you've been caught, and it's over. Let's put an end to this despair. Your reign of terror is over, and any further actions on your part are pointless. Why not save your last disciple's life, give your soul a chance of redemption."

He could see by the smug, teasing expression on Roberts's face that he wasn't going to tell him anything.

"And why would I unburden to you, Khan?" Roberts asked.

"You've sent out your message in the first two attacks, murdering more people is futile. You claim to be involved in a race war, yet you're sending teenage white kids, the ones you're meant to be fighting for, to their deaths," Khan pointed out. "How can you justify killing the people you're meant to be fighting for?"

"I don't need to justify anything, I just need people to know that I did it," Roberts said. "While the Baileys of this world talk a good fight but never actually do anything, I'm at least out there fighting and trying to make a difference."

And what a difference, Khan thought. *Men, women, and children murdered in the name of a dinosaur political movement that has been dead for seventy years.* "You certainly made a difference, all right. The whole of Britain now hates Fascism with a passion that nobody since Mosley has managed to achieve."

Roberts moved slightly in his bed, causing one of the monitors to beep. He adjusted his pillow, his indifference to the new murders he was about to cause, infuriating Khan.

"People like the EPP sit and moan about the state of this country but they never actually do anything, Khan, at least I'll be remembered for doing something."

"And this was all because of Patel having an affair with your wife," Khan demanded. "Mass murder because you weren't man enough to keep your woman," he taunted, deciding to take a different approach. The soft talk approach wasn't working, so Khan now reckoned it was time to try and rile Roberts into making a slip.

Roberts didn't take the bait, but instead calmly looked at Khan and smiled. "Nice try, Khan, but I'm long past the stage where I look at Jill as anything other than an irrelevance."

"You were married for ten years, you must've had some feelings for her," Khan pushed.

"Ten years too long," Roberts reflected bitterly.

"You must've had feelings for her to get married in the first place. If you say you didn't have, I don't believe you."

"Of course, I had feelings. Feelings of loathing, contempt, intense hatred, I think you'll find that over the years, with what she was doing, I developed plenty of negative feelings toward my cheating wife."

"You must've loved her when you married her," Khan said.

"Marcia Bradley said that the affair started when I was in Wales last year tracking down the serial killer, Peter Rivers. While I was serving the people by bringing a dangerous serial killer to justice, my wife was playing around with Patel," Roberts reflected. "I deserved better than that wouldn't you say, Khan?"

Roberts did deserve better, Khan thought, but however much he was wronged by his wife, it was no excuse for mass murder. Just as Khan was going to say something, a young stressed-looking doctor appeared, "He needs to rest," the doctor told Khan.

Khan was about to protest but decided against it. He was getting nowhere with his interview. He badly needed to change tactics if he was going to get anything out of Roberts. There was one last hope. Machin had worked with Roberts closely and longer than anyone else. She knew him better than any other cop did. Roberts liked to play games, as shown in the way he had not immediately shot Machin, firstly taunting her and Bailey with his supposed genius. Because he had been caught, Roberts had shown he was capable of making mistakes. Would he still want to play his games with Machin? Khan didn't know, but he knew there was only one way to find out.

CHAPTER 57

When DCI Khan told her he wanted her to talk to Roberts, Machin was by no means overjoyed at the prospect. "I'm the last person he's going to talk to," she grumbled as Khan pushed her in the wheelchair along the hospital corridor toward Roberts's private room.

The protests from the doctor over moving Machin so soon after her operation were still ringing in Khan's ears, but with another disciple on the loose out there and the urgency of finding them, Khan wasn't worried about upsetting the doctor's sensitive feelings.

"Well, he certainly won't talk to me. We've got nothing to lose," Khan said, as they reached Roberts's room. The police guard on the door told Khan that the doctor and nurse had left a few minutes ago. Khan seized the opportunity. This was the moment to see Roberts, unhindered by the medical staff.

As they entered, a dozing Roberts seemed to immediately become aware of their presence and stirred. When his eyes slowly opened and he saw Machin in the wheelchair, he smiled, with a look that told them he was pleased his gunshot had temporarily disabled his former colleague. "Nice to see you, Sarah," he said.

"I wish Bailey had killed you," Machin snapped.

She wasn't going to play it softly with this killer. She felt more betrayed than all her colleagues by Roberts's evil. She'd worked with this monster for five years and had never had any inclination of the evil that lay within him. After all they'd been through in the hunt for the serial killer, Peter Rivers, Machin never expected the same kind of evil right on her doorstep. She wondered if she was to blame for not seeing the signs. There surely must've have been some evidence of an evil streak while they'd worked closely together. All that time he was meant to be tailing people would need to come under scrutiny now. When he'd allegedly been on the job, instead, he'd been at his lair, torturing his teenage victims, forcing them into unspeakable crimes.

"You know what, Sarah, I'm quite sure you do."

Khan went and sat on a bedside chair, telling Roberts, "I thought maybe DI Machin might get you to see sense."

Roberts shook his head. "And why would you think I'd talk to her if I wouldn't talk to you, DCI Khan?"

"Because I know you better than DCI Khan, Morgan," she said calmly.

"You knew so much about me, yet you didn't know I was doing all this," Roberts said smugly. "It doesn't bode well for your detecting abilities, Sarah, the fact that you worked with me all those years and you knew nothing of what I was doing."

Machin wasn't going to get involved in a slanging match, so she moved on. "You brainwashed those two kids to commit murder. I've been lying there thinking, since my leg operation, trying to work out what kind of man could send kids out to do this? I came to the conclusion that a coward—only a coward who hasn't got the balls to do the murders himself—would send kids out to commit murder," she goaded.

"Every terror campaign needs an organizer, Sarah. For the message to be driven home someone has to remain in the background, organizing and making sure everything goes to plan," Roberts explained. "I didn't send them to commit murder. You could say I directed two young patriots on a noble quest to stand up and be counted in the fight for Britain—"

"You sent them to murder for you," Machin interrupted angrily.

"You know it's not that simple, Sarah."

Roberts had the zealot's glow of recognition in his eyes and was relieved that, in Khan and Machin, he had an audience to eulogize to.

"Mass murder and lunacy, it seems simple enough to me," Khan said.

"Well, you're never going to understand," Roberts said. "How could I expect you to ever understand, Khan? You can never understand the resentment of being passed over for promotion because of the color of your skin. Political correctness has destroyed this nation, Khan. It's why someone like me has to do what he has to do."

"I understand people like you, Roberts. I understand your deep-rooted insecurities, your xenophobia, how you blame everybody but yourself for the manifestations of your own evil."

Khan stared hard into Roberts's cold, merciless eyes, searching for some level of pity in the man, but, after a few seconds, he reluctantly concluded there was no compassion to be found inside of Roberts and that he was a soulless, empty shell.

"You killed Adam and John without a flicker of mercy," Machin reminded him angrily.

"If we're going to build a new Britain, there's no time for mercy," Roberts stated blankly. "Those boys died for the good of Britain, as a warning to other immigrants who dare to come."

"And, what about this disciple who's still out there?" Machin asked.

"What about him?"

"He's now a rudderless ship, without you to direct him. He's now just as dangerous to the people you're supposed to be fighting for, as well as those you're supposedly fighting against," Machin warned. "If you're a true white supremacist, then you can't be happy that your disciple is likely to kill fellow Anglo-Saxons. Is murdering your own people what you're fighting for, Roberts?"

Roberts remained unruffled. "If the training is strong enough, then mistakes can't be made."

"Training! You make it sound like you're some kind of Special Forces army instructor," Machin snapped.

"No, I'm just the man who's been tasked with re-modeling this country's soul," Roberts retorted.

"We know that your disciple is trying to murder Prince Henry," Khan stated. In Roberts's eyes, no matter how hard he tried to hide it, Khan could see a flicker showing he'd been rumbled. "Did you really think that we weren't clever enough to work out your target?" he pressed. "All we have to do is cancel the investiture ceremony, and your last disciple is useless."

Roberts smiled. "You won't do that."

Khan laughed. "Of course, we will, since your attacks in Brighton and Folkestone, we take your threat seriously."

"Prince Henry's stubborn, he'll never back down and cancel the ceremony," Roberts predicted positively, with an alarming insight into Prince Henry's character.

"Save the boy," Machin said, "the ceremony is being

canceled. Why don't you save the boy by telling us who and where he is, Roberts?"

"I don't believe you," Roberts stated coldly.

"We're not playing your games anymore, Roberts. Tell me where the boy is, and I'll do everything I can for you," Machin promised weakly.

"I shot you, Machin. With the hatred I know you must now feel for me after my betrayal, do you really expect me to believe you'd help me?"

"I remember how you were before this sickness took hold of you," Machin said. "You've had a mental breakdown, and you're refusing to accept it, let us help you."

"Machin, the amateur psychiatrist, you tried this once before with Peter Rivers and look what that led to," Roberts reminded her.

She remembered. She'd hesitated before they'd gone to arrest Rivers, and it led to Debbie Duncan's rape and almost her murder. Even though she had saved her by killing Rivers when he came after Debbie, it was something she felt she could never atone for. Roberts, in that one statement—bringing up her past mistakes—showed Machin this was not a man who was going to show pity.

"You need treatment, Morgan," she said.

"I'm sure that's what the system will arrange for me once Prince Henry's dead."

"You won't get near Henry," Khan told Roberts angrily.

"It's not me you've got to worry about," Roberts announced with a smile, and Khan, seeing the smirk on Roberts's face, felt a depth of hatred for him that he'd never felt for a man before. Khan was in a dark place, knew that if they'd got the last disciple's name out of him, he, Khan, would've been tempted to punch him in the face and wipe off that smug look.

Machin moved her wheelchair until it was right next

to Roberts's bed. "You think you're untouchable, Roberts, you think that the legal system that's in place to insure a suspect's rights applies here." She paused for effect. "Terrorism is treated with the disgust it deserves in this country. If you'd committed these heinous crimes on your own, then the world might have shown you some mercy. The fact that you've used kids to carry out your murders, that the Brighton bombing killed children, all these weigh heavily against you, Roberts. When the world sees the evil way you've brainwashed your victims, the world will not be kind to you," she warned.

"Listen to DI Machin, Roberts," Khan pitched in.

"It's all irrelevant. Once my disciple has killed Henry, then my work is done," Roberts said stubbornly.

"That's not how this is going to work," Machin interjected. She smiled suspiciously at him. "Just before we came in here, I made some phone calls, calls to people who are very interested in your well-being."

Roberts suddenly looked twitchy. "What are you blabbing on about, Sarah?"

"This is one of your big problems, Roberts. In all your ranting, the one thing that clearly comes across in everything you say is the fact that you seem to feel that you can kill with impunity, kill without consequence." Machin leaned her elbows on the corner of the bed. "As all good coppers should know, and a fact that you seem to have forgotten, that's not always the case."

Roberts smiled irritatingly, asking, "Is there any point to this?"

"All we need is the name, Roberts, give us the name of your last disciple and then you can go and wallow away for the rest of your life at Broadmoor with the nut doctors," she pressed. The name of the boy would give them something, a chance, she decided. Just one name and this misery could be over.

"You know I'm not going to give you the name, Sarah, why don't you just go back to bed and rest your wounds." Roberts reached out his hand and gently patted Machin on the shoulder. She angrily brushed his arm away.

"Anyway, back to those people who are interested in your wellbeing," she snapped. "When I spoke to John's and Adam's families a couple of hours ago, they seemed to be particularly interested in where you were, so much so that they immediately drove here when I called them. At this moment in time, they're all down the corridor in the waiting room, waiting for me to give them the nod. In a few minutes, DCI Khan and I, plus the police guard on the door, are going away for a coffee break to give them a chance to get acquainted with the man who murdered their sons."

Roberts suddenly looked uneasy.

Machin added, "Still, at least it'll give you a chance to explain why their sons had to die. I'm sure, in the depths of the despair they must be suffering since their sons' murders, they'll be prepared to listen. I wish I could remain and hear how you try to explain why their sons had to die for your warped prophecy. I'm sure your words will get an interesting reaction." Machin said then patted Roberts gently on his shoulder and smiled.

The room lapsed into an uncomfortable silence. Finally, Roberts broke the silence, nervously pleading, "You can't do this to me, I've got rights, I know what a murder suspect is entitled to."

Machin laughed. "I'm sure you do, Roberts, as a cop I'd expect nothing else."

"It's not legal—"

"Now he starts pleading for the police to protect him," Khan laughed. "Can you believe this guy, Machin?"

"I'm a suspect for murder, and legally I'm entitled to police protection to make sure I get a fair trial in court," Roberts stated anxiously.

"In my eyes, you've got no rights, Roberts," Machin said. "All we need to say is that our colleague guarding the door was distracted for a few minutes. No court is going to have any sympathy for you. I think after what you've done to their kids, it's only going to take a few minutes for the parents of the murdered boys to carry out retribution, that's unless they decide on the slow torturous approach."

Khan stood, walked around the side of the bed toward Machin, and grabbed the wheelchair handles on her wheelchair, ready to go.

"You can't do this!" Roberts begged.

"And why can't we?" Machin asked Roberts, as Khan slowly turned her wheelchair toward the door.

"If you believe in the sanctity of the law, you can't do this," Roberts said pathetically.

"Maybe after the evil I've seen you do, I don't believe in the law anymore. If you're not going to be of any help to us, then we might as well let the families have their revenge and save on the hassle of a long trial," Machin commented.

"No court will ever convict any of John's or Adam's families for acting out their revenge on you. I'm sure any member of the jury would've felt like doing the same if you'd murdered their son," Khan added.

A kaleidoscope of thoughts was racing through Roberts's head. Murdered by the families of his victims in this cold, sterile hospital room was not how his glorious Nazi revolution was meant to end. Roberts needed an open courtroom to address his beliefs to an eager press. A speech to justify his patriotic acts was needed to make Britain understand that he was fighting for them. Roberts wouldn't be denied, he couldn't be denied, by Khan and his stooge, Machin. "Hold on!" he shouted, as Khan started to wheel Machin's wheelchair out the room.

Khan stopped the wheelchair, exchanging a look with Machin that said that they both knew that Roberts had cracked.

"This is your last chance, Roberts. No more playing games. After we leave this room, any chance to help yourself is gone," Machin warned him ominously.

Khan turned the wheelchair back around to face Roberts. "We need to know everything about your last disciple," he said.

"I'll tell you, just keep the families out of here," Roberts begged. All the smugness he'd shown since they'd entered his room had now evaporated into blind panic at the thought of being left alone with the relatives of his victims.

Khan produced a pen and notepad and handed them to Roberts to write with. He leaned on a reading table in front of him and wrote. He wrote like a man who needed to write down as much as he could to ensure his path to salvation. The name, Craig Murray, was written down in block capitals on the pad.

They now had a name, Machin thought. From the name, they could find an address from the ranks of teen-agers on the reported missing list. Once they had an address, then they'd be able to get a recent photo. With a photo, they'd have a specific target to look for rather than waste time scrolling through a random list of names on the missing persons' list.

Khan wasn't worried, was optimistic that with a photo of Murray, there'd now be an unbreakable ring of security around Prince Henry, all armed with Murray's photo. Khan was certain there'd be no chance now of Craig Murray breaking through the security cordon.

Outside the hospital entrance, Khan took out his mobile phone and immediately set to work, calling his team to set things in motion. The police's work wasn't just about preventing Prince Henry's murder. Their work was just as much about saving Craig Murray from a cruel, evil death. Saving the soul of a boy who'd been brainwashed to commit the ultimate act of savagery, for the warped political ranting of the lunatic, Roberts, was all that could be salvaged from this mess, Khan thought. Craig Murray was a boy who deserved to live, Khan decided, and if he had anything to do with it, he would make sure that he did.

CHAPTER 58

Machin had discharged herself from the hospital. There was no way she could just lie there calmly in a hospital bed waiting to hear news from the investiture about the whereabouts of Craig Murray. Khan had helped her into his car, and they'd hurried back to Dover police station, a place that had been chosen as the obvious base for the investiture security operation. There'd been no need to get rid of the families of Adam and John, as they were, at the moment, still blissfully unaware of Roberts being their sons' murderer. Machin had shown in her confrontation with Roberts that he wasn't the only person who knew how to play mind games.

She was seated in a quiet corner of the conference room, listening while the security team, headed by Rutherford and Khan, set to work planning the investiture ceremony security operation. In her brief time in the wheelchair, she was starting to realize the invisibility of disability and vowed that, when she was upright and could stand again, she'd view disabled people in a far more sympathetic light. Bailey was still being held by the police, something she felt guilty about, especially now that she knew he wasn't involved in terrorism. He was also the man who'd saved her life, and the whole situation seemed grossly unfair.

Bailey was brought up from the cells so that he could sit and talk with Machin. While Khan and Rutherford were busily engaged in issuing orders, she said, "Thanks for all you did in Roberts's lair, Bailey."

Bailey shrugged matter-of-factly. "There's no need for thanks. I told you the EPP wasn't involved in this. Now at least you believe me."

"You shouldn't be carrying a gun," Machin told him dutifully.

"And if I hadn't been carrying that gun, we'd both be dead, Inspector," Bailey stated pragmatically.

Machin couldn't argue. They'd been moments from death when Bailey had shot Roberts. "You know that you're going to be charged with carrying an illegal firearm," she told him guiltily.

Bailey surprised Machin by laughing. "Whatever I'm charged with, it's better than being dead, wouldn't you say, Inspector?"

Machin couldn't agree more. The fact that Bailey was going to be charged for using a gun to save her life was ridiculous, she thought. "I'll stick up for you in court," she promised. There was something bothering her, "Do you often carry an unlicensed firearm around with you?"

"And that's something I'm going to tell a copper?" Bailey remarked sarcastically.

"You claim the EPP is a democratic party, yet you're carrying a handgun around with you," she retorted.

"I only armed myself after I found out about Red Vengeance. From that time on, I've been worried about my safety and decided I needed to take out my own personal protection policy," he explained.

She decided to let the matter drop. They had pictures

of Craig Murray from a missing person's report. Now photos of Craig Murray had been distributed to everybody involved in Prince Henry's security, Machin was quietly confident that the boy wouldn't evade the security net. She thought that, at last, this was one of Roberts's disciples that had a chance of being saved. Their main worry was whether he was carrying a suicide bomb like the Brighton bomber. If he was, then even if he didn't get near Henry, any bomb detonation could still kill many people in the crowd. They needed to stop Craig Murray before he got anywhere near the ceremony. With all the spotters they had around the castle, she was confident that Murray wouldn't get close enough to do any real damage.

"I'm surprised that you got the last disciple's name out of Roberts," Bailey said. "Fanatics aren't usually that giving."

"He didn't give it willingly. We had to threaten him with letting the relatives of Adam and John into his private room when the doctors weren't around. That seemed to persuade him to cooperate." Machin elaborated.

Bailey liked what he heard and laughed out loud. "So deep down, the man's a coward."

Khan walked over to Machin. "I need to get to the castle. It'll be better if you and Bailey stay here because of the extent of your injuries, and in view of Bailey's firearms charge."

She didn't argue. Although she wanted to be at the castle with Khan and the others, the last thing they needed was for her to become an encumbrance and to get in the way of such an important security operation.

"I'd sooner be with you, sir," she told Khan but could see, by the steely look in his focused, deep-brown eyes, that her boss wasn't for changing his mind.

"I'll give you regular updates over the phone," Khan promised, and then he and Rutherford were gone.

She stared at the door they'd left through long after it had closed. There were now only Bailey, herself, and two busy controllers in the room. She didn't like it. She was a policewoman who liked to be very involved in the action, not uselessly sitting on the side-lines.

Bailey reassured her. "They'll get him," he predicted confidently.

She hoped he was right. This misery needed to end, and it needed to end fast. Bailey pushed her wheelchair over to the window. From the window, they had a panoramic view of the castle towering over the town on Castle Hill above them. She stared at the imposing castle turrets that had, for centuries, guarded the gates of England against foreign invasion. Roberts had shown the castle a new kind of modern menace—a threat not with swords or bows, not a Napoleon with his invading army staring across the Channel from Boulogne or Nazi Panzers waiting by their barges to be unleashed on Britain. This was a threat of hatred and dysfunction. Roberts had shown it was an enemy that the historical ghosts that seeped through Dover Castle's intimidating high stone walls had never encountered before. This was an enemy of the twenty-first century, an enemy of pure hate and division—an enemy, a man with a bad soul—against which no form of fortification could protect you.

CHAPTER 59

Khan, like the rest of his colleagues, was mingling with the bustling crowds around Dover Castle. The security team protecting Prince Henry were alert and ready for anything. The outer security ring was strong and virtually impregnable, Khan was confident that Craig Murray would not be able to get through it. Everyone would be searched, before any of the public got anywhere near the spot where the slow drive past of the royal cavalcade prior to the ceremony would take place. Prince Henry was not being cooperative and was refusing to kow-tow to terrorists. In a private meeting with the royal head of security, Rutherford, Henry had defiantly told him that he fully intended to go on a walk-about amongst the crowds before and after the ceremony.

It was Rutherford's worst nightmare. He wanted a straightforward drive into the castle grounds in Prince Henry's armored limousine. With its Kevlar rubber tires, polycarbonate glass windows, and reinforced steel body, the limousine was more like a tank than a car. While Prince Henry was seated inside the limo, Rutherford knew his safety was virtually guaranteed. Alas, Prince Henry, as an ex-soldier, wasn't a man who skulked away from danger. He was not a coward, but a man who confronted danger head-on. Today that confrontation could prove fatal, Khan reckoned. He glanced at his watch. Henry's cavalcade was only minutes away from the castle, so they needed to find Craig Murray now.

Khan studied the rapidly gathering crowd, looking for a teenage boy who stood out on his own. If Murray slipped through the outer ring, then they had to be ready. Khan looked at the recent picture he had of the boy. There were many teenage boys in the crowd, but, so far, none of them looked anything like Craig Murray. Rutherford rang Khan with a progress report shortly before Prince Henry was due to arrive. None of the security team had reported seeing the boy, and now Henry was almost upon them.

Rutherford got his men to redouble their efforts. Craig Murray had to be out there somewhere, Rutherford thought. If Murray was going to strike, then it had to be soon.

Khan started moving more frantically through the crowd. He wanted to save this boy more than he'd wanted to do anything in his life for a long while. In Khan's eyes, Craig Murray needed to be saved to prove that the Fascists could be beaten. Khan needed to beat them. For all the decent working people out there who lived a life without prejudice, this was a war he couldn't let them win. Khan needed to beat them to avoid the race war that Roberts's dark, perverted mind was somehow trying to cause.

Everything pointed to Craig Murray being in this crowd somewhere. The spectators had been through the security checks and metal detectors, in order to be allowed to line the route Prince Henry's limousine would take. Khan knew that nothing was fool proof. In this high-tech world of the modern terrorist, evil people were always discovering new ways to bypass security. Inside the castle keep, the dignitaries were patiently waiting to start the ceremony.

Khan thought he saw a boy moving near the back of the crowd, just by the slope where the limousine would climb the road toward the keep. Khan desperately pushed his way through the expectant crowd, receiving disgruntled looks from irritated royal watchers. Khan didn't have time to explain he was with the police. The fuzzy mop of blond hair he could see on the boy at the back of the crowd looked similar to the fuzzy blond hair on the photo of Craig Murray he carried.

There were too many people in front of him to get a clear sight of the boy. In the distance, Khan could hear the crowd start to cheer as Prince Henry's limousine started to slowly make its way up the slope toward the keep. It was as it started up the slope, that the limousine stopped—alarmingly for Khan. His mind became a mask of horror as he saw Prince Henry and some of his entourage step out the car and start talking to the crowd. Khan crashed through the people, rushing to the back of the crowd, but when he arrived at the spot where he'd last seen the boy, the boy was no longer there. Khan started frantically searching at the back of the crowd.

Henry was now talking to a mother holding her baby. If the boy who Khan had seen at the back of the crowd was Craig Murray, then the prince was in terrible danger. As Khan desperately searched, he prayed that he would find the boy in time. Prince Henry was at his most vulnerable, standing outside of his car in the open. This scenario of Prince Henry going on walkabout was probably exactly how Roberts had planned it, Khan thought. To his horror, he realized he'd lost the boy and stopped to draw a breath, his eyes vigilant to every twitch and movement. If the boy was going to strike at Prince Henry, then one look at the vulnerable prince standing a short distance away from Khan told him that the time to strike was here, and it had to be now.

CHAPTER 60

Craig stood at the back of the crowd like a bird of prey, waiting and watching. It was a big crowd, bigger than the master had predicted. As his target's car pulled to a halt at the curbside in front of the crowd, Craig started edging slowly around the side of the crowd toward him. He clutched the flowers tightly to his chest. These were the flowers the master had shown Craig how to lace with the deadly concentrated anthrax spores. All he had to do was to brush the flowers against his target's skin and then his target was finished. The master had told Craig this was the only way for him to achieve the path to true enlightenment. The master had neglected to tell the boy that by carrying the flowers so close to his body that he would also be infected, and that anybody who came in contact with the flowers, as Craig elbowed his way to the front of the crowd, would also not survive.

As Craig pushed his way through the crowd, some of the people gave the strange, mesmerized boy, who ignorantly pushed past them, a wary look. Craig was oblivious to their stares, didn't hear their moans and grumbles. All he focused on, through his master's training, was his target, and the target was all that mattered to him. The master had taught him how to remain focused in crowds, had told him not to be distracted by anything going on around him. The flowers brushed against a shrieking woman who was shouting at his target over the top of the front row of people. By brushing the flowers against her skin, the clock was already ticking, draining the woman's life force from her and leading to the horrific death that was soon to come. Craig didn't care. The master had told him he had to harden his heart to pain and suffering. He had to view the crowd as just obstacles that were in the way of him being able to achieve his goal.

His target was engaged in conversation with the lively crowd, barely thirty yards away, and it was at this moment that Craig had to be at his strongest and most determined. Through his complex training, the master had installed the iron discipline that was necessary for the completion of his task, a discipline the master said was sadly lacking in Craig's generation. At twenty yards from his target, the security became more claustrophobic, the security team was now watching for anybody acting suspicious, studying the faces of the animated crowd thrusting against the barriers.

Craig pushed with the force the master had told him would be required, like Moses parting the Red Sea in front of him, and a gap suddenly appeared in the masses. Craig pushed his way into the gap, brushing flowers against more people. As he pushed two women aside by the railing, at last, he could feel the cold metal suddenly upon him. The angry women swore at him, Craig ignored them. To Craig, they were the great unwashed. The master had told him not to worry about collateral damage. That collateral damage was a necessary evil that would be encountered on the path to true enlightenment.

His target was now almost within touching distance.

The shouting and screaming had begun in earnest. The more excited the crowd got, the more observant the police by the barriers keeping the crowds back became. Craig saw a slight gap in the police cordon and stepped forward as his target walked smiling toward the door of a building he was about to enter. The moment had arrived for Craig to prove that the master's teachings had not been wasted. Craig's time for direct action was now. He stepped forward and held out the flowers toward his target's hands. Craig smiled the way the master had taught him, so the target would be at ease and off guard. Craig had the unswerving face of obedience as he thrust the flowers ever closer to his target's destruction. At last, the target looked toward him and smiled. His target then reached out toward Craig to grab the flowers. It was at that point that Craig could feel and smell success as he knew his target was reaching out toward his own destruction.

CHAPTER 61

Khan couldn't see him. He had reached the back of the crowd, and the boy wasn't there. He'd definitely seen him and his unmistakable mop of fuzzy hair. The boy had been there. He couldn't have gone far in the minute it had taken Khan to get to where he'd been standing. He looked frantically around him, scurrying through the crowd in a desperate attempt to find the brainwashed boy. Khan wanted to call for reinforcements, but there wasn't time. Prince Henry was exchanging pleasantries with the spectators at the front of the crowd, blissfully unaware of Khan's desperate search. He laughed and joked with the crowd, one of his endearing characteristics that made him a man of the people, a trait that left him vulnerable and a massive security risk on days like this.

It was as Khan's eyes darted around the front of the crowd that he saw the teenager's mop of hair as the boy slowly worked his way through the crowds toward the front. It was only a matter of moments before he would arrive at Henry's side. Khan hurled himself into the crowd, pushing people aside. The crowd objected, Khan shouting that it was a police emergency. He pressed on, getting ever closer to the boy. As he was almost at the barriers separating the crowd from the royal party, he could see the back of the boy's head barely yards from where Henry was laughing and joking with a young mother.

"Protect Prince Henry!" Khan screamed, adding, "There's an assassin in the crowd!"

In the commotion, nobody at the front could hear what he was saying. The boy was reaching out toward Henry, and just when he was right next to Henry, Khan elbowed his way through to the front of the crowd and forced his way past the barrier. The boy was facing away from Khan toward Henry, Khan started running along the front of the crowd facing him. As Khan ran a worried looking security guard panicked on seeing some maniac rushing toward Henry. The guard rugby tackled Khan and they both crashed onto the hard concrete pavement.

"The boy's trying to kill Prince Henry," Khan quickly told the burly security guard who was now pinning him to the ground. Khan got the guard to look at his police badge, and, on seeing his identity badge, the guard took him more seriously. Khan pointed to the boy standing with his back to them near Henry. The guard radioed Henry's immediate security team who then rapidly formed a shield around him.

The boy stood still by the barrier, unable to comprehend what was going on. Khan and the security guard rushed toward him as Henry was quickly ushered back into the armored limo. As the limo sped away, Khan and the security guard arrived at the boy's side. Now that Henry was safe, all Khan was thinking about was saving the boy. Everybody had been checked as they entered the castle grounds, Khan was convinced the boy's weapon couldn't be a gun or a bomb. Whatever it was, he had to stop Craig Murray before he harmed any of the crowd.

As he reached the boy, Khan put his hand on the boy's shoulder. "Stay calm, Craig, your ordeal is nearly over," Khan said.

The boy turned abruptly, Khan twitched, wondering if somehow the boy had smuggled a bomb past security and it was about to explode. When his face wasn't blown away, and all that could be heard was Henry's car screeching off, Khan was relieved to see that the boy wasn't wired up with explosives. Khan's relief was short lived. As he stared long and hard into the face of the would-be assassin, he looked quickly at the picture of Craig Murray on his mobile phone screen. His relief at foiling the assassination soon changed to horror, for although the boy was the same age and height as Craig Murray and had similar blond hair to the kidnapped boy, one look at the freckled face before him, and Khan could see that whoever this boy was, it wasn't Craig Murray.

Toby Henson smiled at the crowd that had gathered outside BBC radio headquarters to protest at Henson's invite to a political debate due to take place on BBC Radio 4 later in the day. The crowd was a mixture of EPP supporters faced off by militant socialists. A large cordon of police stood in a thin blue line by the barriers separating the two factions. Henson was pleased at the volatile reaction his radio appearance was creating, his appearance on the radio debate was at least sparking an interest in the party and making the event newsworthy. Henson knew, like any good politician did in this advertising-generated society, that lack of publicity for a party was the real killer to any party's chances of electoral success. As the leader of the strongest far right party in Britain, Henson knew that the EPP had to stay at the forefront of social events if they were ever going to get the kind of electoral support that would allow them to make an impact on British politics. Henson had decided long ago that the EPP was all about impact.

The phone call that Henson had received that morning from Ian Bailey, at last, gave Henson something with which he could fight back against his public and media detractors. Bailey was in Dover and had told Henson about the terror campaign that DS Roberts had been engaged in. As Bailey was telling Henson about Roberts's set-up at the lair and about his brain-washed victims, Henson had smiled. Apparently, Roberts had been trying to doctor evidence so the blame for the recent murderous terrorist campaign would be laid at the feet of a militant left group, called Red Vengeance. Red Vengeance—it had a particularly catchy ring to it, Henson thought. He now realized that, thanks to Bailey's call, Henson now had a list of responses with which he could destroy the panel's most virulent questions.

He'd been invited by the BBC to take part in a public slaying. Henson couldn't wait to see the look of horror on their smug faces when they realized that because of Bailey's inside information Henson was going to turn the tables on them. In a day or so all the information would be released by the police to the Press about Roberts's lair, proving that Henson was telling the truth. The inside information gave him a wonderful edge over his political rivals, and, as any good politician knew, an edge was all you required in politics.

As Henson approached the entrance, the press were busy snapping pictures, and film cameras were filming his every move. From the mass of cheering EPP supporters a boy slipped past the barriers carrying a bunch of flowers. The police, seeing the boy carrying flowers and coming from the friendly arms of Henson's supporters, decided there was nothing sinister and ignored him. The EPP gave the boy a rousing cheer as they saw him approaching Henson with the flowers. From the massed ranks of the militant left, the socialist workers booed and jeered the boy's progress.

Henson could see an opportunity, a supporter handing him flowers in front of the press cameras was a good publicity opportunity not to be missed. As Craig Murray reached Henson, he thrust the flowers into Henson's face just as the master had instructed. Henson irritably pulled the flowers out of his face, but not before the contaminated flowers had brushed against his skin. As the cameras snapped away, Henson put a comradely arm around Craig's shoulders and smiled. Even though he had been told to smile, Craig's face remained blank and devoid of emotion. On seeing that he was going to get no reaction from him, Henson ignored him and hurriedly entered the building. As Craig saw Henson go, he had a strange look of contentment on his fresh, youthful face. Craig had been tasked with a mission, a mission that he'd just completed.

The master would be pleased that his disciple had succeeded in doing what he'd been ordered. It was a mission of death, a mission that the master said was going to change Britain and bring renewed hope to the British people.

Craig didn't understand. He had a sore throat, aching muscles, and could feel clogging starting to envelop his lungs. He'd been keeping the flowers close to his chest since he was given them yesterday and had no idea how infected his body had become. As he sat on a nearby wall and watched the crowd commotion all around him, the sweat started to envelop his body. Craig suddenly felt very ill like he had the flu, his pulse rate had quickened alarmingly, and unbeknownst to the disciple, Craig, they were all the ominous signs of his downfall. It meant that, for the disciple Craig Murray, his race was nearly run.

CHAPTER 63

A tired-looking Machin was sitting alongside Bailey in Khan's office. Opposite them, Khan was seated behind his desk. The room was gripped with an uncomfortable, reflective silence as nobody knew how to comment about what they'd just heard. News had just come in from London that Toby Henson, the EPP leader, had just been rushed to the hospital. The victim of a suspected anthrax attack. Now it had been confirmed that Craig Murray, Roberts's last missing disciple, had been the deliverer of the lethal, infected flowers—news everyone now greeted with a mixture of surprise and horror. Nobody had ever considered Henson with his virulent far right views as a target, Khan thought. Roberts seemed to be a Nazi, and yet he had attacked one of his own. Kahn couldn't make any sense of it.

"I thought the target was Prince Henry," Khan openly admitted.

"We all did. That was what Roberts wanted us to think," Machin said, adding, "He was playing another of his evil games."

There was a moment's uncomfortable deliberation until Bailey said, "When you threatened Roberts with letting the parents of his victims loose on him, he was going to tell you whatever he needed in order to prevent that. He probably knew you'd never do it. And, all the time you thought you were playing him, he was playing you, Machin."

Machin recalled how Roberts had looked suitably terrified and had played his part well. The fact that he'd caved in so easily should've made Machin suspicious. Roberts had suddenly become cooperative, had told them the name of his last disciple. Although he hadn't directly told them the target was Prince Henry, he'd let them assume so by wearing the expression of a man that had been rumbled when they'd mentioned Prince Henry's name.

Prince Henry had fit in with what they'd wanted to believe was the target. The lair being in Dover's Western Heights, opposite the castle, had added to the illusion. The discovery of it just before Prince Henry's investiture, as far as Machin and Khan had been concerned, made them assume that the prince was the target.

"How's, Henson?" Machin asked Bailey.

"It's not looking good. The doctors reckon that the amount of anthrax spores that he's ingested from the flowers means he's got no chance of survival."

Bailey would maintain an image of quiet concern when asked about Henson. He'd adopt the persona of a distraught colleague. There was so much Bailey needed to do in the weeks ahead so he wouldn't come across in the press as a man who didn't care about Henson. It was now time for calm transition, a period when dramatic events were about to engulf the party. Nobody could know where this was going to lead. Bailey had intended it to lead to a better future. He'd already been called earlier in the day by some party activists who'd asked him to take over the leadership of the EPP. With Henson lying in the hospital on his deathbed, Bailey wouldn't make an immediate grab for power. To achieve the support for his leadership that he now required, he had to show Henson the due reverence the outgoing leader deserved. He wouldn't alienate future supporters by acting cold and unfeeling. His attitude toward his soon-to-be predecessor had to be always one of honor and respect.

"We should've been suspicious when he told us Craig Murray's name," Khan reflected. "A fanatic like Roberts was never going to give up the name of his last disciple so easily, especially as he would've looked at it as his last chance to make any impact in his campaign of terror."

"None of it makes any sense," Bailey said. "He murdered the greatest far right leader this country has seen since Mosley," he eulogized, though he could see by the cold look that Khan and Machin gave him that the detectives obviously didn't look at Henson the same way.

"Why would he kill the people with whom he's supposed to have some kind of ideological allegiance?" Khan asked.

"The EPP is nothing like this cretin," Bailey retorted. "The fact that he's murdered Henson shows that Roberts was just as much an enemy of the EPP as he was of the public."

Machin didn't comment. In her eyes, none of it made any sense. In the last few days, she was only just coming to terms with the fact of what Roberts was really like. In Roberts's lair, and, by the way he'd played them at the hospital, she'd seen how evil he could be. It made her uncomfortable to think of all those times she'd worked with him in the last few months, and how, in all that time, he'd seemed normal. So normal that, while he was supposed to be doing work for Counter Terrorism Command, he was, in fact, brainwashing kids and plotting mayhem and murder. Roberts had been more like a friend than a colleague to her over the years. It was a friendship that these revelations had now totally shattered.

She knew that the aftermath of this betrayal would have long-lasting effects on her psyche. Her friendship with Roberts had been a false friendship that he had used for his own evil ends. It meant that, in the future, she would now always have trouble with trust issues and with letting friends and colleagues into her life.

"He was intent on causing dysfunction and mayhem, he would've done anything to create anarchy, turn Britain into a land of social divide," Khan forecast prophetically.

"They reckon the anthrax-laden flowers brushed the skin of many in the crowd before Murray got to Henson, Henson isn't going to be the only death in all this," Machin reflected sadly.

"Even at the end of his evil, he couldn't help himself by doing one more evil act," Khan said angrily.

Both Machin and Bailey had to agree with the DCI's summing up.

"The moment Roberts gave Craig Murray that bunch of anthrax-laden flowers, he knew that Murray was dead," Khan pointed out.

Machin thought of the horror of killing a poor innocent teenage boy like this. How could the man with whom she'd shared danger on many occasions turn into this? Roberts, the enigma, whose name, after news of his horrific deeds was presented to the press, was forever going to be synonymous with the likes of history's evil mass murderers.

"None of this makes any sense," Bailey said.

"Evil never does," Khan reasoned. "Nobody but Roberts is ever going to know why he killed all these people. Blaming Patel for having an affair with his wife doesn't cover it. Whatever dark forces caused this madness, only Roberts really knows. Let's hope the psychiatrists can unravel it," he added.

"I need to see him," Machin told Khan.

"And what good is that going to do, Inspector?"

"Probably no good at all," she confessed. Whether it did any good or not, Machin needed to see Roberts, she needed to see him and try to understand this madness.

"I have to go to London to see Henson. According to reports from his family, he's got very little time left," Bailey told them, asking. "Is there anything else you need me for, DCI Khan?"

Khan said there wasn't. Apart from carrying an illegal firearm without a permit, there was nothing else to hold him on. Although Khan hated what the EPP stood for, he wasn't going to push it, Bailey had saved Machin's life. If he hadn't had the gun to stop Roberts, then Roberts would've got away with his evil and murdered countless more people.

When Bailey had gone, Khan turned to Machin and asked, "Considering how close you were to Roberts and how the press is going to view it, is going to see Roberts really a good idea?"

Machin shrugged. After Roberts's deception, she wondered about her judgement on anything. She contented herself with, "Who knows, sir?"

She certainly didn't. She just knew she had to see him and needed to know more about this monster before he was incarcerated in Broadmoor for the rest of his days.

"Shall I come with you?" Khan asked.

Machin shook her head. "This is something I need to do alone, sir."

Khan, to his credit, didn't argue. He went ahead and arranged for a driver to take Machin to Canterbury Hospital to see Roberts, who was completely bedridden, and still under heavy police guard. Khan could see the look of

devastation in her eyes, a look that no amount of camaraderie or hugs would remove. Only one man, Roberts, was
ever going to allow Machin any peace of mind over the
issue of his betrayal. She was going to have to step inside
the mind of the creep one more time, Khan thought. That
was if she wanted redemption and the chance to lay any
future demons to rest. Regrettably, therefore, she had no
other choice.

CHAPTER 64

When the policeman on guard in the corridor slowly pushed Machin's wheelchair into the private room where the police had wisely put Roberts, he was lying in bed asleep.

"Do you want me to stay in here with you, ma'am?" the guard asked as he parked Machin's wheelchair near the bed.

Machin told him she'd be okay, that she'd holler if she needed him. The guard nodded and then stepped outside. Machin just sat and stared at Roberts's calm, emotionless face for a moment and noted every contour for posterity. He hadn't been able to contain his joy in their last interview when he'd seen that his shooting of Machin had temporarily put her in a wheelchair. The surgeon told Machin that it was only temporary and that, after months of intense physiotherapy, the severed muscles should heal and she should be able to walk normally again.

"I know you're not asleep, Roberts," Machin said as she wheeled her chair closer to the bed and stared hard into his face.

Roberts slowly opened his eyes and smiled mischievously. "There's no fooling you, Sarah," he said sarcastically, adding, "You really are a master detective."

"The boy killed Henson," Machin stated angrily, ignoring Roberts's jibe. "He also brushed flowers against several people in the crowd as he pushed through them to get to Henson. The doctors at the specialist biological weapons ward in London reckon that at least five more people are going to die because of you."

"War can be a terrible thing, Machin. Sometimes the innocent get killed along with the guilty, though I doubt that any of those supporting or protesting against Toby Henson and the EPP outside that BBC building were that innocent."

"You're not involved in a war, Roberts," Machin replied angrily. "This isn't a war, this is nothing more than your own personal hate campaign."

Roberts smiled. "Being indoctrinated by police institutions, it's not surprising that you can't understand the war the indigenous people of this country are currently involved in."

"If you'd just murdered Patel, your wife's lover, I could've understood. If in a desperate act of anguish you'd lashed out, I might even have had a tinge of sympathy and understood how such a situation could've backed you into a corner," Machin reflected. "But this evil you've embarked upon, the kidnapping of boys, the killing of women and children with that bomb, and finally, just when I thought it couldn't get any worse, you've used biological weapons."

"It's no good just getting rid of the flesh of the apple when the core of the apple is rotten," Roberts lectured. "The whole of society has been infiltrated, all the top jobs in the media, most health-care professions, top businesses, you only need to take one look at DCI Khan and how he's reached command within the police as proof of my point," he ranted.

"And what is your point?" Machin asked, deciding that maybe this had been a mistake to come here and be subjected to any more of Roberts's madness.

"And that's your problem, Sarah. It's right in front of you, and yet you still can't see it."

"You're not making any sense, Roberts."

"They reach these positions of prominence because their parents subsidized them through university, pushed them on to become achievers so they could take control of Britain's institutions. This country is now completely dominated, in the higher echelons of business and commerce by Asians." As Roberts finished his rant, in his eyes Machin could see the blank stare of the unflinching xenophobe. This was the stare of Hitler, Amin—the stare of men without a conscience.

With his virulent outburst, Machin was starting to understand how far into the depths of madness her colleague had fallen. Now Roberts had been captured, knowing that he'd soon be incarcerated in a mental institution for the rest of his life, his subconscious was now no longer bothering to hide his hate and loathing for mankind. "Asians are in control because they've studied hard, worked their socks off to get the qualifications necessary to make it in their chosen field," Machin told him. "It's not their fault that others don't have the same zip."

Roberts surprised her by laughing. "I feel sorry for you, Sarah. The social media has brainwashed you completely. Believe me, I know how easy it is to brainwash a person and to make them completely susceptible to your viewpoint."

"Those poor kids!" Machin snapped, suddenly recalling the three teenagers who Roberts had sent to do his evil deeds. "They were young, had their whole lives ahead of them. "You've destroyed their families, murdered the innocent. Nothing you believe in can justify what you did."

"I did them a favor," Roberts stated coldly. "At least they won't have to grow up in an Asian-dominated Britain, a Britain where they'd soon realize they'd have no hope of advancement. And, while Asians control everything, that's the way it always will be, Machin."

She didn't buy any of it. "And all this evil came about, all because a man, named Patel, shagged your wife."

Machin could see a flicker of anger momentarily pass through Roberts's tired-looking eyes. It was only there a brief moment, and then it was gone.

"And you really think that's all that this was about?" he said.

"You might try and put a gloss on it, claim you were involved in some sinister terrorist campaign to save Britain, but we both know the truth, Roberts, we both know that you've achieved nothing other than a brief sick and twisted notoriety." Machin tried hopelessly to bring Roberts back to reality, noting by the lack of emotion in his dead eyes that such a feat was impossible.

Roberts laughed again. "I've killed the leader of the EPP, a party that was well supported in last year's elections. Think what's actually happened here, Sarah. A member of Counter Terrorism Command, who is meant to protect the people from such things, has murdered members of the public in terrorist attacks. I've also killed the leader of the EPP, Toby Henson, and murdered the anarchist journalist, Tredwell. Think what a public relations disaster this is going to be for the police. Because of me and my actions, any trust the public might've had in the police has been wiped out completely."

"Normal hardworking police officers won't be blamed for your madness," Machin countered.

"No, they probably won't, but whether they are or not, I've still planted an element of doubt about the police, particularly in the Counter Terrorist Command and DCIs like Khan, in the public's heads," Roberts retorted.

"You underestimate the public—the British people are cleverer than that. The British people will quickly realize that this was the work of a lunatic acting alone."

"Either that or they'll always be wary that the security forces they've grown to trust have sick individuals amongst their ranks who might try to kill them," Roberts commented, and the smirk he gave her somehow made her hate him even more.

"Nobody is going to think such a thing because of the rogue acts of a madman," Machin pointed out.

"After this, the EPP support will grow stronger than ever. They'll be looked upon as victims," he prophesied gleefully. "Bailey will get a new start as leader of the party. After the reports come out of how he saved your skin, of how invaluable his help in the hunt for me has been, he'll be a hero." Roberts paused to let her think about what he was saying.

"You couldn't have been that clever," Machin said, "there's no way you could've known that Bailey was carrying a gun when he arrived with me at your lair, Roberts." She was starting to have doubts. There was something about the smug way Roberts was talking about the increased support for the EPP that Machin didn't like.

Her statement was met with an uncomfortable silence. She thought back to the moment in the lair when Roberts had given his lecture. He had surprised her by not killing them immediately, seeming to unnecessarily engage them in conversation after he'd shot her in the leg. Why hadn't he shot and killed her instead of shooting her in the leg? This was a question that had been plaguing her since it happened. In his lecture, he told them they

were both going to die, a murder he could easily have accomplished the moment they arrived at the lair. Why had
Roberts delayed the act of murder and felt the need to
taunt them for as long as he had?

"I did my research, and I knew Bailey was carrying a
gun when he entered my lair," Roberts explained.

None of this made sense. If Roberts knew that Bailey
was carrying a gun when they'd stepped into the cell to
look at Tredwell, then why hadn't he taken it off him? It
had baffled her at the time, wondering how Roberts had
let Bailey get the drop on him, and how he didn't seem to
notice Bailey drop his hands. "You wanted Bailey to kill
you!" Machin said. The look of fulfilment that suddenly
appeared on Roberts's face told her everything. "You
wanted Bailey to kill you so that, after Henson was murdered, he would look like a hero from the way he'd saved
me by killing you."

Roberts's plan all along meant that he needed to die
at the hands of Bailey in that lair. The fact he hadn't, that
Bailey hadn't killed him, meant that he'd had to adjust
his plan and send them on a false trail with Prince Henry
at the Dover Castle investiture ceremony. He'd played
Machin in the hospital just like he had ever since he'd
found out about his wife's affair with Patel. There was so
much they needed to extract from Roberts to clear this
whole shoddy mess up. When he was better, the interviews and psychological reports would start in earnest,
only then would they start making progress in unraveling
this chaos.

"None of this matters now, nothing can be proved,"
Roberts predicted then picked up a hanky off the bedside
table and blew his nose. There was something about the
satisfied smile that appeared on his face soon after this
action which unnerved Machin. She wheeled her wheelchair away from the bed toward the door. "What have

you done?" she asked nervously, not liking the look that had suddenly appeared on his face.

"I've done something that someone like you could never understand," Roberts commented, then unnervingly smiled at her. "You'll never understand because your heart isn't true, Sarah—because your heart isn't true, you'll never comprehend the heart and mind of a patriot—"

Machin stared at the sudden, glazed look that appeared in Roberts's eyes. Then his body started convulsing. She rushed back to the bed and pushed the panic alarm. Almost immediately a doctor and nurse rushed into the room and hurried to Roberts's bedside.

Frantically they set to work on a suddenly seriously ill Roberts. They tried restarting his heart with defibrillators, injected him with adrenalin. As they worked, his vital signs faded rapidly. They cleared Machin from the room, making it obvious that things were going badly. After various attempts at resuscitation and shocks to try and restart Roberts's heart, the medical team came to the only conclusion they could under the circumstances, and that was that Roberts was dead. After spending some time checking Roberts over and writing up his death, the agitated doctor appeared in the corridor to talk to her. The doctor seemed very disturbed that a patient, apparently recovering with no complications from the operation they'd performed on him, could die like this.

"What on earth happened?" the irritated doctor asked Machin, his tight lined face etched with tension.

"I don't know," Machin said, and she genuinely did not know. One moment Roberts had been lying there, spitting out his poison, the next he'd been convulsing violently in his death throes. She thought about Roberts blowing his nose. He'd become violently ill moments after he'd blown his nose with the hanky from his bedside table. "He was talking to me normally until he blew his nose with the hanky that was on the bedside table. After he blew his nose, he suddenly started convulsing wildly." The doctor was puzzled but knew they wouldn't be able to come to any conclusions until they'd done an autopsy on Roberts. Machin had been speaking to him and nothing appeared to be wrong. Roberts had seemed, to Doctor James, to be a man on the road to recovery. He had shown no signs that anything was wrong until he blew his nose.

Machin concluded that there had to be something in the hanky. He had taken something from the hanky that enabled him to commit suicide. The Japanese called it hara-kiri. In Roberts's case, she called it an inconvenience. It was significant because it meant Roberts had robbed her of the answers she needed—now she would never really know the truth about what really went on that day when she and Bailey were in Roberts's lair.

CHAPTER 65

To get somewhere in politics in the Saatchi and Saatchi world of the twenty-first century, Bailey had long ago concluded that you had to make many sacrifices. Ian Bailey sat at his gleaming mahogany desk in the EPP Party leader's office. The desk still smelled fresh and alive from the pungent furniture polish used to clean it earlier in the day. It now shone as bright as Bailey's prospects. Later today, he was going to give a press conference, in which he would detail his heroic role in stopping the terrorist, Detective Sergeant Morgan Roberts's, evil reign of terror. He'd emphasize the fact that he'd shot Roberts to stop him from causing further mayhem. Due to his possession of an illegal firearm, the police were going to charge him with an offense. But Bailey would make sure he pointed out that, if he hadn't had the afore-mentioned illegal firearm, then he and DI Machin, along with Tredwell, would all be dead. If they had died, nobody would have been any the wiser about Roberts's evil deeds, and the maniac would still be out there murdering people.

Bailey rummaged through the desk drawers, inside of which there were still some of Henson's personal belongings. Bailey would need to get rid of them today so he could put his own stamp on the room. Putting his own stamp on this office also meant making a mark with the party, a completely fresh start for everyone, with him at the helm. On the wall, there was a picture of the poor departed leader, Toby Henson. The picture was a recent one, taken at a rally, and it showed the vainglorious Henson wearing a smart blue pinstripe suit, addressing the mass ranks of EPP supporters. Bailey decided it was a fitting tribute to the martyr, Henson.

Henson had left behind no wife or family. Officially, it was because he was too devoted to the party for him to get involved in relationships. Unofficially, it was because he was nicknamed Ernst Rohm by those who knew that Henson was a homosexual and had a penchant for good-looking blonds. Bailey had personally made sure that Henson's boyfriend, James, was kept out of the public limelight. Bailey decided to keep an aura around the recently departed Henson, as a single, focused leader.

The funeral had been a noisy affair. It involved the usual mass ranks of clamoring press, who, even after Henson's tragic murder, were still unable to leave the EPP leader in peace. Public anger at the EPP would slowly dissipate after Bailey's press conference. Once people realized that the terrorist murders had been committed by a rogue crazy police officer, the same person who had also sent a brainwashed teenager to murder Toby Henson, then Bailey was sure it would make the public much more sympathetic toward the EPP cause.

On leaving Dover the week before, in a quiet country lane just outside of Lydden, Bailey had donned a false-beard-and-wig disguise and had then dressed in a doctor's coat for his visit to Roberts in Canterbury Hospital. Bailey had noted over the years in his police work that security became non-existent if you looked like you belonged and appeared to be doing what you should be. The guard had left the door open while Doctor Bailey had visited his patient, Roberts, in his room. When Doctor Bailey appeared to the guard to be just doing some standard medical checks, the guard had become lax. In his lax mode, the guard had failed to notice Doctor Bailey's sleight of hand, a sleight of hand that had managed to slip a hanky with a cyanide pill wrapped inside onto Roberts's bedside table.

Roberts had smiled at Bailey just before he left the room, as both men realized this was the last time Bailey would see Roberts alive. When Roberts had come to him last year and asked for his help in tailing Jill, who Roberts suspected was having an affair, Bailey had sensed an opportunity. He was a realist and, unlike Henson, understood that the EPP had no chance of making a real impact on the British electoral process unless something dramatically changed.

Bailey had tailed Patel and Jill to a motel room not long after Roberts had returned from Manchester, following up a lead in the hunt for the serial killer, Peter Rivers. After bribing the motel staff, Bailey quickly found that it was a motel room that Jill Roberts and Patel used on a regular basis. It hadn't been difficult for a man with his police experience and underworld contacts to set up the camera to film Patel and Jill in their regular motel liaisons. It was a film that showed that Jill's affair was of the fiery all-consuming variety. It was a passion that had lain dormant in Jill for a very long time, something Roberts had noted in his sexual relations with her.

Viewing his wife's intense lovemaking with Patel had sent a psychotic Roberts completely over the edge. It was at this moment that Bailey had seized his opportunity—the moment when he had come to Roberts with a plan for him to take his revenge on Patel. It was a plan that gave Roberts a chance to vent his anger through terrorism on the immigrants and migrants that he was blaming for all the country's ills. The plan was fool proof and, as far as Bailey was concerned, was unique in its complexity. It was a plan that would catapult Bailey from a position of relative political obscurity into the public limelight as a heroic action figure. After Henson's death, he'd become the new vibrant leader of an up-and-coming party, a man to whom the country could turn to in an effort to reverse its moral and intellectual decline. Roberts was prepared to die so that Bailey could implement that plan. Roberts had realized, after losing Jill, that he had nothing left to live for, apart from revenge on those he blamed for his misery. He'd died the true patriot's death, and Bailey would always remember his sacrifice.

Bailey's opportunity to make an impact on British politics was now. He wasn't sure, after what he'd done, if he was a nutcase or a genius. Whatever his questions on the matter, he was sure of one thing, and that was that he'd entered politics to make an impact. Foiling Roberts's mad terror plot and then becoming leader of the EPP made this all possible now. All good politicians throughout history knew that collateral damage was unavoidable if you wanted to gain a foothold in power. It was a lesson that the DI Machins of this world would never understand as they looked upon the dead and wounded from Roberts's terror campaign with aberration and horror.

Bailey saw them all as necessary martyrs to propel him from obscurity. As he put on his coat to go to the press conference, he reflected on Hitler and Mussolini and the trusted lessons of the dictators of the past. They'd both learned quickly that, to succeed as a Fascist, you needed to rack up the body count. Bailey decided that his faultless plan, whereby Roberts took the blame for Bailey's mass murder plans, had allowed him to do so. The killing of Henson had been necessary. In murdering Henson, Bailey had given the party its own personal Horst Wessel. Henson was now a man about whom songs would be written, a man to give party members something to focus on, and, in whose memory, they would rally around the flag. Bailey left the room, the happiest he'd been in a long time. This was not a time to remain stagnant, but a time to rapidly move forward because, at this moment in time, they were both on the brink of a new dawn—Great Britain and him personally.

The End

About the Author

Paul Howard was born in the Garden of England, in East Kent, and educated at Castlemount Secondary School, a school that closed thirty years ago. He's always felt lucky to be surrounded by such a wonderful coastline and has fond memories of days spent on the beach as a kid. His deceased father, Mike, was a seaman, who often used to regale him with tales from his overseas trips, including catching strange fish in New Zealand and of his friend, Vic, who used to bare-knuckle fight at fairgrounds in Australia.

Howard lives with his partner, Anna-Maria, a German woman, whose great uncle was Max Brauer, a former prime minister of Hamburg. In the 1930s, Brauer was involved in trying to stop Hitler from coming to power. The resultant success of the Nazis meant that he had to flee Germany for Manhattan before he was arrested. Howard's partner's family has an interesting past, with her deceased English father, a special forces commando in World War Two, receiving commendation letters from Winston Churchill for his bravery in the conflict.

In the 1980s, Howard worked for Hoverspeed at Dover International Hoverport. At the time, he never appreciated what a unique job it was. Because of the huge fuel costs, hovercrafts are far too expensive to run these days. The possibility of having passenger-carrying hovercrafts again is something the world will never see. Since 1989 until recently, Howard worked for Royal Mail as a postman, but his partner's disabilities, Ehlers-Danlos Syndrome and other associated conditions, meant he has had to give up work to become a home care-giver.

In his years of working for Royal Mail, he found a sense of community and a level of camaraderie among postmen that you wouldn't find anywhere other than the armed services. Unfortunately, due to his circumstances, it was time to move on, so, alas, he had to leave many friends behind, look to the future, and focus on his writing.

Disciples of Death, which was released by Black Opal Books in 2016, was Howard's first novel, an international terrorist thriller, set against the turmoil of the Middle East. Previously, Howard has self-published a book of poetry, *Invicta Tales*, and a selection of comedy sketches, *Bish, Bash, Comedy Dash*, on Smashwords. In April, 2015, a short play of his, *The Clearing*, was staged at the Waterloo East Theatre, and produced by Whoop 'n' Wail as part of their May Day production. In a UK lyrics-only song-writing competition, Howard's song, "1982," is currently at the semi-final stage. *Soul Mate*, his second novel a thriller set in Britain, about the hunt for a serial killer was released by Black Opal Books in early 2018.